GW00390875

DOMESTIC
AFFAIRS

CAROLYN ALDIS

DOMESTIC AFFAIRS

CAROLYN ALDIS

Dedication

This book is dedicated to my family…firstly my husband Phil who encouraged me to get this book written…and still encourages me to spend time writing creatively. (Mainly because I get grouchy when I don't.)

Secondly, my girls Lauren, Alice, Sophie and Daisy who have helped me to believe in myself and have developed into amazingly creative women themselves.

Thirdly, I thank God for giving me such a great imagination.

And finally, I thank my friends and family for buying this book…thanks for keeping your promise!

Chapter 1
A Different World

"And here is to the next however many years I have left of my retirement! Cheers!"

Bill's voice rang out across the crowded pub, cutting through the hubbub and causing all people, whether party to his special occasion or not, to raise their glasses and say cheers to the elderly man, quaint in a navy-blue pinstriped suit with a cravat positioned perfectly in the breast pocket.

Still smiling, he turned to his wife and gushed, "I wouldn't want to be sharing it with anyone else but you, my love," leaning over to kiss her on the cheek.

Ivy felt tears of both happiness and sorrow fill her eyes as she accepted his kiss and looked down demurely. She rummaged in her handbag for her little compact mirror, not only to make sure her make-up was still intact, but that the broccoli from her roast dinner wasn't stuck in her teeth.

Once satisfied that all was well, she popped it back into her bag and checked her mobile for the seventeenth time. Although she knew in her heart that there wouldn't be any messages, the disappointment still felt as deep as it had the first time she had checked. Sighing, she fixed a smile on her face as she looked around at the people sharing this special occasion - to her left, Gladys and Ernie, neighbours when they were newlywed all those years ago, bringing up their children alongside each other and spending social occasions together. Next to them were Angela and Desmond, Bill's secretary and her husband, a relationship which had endured well considering theirs was a mixed marriage, back in a time when such unions were frowned upon. She had been a great help to Bill, organising his diary, and looking enough like a horse to never be considered a threat. Chatting to her was Terry, Bill's work colleague, who looked like a lizard, all leathery skin on account of the holidays he took abroad, and next to him, his wife Marion, wearing an imitation fur coat and far too much make-up for a sixty-five-year-old. Opposite them sat a younger couple, the neighbours they now had, having moved into a smaller house. They had spent only a little time with them, and although he was fairly obnoxious, she seemed sweet and in need of a friend, so Ivy was pleased they had come along. Such a shame he was so fat, she thought, he would be quite nice-looking otherwise. Guiltily, she jumped as a glass being tapped with a spoon caught everyone's attention again. Terry was getting to his feet, pushing back the heavy wooden chair, and clearing his throat.

"Unaccustomed as I am...." he began, before being drowned out by raucous laughter from those around the table who knew just how very accustomed he was at talking.

"No, listen, really, I just wanted to say how having known Bill for over thirty years, it has been a real treat to be his friend and work companion, and as much as I would like for him to continue working with us, I know the time has come for Bill and Ivy to spend time together enjoying their retirement."

Bill looked at Ivy, who smiled back at him, knowing she should be glad they would now be spending so much time together, and yet feeling that the space left by their son would be felt even more keenly. She had hoped John might have turned up, just this once as it was such a special occasion. Maybe one of their friends had asked him to come and he had declined as usual with some excuse. She felt the type of disappointment that is only experienced by mothers of selfish children.

"And I am sure there will be many more to come. Cheers!"

Terry had finished his speech at last, and the glasses were raised again, everyone smiling at them as they cheered and took a sip. He sat down and the pub settled back into the general sound of chatter.

Lisa drank her champagne down in one, the bitter taste hitting her throat and the bubbles causing a burning sensation in her chest. She looked at Ivy and Bill, the sweet neighbours she had only recently got to know and wondered if they really were happy, or if every marriage was as much of a sham as her own.

Although she had only been married a couple of years, she had been with Mike for eight and the change in him since being married had at first shocked her, and then left her feeling utterly hopeless and wondering how you could be with someone and know them and yet not really know them at all. As if on cue, Mike came back from the toilets and she saw with disgust that his suit was stained from the meal, and that his bottom shirt button was undone, revealing his fleshy stomach. The weight gain had started on their honeymoon, and he was twice, if not three times the man she had married. He bent down next to her and growled in her ear.

"When can we go? I've had enough now of all these old farts wittering on."

Lisa checked her phone for the time, and then reached for her handbag under the table.

Mike was already standing, and pulling on his coat. Lisa went down to the other end of the table to say goodbye as he headed out of the door.

"Are you off now, love?" enquired Ivy, standing up to hug her. Lisa didn't really do the whole hugging thing, especially with people she didn't know well, but found it surprisingly comforting in Ivy's embrace, and to her embarrassment, felt tears prick her eyes. She held on to Ivy longer than she meant to, and quickly blinked and regained her poise.

"Yes, need to get back to let Zippy out," she explained, referring to the Staffordshire Bull Terrier whose barking irritated Bill. "Thanks for inviting us, it's been lovely."

Ivy saw the desperate look in the eyes of the younger woman, and feeling sorry for her, ignored the rudeness of Mike leaving without saying goodbye.

"See you later," was all Ivy said, and sat back down, releasing Lisa to leave without feeling guilty.

Ivy watched as the young woman walked quickly out of the pub, and marvelled at how people managed to stay together, when they so blatantly didn't fit as a couple - Lisa was a slim, pretty girl who seemed to have her head screwed on, so how on earth had she ended up with an oaf like Mike?

"Are you thinking what I'm thinking?" muttered Gladys leaning towards her.

Ivy smiled at her old friend, and nodded.

"Poor girl, so sweet natured with an awful husband like that," she mused, "How does a couple end up so unhappy?"

Gladys looked smug, and linked arms with Ivy.

"She obviously didn't choose wisely like we did with our lovely husbands," she murmured proudly, "Youngsters these days don't seem to consider anything or spend time thinking about anything of value, it's all gimme gimme gimme!"

Ivy smiled and removed her linked arm, and patted Gladys's hand.

"I just don't think it's as simple as that anymore," stated Ivy, "It really is a different world from when we were girls."

Later, when they had made their way home, still high on the comments and well-wishes from their friends, Ivy reflected on what retirement would mean for her. She had always known Bill would retire at sixty-five and the fact that they got on so well was a blessing...she knew many couples didn't even make it to ten years these days, and her and Bill had managed forty-seven years together, having married in their teens. That was the way it was done then...no living together, no practice run, trying it out to see if it would work. She smiled ruefully at the memory of the times her marriage had felt close to the brink of destruction. Nothing had prepared her for the pain and anguish of arguments and harsh comments within the confines of marriage and she was glad those days were over. Ever since John decided not to visit, their relationship had grown stronger, tied by the bond of disappointment caused by another beloved human being. Ivy wondered where he was and if he was interested in the retirement of his parents. She tried to cheer herself up by focusing on the plans they had discussed for the future. A cruise was top of her list, something that she had seen advertised in the magazines at the doctor's surgery. Bill had talked about a new car and exotic holidays and even simple treats like having coffee and cake out, not worrying about the cost. The days of counting pennies were over and she couldn't help but feel a little smug as they pulled onto their drive.

"You're quiet," he mused as he opened his door before walking around to her side of the car to open hers.

"Everything alright?"

She swung her legs round and used the door to lever herself out. Since her knee operation, she had to be careful not to twist it and turning her whole body was the only way to keep it protected. Bill had always been chivalrous, so opening the door for her was a natural act for him.

"Yes, just thinking. Did you enjoy your meal?"

Bill walked to the front door of their semi-detached house, the garden immaculate, with pansies and lobelia in the beds and either side of the front door in hanging baskets. He put the key in the lock and turned to let himself in, wiping his feet on the mat and hanging the keys up immediately.

"It was a nice bit of beef…and the speeches weren't too painful, were they?"

Ivy saw the envelope on the mat and stooped to pick it up. It looked official, with DWP stamped on the front. She handed it to Bill as she went to put the kettle on, putting two teabags into the teapot as she passed it to get to the fridge. The kitchen was old-fashioned with a country feel to it, all wooden cupboard doors and brown kitchen utensil pictures on the tiles. The cream work surface was stained where Ivy had left teabags on the side and not cleaned it off in time, much to Bill's annoyance. She brought the milk out of the fridge and had just put it on the side as the kettle clicked off.

"That is outrageous!" Bill exploded from the lounge.

Ivy jumped, sloshing the milk over the side of the cup, into her saucer. She set it down quickly, before hurrying into the lounge, where Bill was sitting at his writing desk, reading glasses on, letter in hand.

"What's happened?"

Bill had turned beetroot.

"The government have cut my pension massively!"

"What? Let me see."

Ivy moved over to where he was and went to take it.

"It won't make any difference if you look at it, it will still say the same thing!" he countered tetchily.

Ivy was hurt by his tone, but knew it must be bad. Money was the only thing that Bill ever got really angry about.

"I thought I was getting £277 a week and they now say it is £79 due to new government cuts...I just can't believe it."

"Well, surely my pension will help?"

"No, it's the same for you as well...that's what I am saying, it's as if only one of us had a pension, and a lower one at that!"

Bill looked defeated and Ivy wasn't sure what to do. She couldn't believe how quickly emotions could change, how one minute life was wonderful and on the up and the next, things conspired against you and you were down at the bottom of the heap. Ivy knew that with Bill, practical help was best, and she used this tactic to cheer him up, by wandering back into the kitchen, trying to make light of it.

"Well, let's see if we can cut back. There is my painting class and swimming - I could give them up to save a few pounds. And baking, I could bake cakes and biscuits from scratch, it's much cheaper than buying it readymade."

She came in with their drinks and set them down. Bill looked at her as if she had just spat at him.

"You can't be serious...as if a few cutbacks will make any difference, we are really going to struggle!"

He pinched the bridge of his nose, the stress evident in his twitching jawline. Ivy felt helpless as the tears began to roll down her cheeks, turning away to hide her distress. She reached across for a tissue and Bill glanced up at her.

"Look, if you want to make cakes and biscuits, then do it," he reassured in a gentler tone, realising how upset she was.

"You're right, we can at least try to cut back. Pass me a pen from the drawer so I can draw up a plan of money saving ideas."

Feeling glad that she had brought Bill a little way back to his senses, Ivy turned and went to the bureau and opened the drawer. She handed the pen to him and then looked out of the window, concern etched on her face - one measly pension between them? How on earth would they survive?

Chapter 2
All Under Control

Ivy had spent the morning weeding in the back garden,
which due to the recent rainfall, had become overgrown
with dandelions and nettles. Bill had gone out for his
usual morning walk, and wanting to achieve a feeling of
satisfaction, she had put on her old trousers, plus an old
holey jumper of Bill's, and entered the inner sanctum of the
garden shed. Bill had arranged all the tools neatly, spending
last summer painting the shape of each tool on the wall so
that he could see if any were missing; super organised, the
opposite of Ivy. She wondered sometimes how on earth they
could have made their relationship work when they were
both so different, yet theirs had endured where so many had
floundered. Ivy picked out the hand trowel and fork, and
went to where her lap tray was laid out on the grass, upside
down so the soft cushioned side was facing her, perfect for
her to kneel on in comfort. Having been given four as gifts
over the years, three from the same person, she put them to
good use, using only one as an actual lap tray. She knelt and
began attacking the dandelions at the root, knowing that
if she just took the top off, they would be back in no time.

Although it was a cool day, the exertion from digging down soon warmed her up. Moving the tray along and shuffling across allowed her to clear a considerable size of the bed. Puffing, she pulled at the roots and threw them into a pile on the grass, to take to the compost bin when she had finished.

Turning back, she gave a little cry as a huge earthworm slid out from the soft earth, forcing itself out to find a better undisturbed position. The bluish tinge of its body reminding her of the veins in Bill's arms that stuck out so noticeably. She stared at it as it began to burrow down again, and suddenly got an image of John, aged about six, squatting down beside her in their old garden, his little face earnest, looking into his cupped hands. Desperate for the memory, she closed her eyes and remembered....

"Mummy, look, it's hurted!"

She recalled the horror as he had thrust the damaged worm he had found into her face as she knelt beside him on her young knees (no need for a lap tray then).

"Oh John, darling, put it down, it's all yucky."

He continued to study it, now two worms instead of one, the damage to its body separating it into two, writhing on his little palms.

"Why is it still moving?"

"I don't know, it's probably just its nerves. Put it down and wash your hands."

She was always wanting to get rid of anything messy, not wanting to deal with the 'not nice' in life, to keep it all easy.

"What have you got there, young man?"

Bill always seemed to appear after she had managed to say the wrong thing.

"It's a worm that's dying, mummy killed it with a spade!" blurted John, reproachfully, his brown eyes filling with tears.

Bill took the boys' hands, and shook the worm into his

own hands.

"Mind out Daddy, you're hurting it!" John had exclaimed, shocked at the perceived damage being inflicted.

"It's not dying, it's now two worms! Look, if you put them down, they will wriggle into the mud and both will live, see? Don't be sad, Johnny."

John looked at the worms, now burrowing into the earth, and began to smile.

"It's like magic!" he exclaimed, eyes lit up.

"Yes, it is." replied Bill, ruffling his hair.

The memory of Bill at ease with their son caused Ivy's breath to catch in her throat, and she shook herself from her reverie. She had got stiff, having stayed in the same position for too long, and although she hadn't finished the weeding, she'd had enough. She stood shakily, and took the tools back to the shed, having been with Bill long enough to know how irritated he got if things were not put away. Going towards the house, she picked up the lap tray and went through the back door, setting the tray down in the corner of the conservatory. Ivy moved slowly into the kitchen, pausing to pick the kettle up, before taking it to the sink to fill it. She looked out the window, to see Bill chatting to Lisa, who was in the middle of taking the shopping in from her car. He was laughing now, and Lisa smiled, acknowledging the joke, and again, the catch appeared in Ivy's throat. It never ceased to amaze her how happy Bill was, how he could laugh and joke, even after all the heartache that had clouded the last few years. Since they had last seen John, at that awful Christmas, when the conversation of children had come up and been shot down by John and his wife Katy, their relationship had been reduced to cards at birthdays and Christmas. She knew his career was important to him, but never imagined that the little boy who adored her would have no real input in their lives. She went to the cupboard and reached for the Bourbon biscuits, her favourite, and took a knife from the drawer, cutting the packet open. Bill came in to see Ivy eating them straight from the packet and knew that she had been thinking of John. He even put the biscuits into the tin without saying anything after she had left the pack on the side.

"Do you want a tea, Bill?"

He washed his hands and dried them on the hand towel, looking out of the window.

"I saw Lisa" he chattered, "She is such a lovely girl, really friendly. We have been very fortunate with our neighbours, haven't we?"

He was wittering and she knew it was to avoid real talking. Ivy went through to the lounge, the afternoon sun filtering through the lead lined windows, casting a homely glow over the brown sofa. She made a beeline for it, balancing her cup of tea on her new book, with three Bourbons stacked on it too, wishing she had remembered where the real lap tray was as this would have made the task easier. Flumping down onto the sofa, the movement sloshed the tea onto the book and biscuits. Annoyed, she grabbed a tissue from out of the floral box on the coffee table, and mopped her book. Having settled again, she bit into the biscuit, now soggy and cold, and felt sickness inside her that had nothing to do with what she was eating. She stuffed the tissue up her sleeve, and brushed the crumbs onto the floor. Bill had been clattering in the kitchen, tidying up the surfaces. Realising the noise had now stopped, she looked up to see him reading through some paperwork, although what he had to do since leaving work she had no idea. She had just started to read the next part of her book, having read the same paragraph four times, when the bell rang. Thinking it was the neighbour, Ivy stayed in her book position, feet up on foot stool, semi lying down. She hadn't the energy to invest into a new relationship, and people always expected her to be so happy now they were both retired, and some days she didn't feel it. To her surprise, she heard Gladys speaking to Bill.

"I am just so thrilled, I thought it was never going to happen, and then he just came out with it!"

Her voice was so shrill and excited, Ivy got up, flinging the book down, and met Gladys as she bounded into the room, Bill and Ernie coming in behind her.

"What's happened?" asked Ivy, smiling at her old friend "Sounds like good news."

"It's George! He's getting married at long last!" Gladys gushed, her eyes shining.

Ivy hugged her friend and was genuinely pleased. For years, Gladys had been convinced her George was gay, and that he would never marry, which for Gladys meant no grandchildren, even though Ivy had explained that this wasn't necessarily the case.

"Oh, that's wonderful news!" exclaimed Ivy, as Bill shook Ernie's hand.

"Congratulations," said Bill, "Shall I put the kettle on, or do you fancy something stronger? There's sherry in the fridge?"

"Oh, tea will be fine, thanks Bill," interrupted Gladys, taking up Ivy's position on the sofa.

"Is there any of that Victoria sponge cake left, Ivy?" called Bill.

"In the Roses tin in the cereal cupboard," she replied, smiling at Gladys.

"It's going to be at a church called St Mary's in a village in Norfolk. That's where she is from, although she doesn't go to church there, just always had a dream to get married there, she is such a lovely girl, though he has only known her a couple of months -.”

"Four months, dear, and he did work with her a couple of years ago, so he has known her a while…” interjected Ernie from the kitchen.

"Well, anyway, it doesn't matter because he says she is the one and that's it, he is marrying her and I just can't believe it, the speed of it!”

Bill came through the archway into the lounge with the cake on a plate and a knife.

Gladys looked at it with horror.

"Ooh, none for me, I've got a dress to fit into!”

Ivy smiled, confused. "Surely you can have a little, there's plenty of time...?”

"But that's just it! They are getting married on March the fifteenth - that's only a month's time!”

Bill and Ivy looked shocked, and Ernie, who had just walked in with his tea, sat on the armchair.

"It is quite soon, but that's George for you, never one to hang about," said Ernie, "I'll have a piece of cake, thanks, no need for me to slim!”

Ivy recovered herself enough to say something.

"At least you won't have long to worry over it. Have they managed to get all the preparations done?”

Bill cut a slice of cake for Ernie, who went and helped himself to a fork from the bureau before returning to his seat.

"Well, he says it is all under control, and everything is booked, but I do wonder if he has thought of everything," wittered Gladys, looking perturbed.

"You worry too much," mumbled Ernie through his cake, and Ivy watched as a fleck of cake arced through the air and landed on the coffee table, unnoticed by Ernie, who went on

"Just be thankful he doesn't want us to pay for it!"

Ivy looked at the speck of cake, and imagined that over the weeks, lots of specks of cake would land on the table, and create a soft table cover, pretty and colourful, and people would come around and ask where she got it from, and she would have to lie and say it was a present from their last holiday, and no she didn't know what the fabric was, and the smell, well, you just had to put up with it as it was such a wonderful piece and...

"Did you hear me, Ivy?"

Gladys's face, marred with irritation, was staring at her. Dazed, Ivy smiled weakly.

"Sorry, I was miles away."

"I should think you were; I was just saying how George has allowed us four friends to come along to the wedding and I would like you and Bill to come!" announced Gladys, who was now cutting a large slice of cake for herself, the problem of the dress forgotten.

"Oh, that would be lovely," replied Ivy, "I love weddings. It's been ages since we went to one, must have been when John-."

She stopped mid flow, but not in time for the awkward feeling to disappear. Ernie cleared his throat, Gladys was examining her cake intently, and Bill laid his hand on Ivy's shoulder. She put her own hand over his and said too brightly

"Well, I shall need a new dress, and shoes and a bag..."

Bill stepped in.

"Oh, right, so it's not costing you, Ernie, but I am having to fork out for it!"

They all laughed, relieved that the moment of embarrassment had been covered, and Ivy gratefully squeezed Bill's hand.

"I just hope we get on with her parents," said Gladys finishing the last bit of her cake, "We have to be on the top table with them, and apparently, she is quite posh... buys everything organic!"

She suddenly looked stricken, and grabbed Ivy's arm.

"What if she wants all the wedding food to be organic? That will cost a fortune!"

Ernie looked irritated and cleared his throat again.

"Oh, for goodness' sake, Gladys, what does it matter? George is paying for it, so it doesn't involve us anyway."

Ivy patted her hand, and smiled.

"I'm sure whatever they have, it will be wonderful, and I for one will be happy just to share in their happy day." ventured Ivy graciously.

Bill stood up as they put down their plates, and moved forward to clear them away. Gladys picked up her bag, and rummaged through it, taking out some paracetamols. Ivy watched as she popped the pills through the foil, and put them both in her mouth. Grabbing the cup in front of her, she quickly drank the remnants of her tea and gave a little shudder. Ivy looked at her sympathetically, as Ernie and Bill went through to the kitchen.

"What is it this time? You know you really shouldn't be on painkillers all the time, it can't be good for you."

Gladys smiled ruefully, and put the pack back in her bag.

"It's my back now. After last year, with all the trouble in my hands, then my elbows, and now it's in my back, it's just so irritating. Some days it's bearable but today it has just ached and ached. I think it's stress-related!"

Ivy smiled at her. For as long as she could remember, Gladys had been a moaner, a glass half-empty type, always looking at the negative of every situation. Ivy often had to get her to see the positive side and usually Gladys would reluctantly admit that there was a silver lining in the dark cloud. It was one of the reasons they were such good friends, the whole opposite thing. The arthritis that had initially started off as mild, now caused her friend so much pain that she knew she just had to be sympathetic and allow Gladys to take the pills and offer practical help in any way, which is what she did now.

"Can I help at all? I know you said George has sorted all the preparations, but what about coming with you to buy the new dress? I could get mine as well, make a day of it."

The thought of the cost of a new dress made Ivy feel a pang of fear, but she reasoned she could get out of buying a new one with the excuse of not being able to find the perfect one. Gladys smiled and stood up to check her reflection in the mirror and Ivy knew she had won her over.

Ernie sauntered through from the kitchen.

"Are we off then, love?"

Gladys turned to him, linking her arms with Ivy.

"Ooh, yes, we are, and next Saturday, Ivy and I are going shopping!"

Ernie and Bill exchanged groans. This was turning out to be something that was going to cost them dearly.

Chapter 3
A Choice Between
Sawdust and Cardboard

The room is dark. The illuminated number on the clock says it is 5.32am and John is suddenly aware of a strong urge to take a pee. He rises to the top of his subconscious, like a diver coming up for air, and gasps awake, seeing the time, and sighing heavily. His wife murmurs something, probably moaning at him, he thinks gloomily, even in her sleep. He sits up slowly, and puts his feet down onto the cold wooden floor, another bloody stupid idea of Katy's to get rid of the thick carpets that kept the room so warm and cosy. A stretch as he wandered to the en-suite, not Katy's idea, but stupid anyway, he always feels like he is crapping in his bedroom whenever he goes. Having relieved himself, he pulled the mini light switch above the sink. His face, grey and pasty, hair askew, stares back at him. His brown eyes, although bleary and worn, were still his best feature. John could never get over how much he had changed over the years. First blonde hair, then dark brown, now flecked with silver, his initially perfect chiselled jaw, now sagging with age and the wrinkles that appeared deeper as the years rolled on, filled his forehead, the sands of time marked out for all to see.

Another sigh as he turned the shower on and removed his boxers. Stepping into the hot flow, he was irritated to see his wife's various bottles of potions scattered all over the bottom of the shower, and angrily kicked them out of the way. As he washed his hair, the water gurgled round the plug hole and the tray started to fill up with water. He washed himself, and rinsed off, and having turned off the water, bent down and drew his finger across the plug hole. The mass of thick long hair that attached itself to his finger made him gag and he opened the screen and threw it down the toilet, disgusted. Dripping, he walked into the hall to the airing cupboard for his towel, and wrapped it round his shoulders before going back into the bedroom. It was now 6.00 and he wanted to be out of the house by 6.45 at the latest- that way, he could get to his office early and avoid speaking to Katy until the evening, when he would be more inclined to be civil.

Going around to his side of the bed, he sat down, taking his phone off the side, and checking for messages. There were eight emails and six texts – all sent in the space of time from midnight when he had finished working, until now. John moaned slightly, and still feeling damp, dried himself off. Walking to his side of the wardrobe to get his suit and shirt out, he picked out the pale blue shirt bought as a treat for himself only a week ago. Feeling the crispness of it against his shoulders gave him a false sense of being in control and confident. He smiled wryly at the memory of the training course he had recently been sent on to become more focused and confident, all within your grasp. The trainer had looked about twelve, with the life experience of a hamster, cocooned within a world of fluff. From that, he had come away feeling nothing but a touch of guilt at the way he had answered every question cynically, and reduced the trainer to a quivering wreck in front of his colleagues.

John put the tie on, and sat on the edge of the bed to put his trousers on. Katy stirred and turned over, and he willed her to stay sleeping, pulling his trousers on quickly and standing up. He draped his jacket over his arm and paused to check his reflection in the full-length mirror. Some of the puffiness of sleep had reabsorbed back into his body and his hair was now smoothed down, but misery still sat on his face, the furrowed brow heavy with the stress of being an MP, and he quickly left the room, pausing only to close the door quietly.

Softly treading on the staircase, he went down, checking his phone for the time – 6.23 – not enough time for porridge, or eggs, so it would have to be cereal. He went through the hall into the kitchen, and took a bowl out of the cupboard. Always desperate for some caffeine but knowing the machine would wake Katy, he planned to make a detour to Costa to get an espresso. He had read somewhere that by buying a coffee daily meant that £720 of his money was being spent every year on coffee, and what a dreadful waste blah blah – who really cares? Like the other MPs, he could always put it on expenses anyway, he certainly needed caffeine for the job, the hours that he was expected to work.

Opening the cupboard, his heart sank. The only cereal was All Bran or Special K; in his mind a choice between sawdust or cardboard, neither of which appealed to him. He was annoyed that Katy had only thought of herself as usual and not bought any type of cereal that he liked, pushing away the fact he hadn't eaten any for months as he usually had porridge. He wanted to feel angry at her, and God help whoever bumped into him first in the office today… the need to vent was too strong. Padding to where his shoes had been tidied away, he slipped them on, using the back of his trousers to shine the front. John opened the fridge and saw the fresh orange juice that Katy had most days. Taking it out, he unscrewed the lid and swigged straight from the bottle. Startled by a noise overhead, a sneeze signalling that Katy was awake, he spilled some down his cheek and neck. Cursing, he grabbed the kitchen roll and pulled some off to wipe it. Leaving the juice out on the side, knowing how irritated Katy would be with it lukewarm, he threw the kitchen towel into the recycling bin.

Crossing quickly to the hall, he took the keys off the hook and then went to his study to get his beloved briefcase out from under the desk before heading for the front door. John slammed it, getting some satisfaction from the irritation he knew Katy would feel hearing such a loud noise early on. The sun was bright and low, the air fragrant. The honeysuckle round the door was in full bloom and filled his nostrils with sweetness as he headed to the car. Pressing the button on his key fob, he opened the boot to his Mercedes, and laid the briefcase down in it. He opened it to remove his wallet so that he would have it ready to pay for the petrol and coffee he needed to get on the way. The suit jacket was slung on the back seat before he opened the door and slid into the front seat. Gunning the engine, he fumbled for his shades in the glovebox. Do people keep gloves in a glovebox, assuming that's how it got its name, he pondered as he slid on the sunglasses and pulled off the drive, checking the road as he went. Pushing his foot down, he allowed his annoyance to affect his driving, zooming along the main road, up to the traffic lights. He nearly hit a cyclist as he moved forward, the lights turned to amber and the cyclist shot across his path.

"Nob!" he shouted, cross now, and cut up the person behind him as he approached the petrol station. He jumped out, and went around to the passenger side and, having checked it was diesel, filled up, then slammed the pump back into its slot. Going into the shop, he was surprised to see a queue. It was only 7.15 and there were four people in front of him. He looked at the shelf, scanning the chocolate bars in search of some mints. He picked up a packet of Polos, and went to the coffee machine to get himself a double espresso. Once the cup was filled up, he walked towards the cashier, who was now free having served three of the customers; the other was still deciding which oil to buy. The cashier was young and, in his opinion, would have been quite pretty if she hadn't been so obese - her legs hung way over the chair and it looked very uncomfortable to be sitting like that. John tried not to stare at her, marvelling at the sheer size of her face, with its additional folds of skin either side; a face within a face. He wondered what she would look like slim. To him, all fat people had a similar look, a piggyness to the eyes, indents along the cheeks and a general air of heaviness. He paid and smiled at the girl, but as if she could read his mind, she scowled at him and swivelled round in her chair, busying herself with something under the counter. He left hurriedly and once in the car, popped the cup into the cup holder.

When he was on the road again, he drank the espresso, enjoying the rush of caffeine as he drove to the office. Today was not a day for him to be in the House of Commons, so he was able to go and do what he enjoyed; paperwork, dictating to his secretary letters of great importance and a meeting, which he would chair, on family values. He pulled into the car park and noticed, with a growing sense of irritation, that the new employee who had started last week had parked in his parking space. She was a nervy girl, who always looked like she was on the verge of tears, and overweight too, so as far as he was concerned, didn't have much going for her. Parking in the disabled bay near the door, he got out of the car and took the now empty cup out and threw it in the bin. Walking around to the boot, he took the briefcase out and caught sight of the other members of staff in his office looking down at him, smirking and pointing, aware of the fact the girl had taken his spot, knowing how angry John would be and not having told her to move.

This angered him more and he considered not giving them what they wanted, but decided that he needed to vent. His mother always used to say how you must let your feelings out, very important or else you might, as she put it, end up 'do-lally'. He shook off the image of his mother and strode into the foyer. The receptionists on the front desk looked up as he swept past, up the stairs and straight into the open plan office, heading for the new girl sat at her desk. She had her back to him and, having dispatched his briefcase on the floor outside his office, he spun her chair round so that she faced him, causing her to wobble momentarily and then grip the sides of the chair, looking up, terrified. He lowered his face down to her, getting as close as he dared without being repulsed.

"Why is your bloody car in my parking space?"

She got flustered and started to stammer. "I-err, oh, I didn't know..."

"No of course you didn't."

He straightened up and turned quickly, just catching his colleagues off guard as they quickly looked down at their keyboards.

"You wouldn't have known it was my space because none of these bastards told you it was mine...isn't that right, Mr Jones?"

Mr Jones was all innocent looks and raised shoulders, but John wasn't buying it. He was suddenly tired of it all, the people who got in the way, the annoyingness of the world around him, the sheer apathy of so many of the faces that surrounded him. He sagged, turning away towards his office.

"Just move it, and don't let it happen again."

The girl quickly stood up, humiliation turning her pale made up face red and hurried out to the car park, realising once there that her keys were in her jacket on her chair. She tried to creep in, but her breathing was laboured from all the exertion and too many of the others in the office had been watching anyway and they all smirked as she came in and went out for a second time. John had gone into his office, sat himself down at his desk, switched on his computer, the girl forgotten, and settled down to the day ahead.

Still Chapter 3
Tell-Tale Ache

Katy lay still for some time, enjoying the warmth, and luxury of not having to get up. She looked at the clock and smiled - 6.45am and a whole day off to herself. She knew that work was her baby and felt the satisfaction at the end of a good day, of having done her job well. This didn't stop her loving her days off, especially without John around - his constant criticizing, much as it didn't bother her anymore, was draining none the less. Working as an accountant was something she really loved - she had always enjoyed maths, and to be paid vast sums for doing sums made her feel warm and happy. If only she could feel like this always, she mused but being married to John was far too depressing to ever feel happy about. She turned onto her side and cupped her hands round her mouth, blowing out, and then realising how bad her breath was, moved them and sighed. She knew some of the relationship breakdown was down to her, that she could be just as mean as he was, but she didn't have the energy to try anymore. He had become like all the other pompous, up themselves MPs, who talk down to their wives, and make them feel like shite. They had talked on numerous occasions, but it just led to more tears and hurt and frankly, she couldn't be bothered...she certainly didn't want to waste any more time thinking about it.

Katy sat up and swung her legs off the bed, feeling the warm hard floor under her feet, and enjoying the sensation...under-floor heating was such a good invention. She sneezed, a common occurrence first thing in the morning due to having a dusty room - it was one of the reasons she got rid of the carpet; the room felt cleaner without them. Moving over to the en-suite, a noise from the kitchen stopped her dead – John must still be here, she thought, and carried on walking into the shower room. As she pushed the door to, she heard the front door slam – as inconsiderate as ever, she thought wryly, and sat on the cold seat, kicking her underwear off. Wrapping her dressing gown around herself, she flushed and washed her hands with the fruity soap her mother had sent, all the way from Canada, for her birthday. What age was it that you first get soap as a birthday present? She quickly glanced in the mirror, and smiled at herself. Having once read that a woman was never more beautiful than when she smiled, she liked the way her face lit up when she did. Picking up her toothbrush, she paused and considered having breakfast before brushing, knowing how the orange juice would taste gross, but squeezed the paste anyway. Simultaneously brushing and turning the cold water tap on to wash away the spittle, turning it off again until she needed it to rinse. Couldn't leave the tap running...it just felt wrong. Contemplating washing her hair and freshening up, she remembered her need to go for a run. Keeping fit and toned was important to her and more than once she had thought that if she ever left John, she would need to keep a good figure to be confident enough to get a new man.

A new man - what a thought. As if that would happen. No, she would grow into a bitter old woman, enjoying her own hobbies as John would no doubt find his own, keeping out of each other's way in their parallel universes. Katy went to her bedside drawer and rummaged around for a pair of plain cotton black knickers – she liked to be comfortable while running, having learned the hard way that not all knickers stayed where they were meant to. She dressed quickly, pulling the Lycra leggings on before donning knee supports and struggled into her sports bra, such was its high support. Slipping her Nike t-shirt on over her head, she went downstairs. The sun was coming through the French windows at the back of the house and the warmth of it filled the dining room. Katy saw the butter John had thoughtlessly left out on the side, with dirty plates and cutlery left from last night...she had been ironing and thought the clinking noise was him tidying up...instead he had made a late-night snack of cheese and biscuits, with pickle smeared on the plate and had left it all for her to sort out. Feeling the anger rise, she opened the cupboard to get her water bottle. Turning the tap on full to fill it, she swore as the water splashed her top. She slowed the flow and finished filling it. Katy went into the hall and took her hoodie down from the peg, zipping it up and turned to the bureau to get a hairband. Scraping her hair back, she finger-combed it into a high ponytail and pulled it tight. She was hungry, but wanted to run first, get it out of the way and give her teeth a chance to wear off their minty freshness ready for her glass of juice. Strapping her phone to her arm, she twisted it around and touched the screen to set up her running app. She opened the door and felt the cool of the morning on her face, before taking her keys off the hook and locking the door behind her. With the keys tucked into her back pocket, she struggled to zip it up before finally setting off.

Katy ran easily and fluidly, glad that the breeze was cold as she soon warmed up. She couldn't imagine how people lived without exercise; the feeling of renewed energy that came to her after running was better than anything else she had tried and boy had she tried...yoga, swimming, Zumba, aerobics. Smiling, she cast her mind back to her time in a hall, with countless other women of all shapes and sizes, leaping around just to try and get fit. The awkwardness of the others talking to her afterwards, wanting to meet up for coffee and talk about all the things they had in common, which in her case amounted to not very much; just because she exercised with them didn't mean she was their best friend and she ended up feeling mean making excuses and so stopped going. Running became her favourite type of exercise, solitary and with minimal preparation, allowing her time to think and work through anything bothering her and meant she could eat pretty much whatever she liked. Win-win. The app told her that she had hit 5k and so she slowed her pace a little, the sweat beading across her forehead. She ran past the local park, usually full of little people, but at this time in the morning, the swings stood silent, the climbing frame an art sculpture, all angles and colours. Slowing down and looking across the playing field, she eventually came to a stop, taking hold of the railings around the park and stared out, panting.

There used to be a time when she was first married that she wouldn't have been able to go past the park, let alone stop and look at it. The pain of their inability to have children had been so acute, it almost winded her to see anything to do with them. Thankfully, as she had become more set in her ways and saw the effect her friend's children had on their parents, ruining relationships and damaging bodies irreversibly, she had come to terms with it. She knew she would never completely be over it but it became more bearable as each year passed. As John had gradually become more distant, she was almost glad to have never inflicted him as a father onto their child. This didn't stop her wondering what their children would have looked like; if they would have been a mini-her or a mini-John, little versions of themselves, like so many of the children born to their friends. In the past, when there had been occasions for them to meet up, the children were so annoying, it made her glad that she didn't have them in her life, that she didn't have the constant demand for attention...it was bad enough with John.

Katy took a swig from her bottle and set off again at a quicker pace, feeling her stomach start to contract with hunger, wanting to get back for her porridge. She thought back to being a child, hating porridge; the gloopy consistency making her want to gag as she swallowed. It was the salt that her mother insisted on putting in it that she could never understand, that saltiness with something creamy like that. Much nicer with syrup. She focused on her breathing as the tell-tale ache started in her calves, always burning after four miles, no matter how often she ran. Katy had thought that in time it would get better for her, the muscles would adapt to being used more often and that she wouldn't ache so much after every run but no, the pain told her that it was time to slow down and head for home. Arriving back, warmed up and achy, her mood had lifted and the endorphins were doing their job and giving her the boost of energy she would need for tackling the house. Katy spotted Brenda by the fence and waved as she came to a stop.

"Morning dear, had a good run?" cooed Brenda in her soft, Scottish lilt, scuttling through her gate so that she could join Katy on the path.

"Yes, just a quick one this morning," replied Katy, undoing the phone holder to pause the workout, "I've got loads to sort out this morning!"

She laughed and just caught sight of Brenda's face as it fell and quickly followed up with "But I've got time for a cuppa, if you are free?"

Brenda beamed and scurried up the path, her nylon dress catching on the miniature rose bushes that lined the path.

"That will be lovely, I just fancy one."

Katy smiled as she carried on up the path. "As long as you don't mind me eating my breakfast."

"Oooh no, dear, that's fine, I'll just have a biscuit or two..."

Chapter 4
Doesn't It Hurt?

Bill straightened his tie in the reflection and combed what remained of his grey hair. He popped the comb in his back pocket and took his jacket from the hanger. It was an old business suit that he had nearly given to charity, but decided against it at the last minute. Good job too, he thought, seeing as he couldn't afford to buy a new one. The shock of the government cuts had subsided, but he still worried about how he would pay for everything. They might not have a mortgage anymore, hadn't for a long time, but he had got used to a certain level of living while he was working and hadn't banked on retiring on such a small amount a week. He sat down on the bed, rigid and upright and looked out of the window, up at the tree that grew outside their room – John had warned him the last time they had spoken that he should get it removed, as it could cause subsidence, informing him that the house would crack as the ground shifted. He had ignored this advice, much to John's disgust, as he liked to look through the leaves when he was thinking…plus he regularly inspected the walls and was pleased to see there was no evident damage. With a jolt, he remembered what he was meant to be thinking about. He had a lump sum, but he knew only too well how easy it was for this money to disappear on everyday necessities and his dream of taking Ivy abroad a couple of times a year was now completely redundant; the cost of everyday living would be a struggle, let alone any luxuries. He was glad he had never shared his dream with her as now she wouldn't be disappointed; the one thing he knew she didn't handle very well. It's what had caused her to break down years before and he didn't want to go there again.

"Ooooh, you do look smart...all ready for the big day?"

Bill turned to look at the doorway that Ivy was framing, clad in her white towel robe, the shampoo that she had gone downstairs for now in her hand.

"Yes, I'm ready, although I think you are going to take a lot longer than me." he chuckled, getting up and crossing to the chest of drawers. Taking a burgundy cravat from the top drawer, he put it in his top pocket and fixed a smile on his face.

"No, not long, only got to wash my hair..." replied Ivy, her voice trailing as she went into the bathroom and closed the door.

"And dry your hair, put on your makeup, clothes, shoes etcetera" muttered Bill as he went downstairs to put the kettle on. It was only 11.30 and the service didn't start until 2.00, plenty of time for a cuppa he reasoned.

Ivy got out of the shower and pulled on her robe, the towelling catching on her wet skin. She did up the belt, never liking to look down at her body, the sagging skin on her tummy depressed her too much and the papery look of it reminded her that she was no longer young. She much preferred looking at herself with clothes on and went to the wardrobe to decide what to wear. The shopping trip with

Gladys had gone well; she had acted well enough, trying on lots of outfits that she couldn't afford and saying they didn't feel right and that she would wear something from her old stock, only one hairy moment with a pushy shop assistant, where she had had to resort to rudeness to get her to back off. The memory of the woman recoiling from her after she said, 'For crying out loud, I'm not buying it!' made her blush. Gladys couldn't understand why the assistant was shirty with them after that and so they left. She looked at her dresses and sighed, wishing she could just pop on anything but knowing it had to be something special. Pulling out a turquoise dress, simple, with a round neck and A-line skirt, she placed it on the bed and then took out a red floral dress and did the same. There was one more outfit that might do, a beige trouser suit that she hadn't worn in a while. She tried this on first and was dismayed to discover that her waist had grown too much to do the button up. That's because I'm not swimming anymore, she thought bitterly, pushing away her conscience that tried to suggest it was the home baking that was more likely the cause.

So, on with the turquoise. It looked nice, but not special enough. She struggled out of it, feeling hot and bothered, and took the floral dress off its hanger before stepping into it and pulled the sleeves up, thinking it felt a better fit than the turquoise one. She looked in the mirror, and saw what the other guests would see.... a plump older woman in a dress that was too young for her...not exactly mutton dressed as lamb, but not a good enough look to get away with. Ivy pulled the dress off and looked at the turquoise one again; with a pretty scarf, she could jazz it up. Hunting in the bottom of her wardrobe for the array of scarves that lived there, she pulled out first a silvery one and then a pale blue. Putting the dress on, she tried the scarves, settling for the silver one before looking in the mirror and sitting down in front of it, reaching for her trusty make up bag. She didn't often wear make-up, but as it was such a special occasion and one where photographs would be taken, she knew she was going to need some help. Her face, moonlike, due to the roundness of her cheeks, left her feeling dejected - her mother had always said it was good to have a chubby face as it plumped out your skin and got rid of wrinkles, but she had never liked the shape of it. Only for so long, thought Ivy wryly as she patted the pressed powder on with a sponge, covering the fine red veins that troubled her cheeks. Her eyes had always had what she called laughter lines around them and although she had religiously used Oil of Olay for decades, she looked every one of her sixty years. She finished putting on her eye makeup, opting for a turquoise shade to match the dress and finally dried her hair. It needed a lot of spray to keep it in place and she combed it as it dried, persuading it to curl under...so often it curled under one side and not the other, irritating her greatly, but today it behaved and curled under beautifully.

"Not bad," she murmured and went to the top of the stairs. She could hear Bill humming to himself in the lounge and as she came down the spiral staircase, he appeared at the lounge door.

"Well, don't you look lovely," he said, admiringly.

"Why thank you." Ivy replied, turning to take her handbag off the coat hook.

She rummaged around as Bill took his cup into the kitchen and put it in the sink.

"Shall we go?" he enquired, getting his keys out of his pocket, "Best to get there in good time, we don't want to be late!"

Ivy checked she had the confetti and tissues she knew she

would need for the service.

"Yes, better to be early than late. Do you remember Great Aunt Brenda at our wedding? I must have been driven ten times around the block while she made her way up the road!"

He laughed at the recollection.

"Well, we don't want to be 'that couple' do we?" he replied as they went through the front door.

At the church, quite a number of people had already arrived, the cars lining the street. Bill had managed to park the car nearby and walked with Ivy, her arm linked with his, along the road to the church. It was a classic Anglican Church with a tall steeple and stained-glass windows, beautiful, ornate architecture and utterly freezing, even on this warm day. As they approached the door, a large woman, dressed in fuchsia pink, the dress much too tight and wearing a navy-blue hat was pinning a button hole onto a man that Ivy recognised as George's best friend and presumably best man. He smiled at them as they entered the porch way, hand outstretched.

"Hello....it's Bill, isn't it?"

Bill smiled, offering his left hand and shook the outstretched hand "That's right...and this is my wife, Ivy."

The young man smiled warmly.

"Lovely to see you both."

"Come on, Henry, no time for chit chat!"

The large woman's voice boomed across the porch and the unfortunate Henry was manhandled into the church. Bill looked at Ivy and they both raised their eyebrows and followed them in, through to the inner door. A young man who resembled Chris Evans was handing out the order of service. He smiled, revealing a gap in his teeth where his left front tooth should have been. Seeing their look of surprise, he pressed his lips together and grinned.

"Bit of an acthident on the sthtag nighth." he lisped.

Bill looked at him incredulously.

"What happened?"

The young man sighed and looked down at his feet.

"I wisth I knew...I remember getting home and crawling up the sthairth...the nexth thing I knew I woke up with my head under the bed and a pain in my mouth."

Ivy stared at him, with her hand on her mouth.

"Doesn't it hurt?" Ivy asked, remembering the screams of pain when John had taken a cricket ball to the mouth, knocking his front tooth clean out.

A sly look came over his face as he reached in his pocket for a blister pack with four large tablets in.

"Theecret rethipee," he said lowering his voice "Trhamadol....I can'th feel anything."

Some more people were coming into the church and he quickly popped the pills away.

"Bride or groom?"

Bill cleared his throat.

"Groom."

They took the order of service and made their way to the left side of the church. Gladys was looking frantically up and down the church and when she saw them, hurried up to Ivy, the lilac dress set off beautifully by her cream hat.

"Oh, there you are, I was getting worried...there's hardly anybody here!"

Ivy looked around her - the church was half full.

"I'm sure people will turn up soon. They have got another half an hour before the bride arrives." she reassured, patting her friends' arm.

Gladys linked her arm with her friend. Ivy felt the tremor from her body through her jacket and squeezed her arm.

"It's going to be fantastic," she stated firmly, "You worry too much."

Gladys managed a weak smile as more guests started to appear. Ivy walked down the aisle and joined Bill, picking some fluff off his shoulder before she sat down. She settled down next to him, linking arms with him affectionately and watched as more guests came in. So many different styles of clothes and so much youth. It had a been a long time since she had been around so many young people and it made her feel alive and on the edge of mortality at the same time - bittersweet. It also made her acutely aware that she missed John and Katy, even though they hadn't got much in common with them anymore. Ivy was determined to enjoy the day and not think too much of anything except the miracle of a young couple getting married. She caught sight of Chris at the door giving her the thumbs up and smiling a goofy smile, the missing tooth making him look like an overgrown baby. She smiled back and settled down for the service.

* * * * *

The wedding had been beautiful; the bride, although dressed in quite a plain dress in Ivy's opinion, still looked radiant. People always said that about brides - 'looked radiant'; the happiness shone out, the hours of makeup and hair styling, turning the ugliest of ducklings into a swan-like beauty. The photographs had taken ages, the best man having disappeared for half an hour so nobody knew what was going on. In the end, it took over an hour for all the photos to be taken by a photographer dressed in jeans and a t-shirt, which surprised Ivy as she thought that Gladys would have had a more formally dressed young man. She later found out he was George's friend from way back and was new to the business, so he was forgiven for wearing such casual attire. He was also fresh enough when dealing with people to ask them nicely and politely if they wouldn't mind being in the next photo. The downside to this was that it took an age to get everyone in position and led to everyone being late for the reception. Bill followed a friend of Ernie's to the reception as he wasn't sure of the route and was irritated that at the traffic lights, the guy went through an amber light, meaning that Bill had to stop and would have no idea where he had gone.

"Can you reach my map? It's behind my seat."

Ivy leaned round, feeling queasy. She hadn't eaten since breakfast and it was now 4.00pm. She located the map just as the lights turned green.

"Oh, where did he go? Could he not have waited five minutes for me to catch him up...can you open it so I can have a look?"

Ivy obeyed and Bill flicked the pages irritably.

Why don't you just pull over and have a look, she thought, knowing that if she said it, he would be even more cross. She waited patiently as he fumbled about.

"It's no use, I shall have to pull over." Bill said, indicating as he came to a turning on the left.

Pulling up, he took the map on his lap and studied it. Ivy looked out of the window, at the houses in the road, wondering who lived behind the net curtains...she liked to imagine all sorts of families living alongside each other. What was that dreadful programme all those years ago, the man with the nasal voice, and the catchphrase 'Who lives in a house like this?' She imagined herself asking the question and then being shown round the house, guessing from the various furnishings what the owners were like.

"Right," said Bill, "I know where I am now. We shouldn't be too late, it's only around the corner."

When they got to the golf course, the car park was full... evidently, people were still playing golf and the club hadn't allowed for the sheer numbers from the wedding. Bill dropped Ivy off and said he would find somewhere to park. She was glad as she was not only ravenous, but desperate for the toilet. Ivy went into the foyer, and was greeted by a waiter with a tray of champagne, smiling at her. She smiled back, and declined the drink, knowing the toilet had to be the first stop.

"Can you tell me where the toilets are, please?"

The waiter looked very concerned, as if he was worried she was about to pee all over the floor, and hurriedly put the tray down.

"It's down here on the left." he replied, guiding her unnecessarily down the corridor, steering her with her elbow.

She smiled as she unhooked herself from him and escaped into the ladies, laughing as she went in. It was very plush, all burgundy and gold; mirrors surrounded her and she saw herself as the young man had seen her...old. It didn't matter that she had nice clothes on, or her best make up. She was old and that meant she was of no use to him, in fact, she might even be a problem, especially if she did wet herself. Ivy went into the cubicle, locked the door and sat down. Sometimes she felt like doing something outrageous, just because she could get away with it, claiming senile something or other to get her off the hook. Pulling off the toilet roll, she gave her nose a good blow before standing up again, relieved. She flushed, tugged her clothing into place and went to unlock the door. For a moment, the lock wouldn't budge and she had visions of herself having to be rescued, and being made to feel daft by the young waiters.

She looked to see if there was some way to climb under or over the top. Her thought process took her on a crazy journey where she got wedged under the door and needed rescuing and then took her over the top, falling from the top of the door and cracking her head open. The thought of the young waiters finding her and bemoaning the extra work made her try harder to find a solution. Ivy tugged the lock again and felt it move slightly. Leaning against the door, she was relieved to see it eased the lock and enabled her to slide it smoothly across. She went to wash her hands, using the soap and the hand cream at the sink, and could tell by the smell it was expensive. Feeling faint, she remembered her hunger. Food was the next thing to sort out, thought Ivy as she opened the door. She was surprised to see the young waiter still in the position she had left him in.

"Oh, I'm glad you are here, I was worried you might have got locked in..."

Ivy looked at him.

"What made you think that?" Ivy bit back.

Not sensing the danger, he breezed on.

"Oh, one of the waitresses said last week the lock was a bit stiff, so I thought, if she is struggling to undo it, you... might..."

His words dried up as he looked at Ivy's face. She was feeling a multitude of emotions and couldn't decide which one to settle on - anger, hilarity, indignation, sadness and pride. She decided on indignation.

"You thought that with my decrepit old hands I might have a job to open the door, did you?"

The boy looked uncomfortable "I didn't mean it like that..."

"No, dear, of course you didn't. Maybe next time, you should think about what you really mean before you say it, hmm? Aaah, here is my decrepit husband to rescue me."

The boy had turned red and rushed forward to offer the tray of champagne. Bill looked fed up and took two as Ivy joined him. They walked into the reception room, a vast palatial affair, thirty feet high with huge chandeliers, the décor gold and cream. The flowers had been brought from the church and were the centrepiece on every table. Everyone was already seated, and chatting to each other, drinking and laughing and Ivy's heart sank as she realised the meal was nowhere in sight. The bride and groom were doing the rounds and chatting to the guests seated at the tables, George had his back to them and Suzie, his new wife, moved towards them, putting out her hand.

"I'm sorry, but I don't know who you are…are you an uncle of George's?" Suzie enquired politely enough, before George turned and seeing them both, guffawed loudly.

"Darling, these are my parent's oldest friends, Ivy and Bill…known each other for years."

"Oh, I'm so sorry…" she started, as Bill raised his hands, holding the champagne aloft.

"Don't be, they're not all that bad!" he chortled and Suzie laughed, revealing a perfect row of white teeth. Ivy smiled faintly and pulled at Bill's elbow to move him over to the seating plan.

He found their names and carried on over to the table, before putting the champagne down. They sat and smiled at the other guests, introducing themselves and then waited for the waitresses to come over. The woman to Ivy's left looked familiar to her and she stared for a few minutes, taking in the clinging red dress, 1920s style headband, with an actual peacock feather sticking out of it and what looked like a fur stole across her shoulders, before realising who she was.

"You're Gladys' sister, aren't you?" whispered Ivy, almost in wonder.

"That's right, darling, I'm Beryl, the crazy one!" she exclaimed wickedly, grinning and showing her catlike teeth.

Ivy continued to stare, this creature before her the myth of legend in the flesh, the older teenage sister who had gone to find her fortune in America, with a man twice her age, disowned by her parents and only the odd postcard turning up every now and then to let them all know she was still very much alive and kicking.

"Surprised to see me?"

"Well, a little, yes." Ivy flustered, trying to be polite.

"It's a wedding, isn't it? It's when all the old, crazy relatives appear, even the ones that everyone thought had died."

"Oh, I knew you were alive. I just thought Gladys didn't see anything of you."

Beryl took out a long cigarette holder and proceeded to put a cigarette into it. Looking again at Ivy, she grinned again.

"She doesn't. But Facebook is a gift, isn't it? I found George and he seemed a sweet boy, keen to make an acquaintance of his aunt." Tapping the end of the cigarette with her fingertip, the woman slyly turned her green eyes on Ivy before adding "It was him who invited me."

Ivy looked amazed at this information and then a new thought came into her head as Beryl got up, gave a little laugh and then looked down at her.

"I know what you are thinking and no, Gladys knew nothing about me coming until I appeared in the church."

With a tinkling laugh, she glided out of the room, clamping the cigarette holder between her teeth and causing every eye to be on her. Gladys was nowhere to be seen and Ivy decided to try and find her. She didn't have to go far. Making her way to the ladies' toilets, she pushed the door open and was met by the unmistakable sound of weeping. One of the stall doors was locked and she stood outside, before gently knocking.

"Gladys? Are you ok?"

The sound of a nose being violently blown came through the door before it was opened to reveal Gladys in a very sorry state, her hat askew, her hair plastered against her head and the makeup that had taken an hour to be expensively applied had run in rivulets, following the deluge of tears.

"Have you seen her? How could she just swan in on George's wedding day, I mean really! So inconsiderate of her, typical Beryl..."

Ivy got some more tissue out of the toilet as fresh tears ambled down Gladys' cheeks.

"I mean, what right does she have? She hasn't seen any of us for twenty years!"

"Well, George did invite her," Ivy offered, but Gladys was too caught up to notice.

"....and then, without warning, she appears on a day that is meant to be so special, all smiles and looking amazing and l-l-lovely and - and so bloody SLIM!"

She used the tissue to mop her eyes as she sobbed, her whole body shaking with rage and Ivy, feeling helpless, put her arm across her shoulders. When the sobs had subsided enough, she spoke gently but firmly.

"You are right. She could have let you know that she was thinking of coming. But she didn't and she is here now and you are going to have to deal with it quickly or ruin your son's special day yourself."

"But it's not fair!"

Ivy caught Gladys' eye in the mirror and stopped the protestations with a look.

"Today is not about Beryl, or how good the food is, or

how lovely the flowers look, it's not even about you." she reminded her friend gently.

A moment of upset passed over Gladys' face but was quickly replaced by guilt, the realisation that Ivy was right.

"What shall I do?" she whispered, her eyes puffy, her cheeks aflame, using the final crumpled remnant of the tissue to dry them off.

Ivy rummaged in her handbag and took out her stick of concealer and red lipstick.

"First of all, we are going to fix your face." she commanded determinedly as Gladys gave a wry smile "It won't be as good as the make-up artist but it will have to do."

She rubbed the concealer between her fingers and got to work, covering the redness and getting the giggles when Gladys closed her eyes and looked so serious.

"What's funny?" barked Gladys opening one eye, reminding Ivy of Basil Fawlty and she leaned against the sink, laughing so hard she began to feel light-headed.

"Why are you closing your eyes, I'm only doing your cheeks!" she giggled, "Here, put the lipstick on yourself."

She handed her the lipstick and felt faint again.

"I need to eat, I'm starving!" she moaned and straightened her hair, ready to go back and join Bill at the table.

"Right, that's better." remarked Gladys, smiling at herself in the mirror. She washed her hands and used the hand cream, twisting her hands vigorously. Turning to Ivy, she said 'Showtime!' before linking arms with her as they went out of the door.

Chapter 5
They Look So Happy

A week after the wedding, Ivy was standing at the kitchen sink, washing up the lunch things and dreaming. It was a reoccurring day dream she had where John had a son and daughter that he dropped off every day at her house to be looked after while he and his wife worked. They were twins of about seven now, having started in Ivy's mind soon after John married, before she found out he couldn't have children. Ivy would have wonderful adventures with them, often seeing them next to her as she went about her daily tasks. Today they were playing on the grass at the front of the house, throwing a ball to each other and calling her to watch them...she could almost hear them. Ivy had never told Bill about them, worried that he might think she was losing the plot...is that what they called it these days? Years ago, it was a woman's nerves that were blamed, women being viewed as weak and in need of smelling salts and bed rest. Now it was all medication and touchy feely counselling and although she had used a counsellor, she had never mentioned the twins, fearful that if she did, she might lose them. And they were doing no harm to anyone, so why shouldn't she imagine them? Bill suddenly appeared rounding the corner of their path with a paper tucked under his arm. She looked at him guiltily and quickly dried her soapy hands on the towel, the children safely stored back in her mind.

"Are you alright? You looked as if you were up to something." he enquired, as he came through the door and hung up his keys and hat.

"Oh no, I am fine, just washing up and wondering what to do for tea."

"Well, look what I have spotted in the paper...on page seven."

Ivy took the paper from him and going into the lounge, sat on the pouffe and opened it to page seven. There was George and Suzie, looking lovely in their wedding clothes, smiling, so happy. She was filled with a warm glow, remembering the feelings she had on the day, people chatting to them, asking advice, showing interest. And the food, so wonderful to have a lovely cooked meal. The jacket potatoes and beans that they would have for tea that night was hardly exciting by comparison.

"Lovely picture, isn't it, pet?" said Bill.

"Yes, they look so happy. It was a wonderful day, so much food and good company...I can't remember the last time I felt so happy."

Bill smiled at her. "I really enjoyed it too. Shame we can't do it more often, free food and all."

Ivy was suddenly looking intently at the paper, a realisation dawning on her face as her mind began to form an idea. She looked at Bill.

"Say that again." she half whispered.

"What?" exclaimed Bill, surprised

"Say what you just said again."

"I said it's a shame we can't do it more often." he repeated, strolling through to the kitchen.

"But we can," countered Ivy, "Look!"

Bill came back in and stood next to her. She turned the paper so that he could see what she was looking at. A list of forthcoming weddings was printed, with details of the venue. Bill looked at her and Ivy smiled.

"What?"

"Don't you see? We could go to one of these weddings! Dress up, claim to be a distant relative, you saw how Suzie didn't know who we were, we could have the whole fun experience again!"

Bill looked at Ivy as if she had gone mad.

"Have you lost your mind? We can't just turn up to every Tom, Dick and Harry's wedding!"

Bill went to put the paper down but Ivy laid her hand on his and took it back. She knew how important it was to get him to see it from her point of view while the idea was still fresh and soft, pliable and able to be worked on and formed into something real. Mustering up her willpower, she mentally grabbed hold of every thread of thought that was floating around and pulled them together to make her case.

"We could go to the weddings and be the elderly relatives that nobody remembers," she stated calmly, opening the page up and studying the names. "We turn up, well dressed, sit in the church for the lovely service, follow another guest to the reception and have a lovely day out."

Bill turned and went into the kitchen. She listened as he filled the kettle up. Looking out of the window, he started to protest.

"But Ivy, how can we? It's dishonest for one thing and if we got caught, we could be in a lot of trouble."

"Think of how happy we felt at George's wedding, so loved, chatting to people we didn't know and yet feeling a part of the family; we both had such a good time."

Bill popped a tea bag in both cups, even though he hadn't asked her if she wanted one. She felt the prickle of irritation round her throat, but mustered the calm she knew she needed to get her own way. It dawned on her what he needed to hear to persuade him.

"Think of the food...a whole days' worth of eating that we won't have to pay for, entertainment, we won't need to go out socially ever again, plus the free alcohol. We would be warm, we could turn the heating off here as we would be out for a whole day and night! You said yourself we have to be careful with our money...well, this is a good way."

Bill still hadn't acknowledged her and focused on the tea. Once he had made it, he put a cup on the table and went into the lounge, muttering 'I don't like the sound of this' and Ivy smiled. He always said it when she had come up with some hare-brained idea that turned out to be a success. She picked up the cup of tea and went into the lounge with the paper. She had some wedding planning to do.

* * * * *

Ivy had worked out when and where the first wedding was to be held. It had to be fairly local so that the fuel wouldn't be too costly, but not so near that anyone would know them. The wedding had been announced in the paper a week ago and she knew she had to get a plan in place so that they were both confident to turn up and chat to people. She sat in her chair in the lounge, looking out of the window, with an open notebook on her lap, chewing the end of the pencil trying to think of how she would get all the information that she needed. Bill came in with the paper and sat down with his cup of tea, looking over at her as she sighed.

"What's the matter?"

"What?" she exclaimed, looking surprised.

"You only sigh like that when you need something," he went on, "So what do you need?"

Ivy sighed again.

"It's just proving more difficult than I thought it was going to," she complained, "I was thinking about all the scenarios that one elderly couple could be at a wedding…maybe elderly neighbours that they have lost touch with? Or old relatives that nobody can remember? How are we going to know their names?"

Bill opened his laptop and began the process of setting it up.

"Pass the paper over here, come on, come and sit with me." he commanded and Ivy travelled over to where he was. He peered over his glasses at the names in the paper and then went onto the Facebook account that John had set up for him, years ago. He typed the name into the search box and found a few dozen results. Picking one he checked on the profile, disregarding it before picking another one and then another one until he found what he was looking for.

"Bingo!" he enthused, "Look, they're friends with someone with the same surname as the bride… so it has to be him, he has to be the right one."

He rubbed his hands together, pleased with himself.

"This is how we will get the info we need, through Facebook and LinkedIn. I've got my profile on there so I can check that out. I haven't used it in ages but I can see if I can find people."

He turned to look at her.

"Don't worry, pet…we'll make it to a wedding!"

Ivy cheered up at this prospect. Suddenly it looked like it was going to happen.

Chapter 6
So Bloody Petty

The sound of the birds singing outside her window were what woke Katy that morning. Nothing remarkable in itself, except that the noise that should have woken her was her alarm clock, set for 6.15am. It was a work day and she needed the time to have a run, to shower, get dressed and eat breakfast. Unbeknown to her, John had come to bed late and found his wife had fallen asleep with her clock radio on - it irritated him that she left it on, regardless as to whether she was listening to it or not and in anger, he had pulled it out at the plug. He was long gone, out for the day to play golf with a colleague and Katy was still blissfully unaware of this development and the ensuing stress she was about to feel once she woke up. She was dreaming; a reoccurring dream that she had woken and was getting dressed, doing up her jacket, her fingers twisting in her sleep. But when she looked at herself in the mirror, she was an old woman and as she opened her mouth, realised she had no teeth. The sensation was so unpleasant she woke suddenly, and using her tongue, made sure her teeth were still in her mouth. She lay there for a moment, disorientated...what day was it? Why was it so light? The birds were loud for this time in the morning. She rolled over to look at the red lit numbers of the clock and stared in disbelief at the vacant impotent screen.

"Oh CRAP!"

She leapt out of bed, the chill of the floor telling her the heating had gone off long ago and swore again, scrabbling in her bag for her iPhone. Swiping the screen, she was horrified to see that it was 9.23 and with fumbling fingers, quickly found her boss' number. She pressed the dial button and putting the phone under her chin with her shoulder, got her clothes out of the wardrobe, laying them out on the bed.

"Good morning, Katy."

"I am so sorry, Martin, my alarm clock didn't go off!"

"That old chestnut.... surely you could have come up with a better one than that?"

Katy held the phone and bent to get her underwear out of the drawer.

"Seriously, I don't know what's happened..."

As she stood up, her eye fell on something not quite right with the familiar scene, a little something out of place. The plug that hung redundant down the side of the bed explained everything. Katy's eyes widened and then narrowed with fury.

"Bastard!" she spat down the line to the unsuspecting Martin, who was in the process of telling her not to worry.

"What's happened? Are you okay?"

Katy picked up the lead dumbly and pushed it back into the wall, the red 00.00 flashing at the connection, fury clouding her vision.

"He bloody well pulled the plug out, the bastard, can you believe that?"

Martin inhaled and went to say something, but Katy ploughed on.

"I mean, he knew I needed it for my alarm, I can't get up without it, I've not got time for a shower, run or anything - aaaargh!"

Katy clenched her jaw together, and sank down onto the bed realising who she was talking to as the silence the other end bounced back at her.

"Martin?"

"I'm still here."

"Sorry, I didn't mean to go on...it's just so frustrating."

She felt deflated, yet furious but suppressed the anger long enough to continue the call.

"Look, get yourself sorted and I will see you when I see you, okay?"

Martin was pitying her and she felt small and awkward. Tears pricked her eyes at his soothing tone and she steadied her voice and swallowed before replying.

"I'll get there as soon as I can and stay late to catch up."

Martin chuckled "Okay, we can chat once you are here."

"Thanks...see you soon."

Katy ended the call and sat on the bed, the rage and indignation beginning to build, causing her stomach to ache. She couldn't believe he had been so thoughtless, so bloody petty! She considered resetting the clock but knew it would take time and that was too precious this morning. Pulling her t-shirt off over her head, she ran to the en-suite and stepped into the shower. Turning it on, not caring how cold it was initially, she got to work soaping herself and washing her hair. Once finished, she nipped across the landing to get a towel from the airing cupboard and not allowing herself the luxury of wrapping it round her, roughly rubbed herself dry. Still damp, she ran around to her side of the bed and grabbed her underwear, pulling it on and growling when it stuck to her skin. By the time she had shimmied into it, she was so angry the tears began and she allowed herself to have a good cry, thankful she hadn't put her makeup on yet. The hurt and disappointment of his actions came flooding into her chest and she put her head in her hands, the coolness of them soothing her pounding head. She knew this was a line in the sand, a moment in time that couldn't be forgiven or swept away... there had just been too many scenarios like this. Catching sight of herself in the full-length mirror, her eyes puffy, her cheeks red, looking quite ridiculous in just her underwear, she stopped crying as quickly as she had started. With a determination that had grown since being with John, she took a makeup wipe and cleansed her face of all upset. Katy pulled out her navy and cream dress, one that screamed 'power dress' and stepped into it, pulling it up and awkwardly fastening the buttons. She put her face cream on and then took her time over her make up. There was no point rushing and she knew that she needed to look good, to try and win the day back, to feel calm. Finishing her make up routine, she grabbed her phone and work bag, and went downstairs. She dumped the bag by the front door, and taking her cream high heels off the chrome rack, slipped them on, the back of one of them catching her corn and she inhaled sharply and forced it on, knowing the pressure would stop as it would distribute itself and settle down. She went into the kitchen and took a banana out of the fruit bowl knowing there wasn't time for cereal. Her coffee, usually decaffeinated, although this morning was likely to be a strong, full caffeine kind, would have to wait until she got to work. As usual, John had left evidence of his presence around the kitchen and she began to get cross as she saw the crumbs, open cupboards and general clutter on the work surfaces. Things needed to change and she was the woman who would start those changes. It couldn't go on like this...

Chapter 7
Mentally Made A Note

Katy was rummaging in her desk for her snack pot. She knew it was still in there as she hadn't finished eating the almonds from last week and was getting hunger pangs. Finding it under her diary, she lifted the box out and onto her desk, opened it and put a couple into her mouth, annoyed at the chewiness of them. She finished typing an email to a new company whose loan had been accepted by the bank and then flicked through her diary. It had started to get dark outside and she had watched her co-workers leave one by one until she thought she was the only one left. The heating had been turned off and looking out into the darkness, she shivered...she could hear the hoover on the floor below that Linda the cleaner was pushing over the carpet and sighed. This was the signal for her to go soon as her room was next to be cleaned and she found the noise too irritating. She got up and bent over to shut down the computer, taking her jacket from the back of her chair. Katy went into the cupboard for her handbag and as she shut the door, was startled to see a man's face looking at her through the glass door of her office. He smiled as he opened the door and she recognised him and smiled back.

"Sorry, I didn't mean to startle you," soothed Luke, the new Coke ad man.

"Th- that's okay," Katy stammered, "I didn't realise anyone else was still here."

Luke grinned.

"I had some typing up left to do for Roger. I can't always get stuff done when there are so many people talking in the office...I've got the attention span of a gnat!"

He smiled easily, revealing a row of pearly white teeth; she doubted he ever drank the Coca Cola like the real Coke ad man. She wondered which of the girls in the office he was with...rumours were already flying around that all the girls fancied their chances with him. Katy suddenly realised that she had been staring at him and not saying anything and that he was now staring intently at her. She looked away, feeling awkward and started to rummage in her bag, talking to but not looking at him.

"Well, I often work late, as there always seems so much to do and not enough hours in the day."

"I know what you mean...the workload here is crazy!"

Katy strode to the door and pulled it open to find Linda making her way up the corridor with the hoover. She held the door as Luke went and helped Linda to wheel it into the room.

"Thanks, love," said Linda in her raspy voice, the result of years containing a sixty-a-day habit.

"You two lovebirds off out together?"

Luke smiled again as Katy started to protest.

"Oh no, we both just so happened to be working late..."

Linda smiled a knowing smile and Luke took his bag from his desk.

"Come along, dear." smirked Luke, strolling down the

corridor towards the lift.

Katy closed her gaping mouth and quickly caught him up as the lift opened. They both got in and, as the doors closed, Luke hit the lower ground button. There followed an awkward silence, one in which Katy began to feel more embarrassed by what had just been said and Luke smiled, enjoying the effect he knew he had on most people. Katy felt hot and opened her top button. She caught Luke looking at her with interest and immediately wished she hadn't met his gaze. Thankfully the phone rang and she answered it quickly, instantly regretting it as John's voice cut through the silence.

"Where the bloody hell are you? I thought you were back at six, I haven't eaten all day and there is sod all in... where are you?"

Katy had turned crimson, the memory of the morning flooding back into her mind, causing her to feel angry all over again. Luke had stopped smiling now and she noticed that bizarrely, he looked annoyed too. The door of the lift opened and they walked through them, out into the foyer.

"Well?" John snapped.

She took a deep breath and levelled her voice.

"Right, well first of all, I am still at work because some arsehole unplugged my alarm clock so that I didn't wake up in time to get to work early and have had to make up my hours. Secondly, if you haven't eaten all day that is your own fault, not mine and thirdly, if you opened your eyes, you will find pasta and a sauce in the cupboard that will be adequate for your tea. Finally, I will be back late tonight as I am going out for dinner, to treat myself....I earn money too, John and if I want dinner out, I am having it...oh, grow up!"

She ended the call and stuffed the phone back into her bag. Luke had walked over to the door and swiped himself out, holding it open as she came and did the same. He looked at her sympathetically.

"Trouble?"

"My husband being his usual self," she smiled bitterly, "He can be a real pain in the backside and seems to enjoy making my life difficult...oh, I don't want to bore you with the details."

Luke looked at her intently again and she had to look away; she felt uncomfortable under the scrutiny of his gaze and couldn't understand why she felt anxious.

"You aren't boring me," Luke countered smoothly, "I could listen to you tell me all your troubles over a drink?"

This threw Katy completely. She hadn't expected him to say this, and she was unsure of how to reply.

"Uh...no, that's very kind of you, but I am fine, really, just moaning as usual."

Luke still held her gaze.

"Well, the offer is there if ever you need a chat. Men can be such bar stewards."

She laughed and again, the anxious flutter in her heart started up.

"Is it ok if I walk you to your car?"

"Of course."

She smiled and started to walk up the road, the cold air of the evening causing her to wrap her scarf round her face. She dug her hands in her pocket and her phone rang again. She saw it was John and gritted her teeth, answering it with a smile.

"Yes? ....no, I said I am eating out.... well, you will have to iron that yourself, won't you? John, I said I will be home late and I won't be ironing at midnight.... I can come back when I like, thank you, I'm not in work tomorrow so, no, I don't have to be back earlier...John please.... don't be like that.... John? John?"

She looked at her phone and saw that he had ended the call. Luke was ahead of her and had stopped by her car. She found it amusing that he knew which car was hers. Another time she would have been perturbed but Luke had made her feel at ease and she realised what the feeling in her chest was...it wasn't anxiety, it was excitement. Luke had asked her for a drink, he seemed to actually like her and even though she wasn't in a position to accept his offer, it made her feel better.

"Thanks, you didn't have to walk me here. I'm quite used to walking up here alone."

Luke smiled again, and shrugged.

"It wasn't a problem and my mum always taught me to be courteous to ladies."

"A lady? After what I just said to my husband? You really don't know me."

He stopped smiling again at the mention of John and Katy immediately wished she hadn't mentioned him; she liked the way he smiled at her.

"He sounds very mean...and he also sounds like he doesn't appreciate you."

Katy sighed and leaned against her car, Luke moving into position so that he faced her.

"He is mean," she said wearily "He does petty things all the time, just to piss me off and then wonders why I don't want to spend time with him."

She felt a spark of something buried deep as he casually moved closer to her and held her gaze.

"You are too good for him."

She laughed and folded her arms against the cold.

"I don't know about that; I can be a cow too I'm sure he would be quick to say."

"I don't believe you...who would call someone as beautiful

as you a cow?"

He almost whispered the words and Katy had to keep her arms folded to stop herself touching him. She could sense something between them, his face seemed closer to her now and the sensation to touch him was overwhelming. He stepped back abruptly and put his hands in his pocket.

"Well, I had better be getting back...bus to catch, cat to feed...see you Wednesday."

He turned abruptly and walked away and she stood and opened the car door. Realising what he had said, she turned around.

"Where do you live?"

Luke who was halfway up the road, turned and looked at her.

"What?"

"Where do you live? I can drop you off, save you getting the bus..."

She couldn't keep the desperation out of her voice... she wanted to spend more time with him. Luke smiled to himself and walked slowly back.

"Only if you are sure. I live in Greenwich."

Katy held the door open for him, having put her bag on the back seat.

"That's fine...I love Greenwich, there's that Greek restaurant near there in Blackheath that does amazing food, so my dinner is sorted."

She laughed and Luke smiled again. Oh, he really is gorgeous when he smiles, she thought as she got in the car, feeling the flutter in her chest at the thought of sitting next to him...get a grip and don't make a fool of yourself...he's just a work colleague, plus he is far too young and you are married, she thought gloomily, concerned that this fact was the last one to come to her mind. Luke began to chat to her easily about himself. She found out on their journey that he plays the piano every day, he lives in a flat with a cat called Jimmy, his father died when he was five and his mother had moved to Yorkshire where she had been born and he visited her every other weekend...the train journey was a pain but he had to see her as they had always been close. No siblings so she was all he had and all she wanted. He went quiet after this conversation and she felt obliged to talk about her life; the friends she had, how she enjoyed keeping fit, something he said he enjoyed too. She flitted over John and talked about how they never saw his parents as it was too painful as there were no grandchildren to share with them. Katy could chat about it now without any tears mainly because the marriage was in such a state, she realised that it would be an awful environment for a child. As she prattled on, she felt Luke watching her in the darkness and found herself feeling good about herself for the first time in a long time. Again, the urge to touch him was there and she was glad she had to drive, that her hands were gripping the wheel. As they neared Blackheath, an idea came into her head that she had at first batted straight out of her mind. She really didn't want to eat alone but couldn't ask him to eat with her, having refused to have a drink with him; what would it look like if she wanted to eat with him? As if he could read her mind, he asked if she could drop him off by the chip shop.

"I can't be bothered to cook and I can eat them walking home."

She pulled up on the green and turned to look at him.

"You can't walk all that way."

"I can, I often do it."

"I don't doubt that, but I would feel bad about not getting you back to your flat and to Jimmy."

Luke gathered his bag onto his lap and turned to smile at

her again.

"Ah, then we have a problem. I need to eat and you need to drop me off. I suppose you could wait while I order them and then drop me home?"

"What like a taxi service? What a cheek!"

"No no, of course not," he stammered hastily, "I just meant..."

Katy laughed, "It's okay, I'm only kidding. I quite fancy fish and chips myself. If you order me some, I can drop you off and then sit in the car, overlooking the green eating mine."

Luke stopped and turned to her with an incredulous look on his face.

"I wouldn't expect you to do that, you can eat in my flat. Save you getting into a mess in the car."

She went to protest and he stopped her by raising his hand.

"Don't be daft, I'll get the fish and chips and you can join me in my humble flat to eat them. I only wished I had tidied it up now. If I had known you were coming..."

He got out of the car and crossed the road to the fish and chip shop. She laughed and relaxed again...eating fish and chips seemed innocent enough. It wasn't like she was going out for a meal with him; her only concern was what she would tell John. She could say she had dinner with a work colleague but then he might ask questions about it and she wouldn't be able to lie and it wouldn't sound good; 'I had fish and chips in a young, good-looking man's flat.' No, she would have to brush over it and pretend she had eaten alone. It wouldn't be that hard. She looked out into the dark sky. Katy often felt a sense of wonder at the world around her, looking at the stars, feeling insignificant and yet singled out at the same time. Not tonight though. She couldn't quite put her finger on what she felt, trying not to feel anything and keeping it cool and relaxed but the fluttering in her chest wouldn't stop and she knew she was going to have to keep herself steady so that she didn't embarrass herself. She could see Luke in the shop, waiting to get the food. When he was out there, she could think clearly and be realistic... but in his presence, she felt out of control and unable to hold it all together. She decided that once she had eaten, she would leave straight away, that way, she wouldn't make a fool of herself and she could always say she had work to do, to catch up on. She watched as Luke came out of the shop, holding the door open for a young woman going in. He flashed a smile at her and the woman smiled back. Katy was shocked to feel a spurt of jealousy shoot up into her throat, the strength of her feelings causing her utter dismay... she couldn't be in this deep already, surely? Luke opened the door and sat heavily on the seat, his aftershave wafted across to Katy, causing her another wave of dismay.

"Sorry, it took forever! I got large cod for both of us, is that okay? Are you alright?"

Katy swallowed and forced a smile "Yes, fine, just a bit tired...where do I need to go?"

Luke directed her to his flat which was part of a street full of large ornate houses. They pulled up outside his and he got out, carrying the food and his bag. Katy got out and took her bag off the back seat. Locking the car, she was touched that Luke waited for her to join him before walking off. How long had it been since John had done that? They walked up to the front door and Luke got out his keys. Holding them in his mouth, he found the right one and opened the door. Katy followed him in and noticed how tidy and minimalistic his flat looked.

"Go on through while I get some plates." he suggested,

heading left into the kitchen. She went right into the lounge and was greeted by Jimmy, walking up and rubbing her legs. She bent down to stroke him, while looking around at the décor; one wall painted blood red, the others cream, the high dado rail and small, mock chandeliers gave it a regal feel. A piano was in one corner, a double sofa in another. Katy realised, with a sense of dread that there was nowhere else to sit, that she would have to sit next to him and began to feel uneasy. She didn't really know him and now she was in his flat. She jumped as he appeared at the door, looking bemused.

"Jimmy, leave her alone, you tart."

He swept the cat up and holding him, looked at her in his disarming way, smiling and relaxed. "Would you like to eat at the table in the kitchen? Probably be easier - and I have a bottle of Shiraz which would go well."

Katy smiled and relaxed again. She was being daft. Luke was a nice bloke who was being kind to a work colleague - she couldn't believe how silly she was being. She accepted a glass of the Shiraz and sat at the little IKEA dining table in his kitchen. The kitchen itself was huge, with black units and granite surfaces that sparkled under the light and a huge wall mural of a city skyline, simply done with a marker pen, but very effective.

"Did you do that?" Katy pointed at the wall politely as he set out the food on two plates.

"I wish," he said, "It was already here when I moved in. Cheers!"

Luke raised his glass and she clinked hers against it, feeling foolish at her earlier thoughts. He was a lovely young man and was being very kind to her. She ate without feeling self-conscious and realised how hungry she was, grateful that he had bought large cod and chips. They ate in relative silence, and having eaten her food, she leant back in her chair and drank her wine. He chatted about the journeys he had made to see his mum and was very comical about the other passengers, making her laugh. He kept looking at her, keeping eye contact and she enjoyed the thrill it gave her to have someone to talk to, to listen to and to laugh with. He filled her glass with more wine and she mentally made a note not to have any more but as the evening went on, the wine glass never seemed to empty and after she got up to go into the lounge, the room took a while to catch up with her eyes and she realised she had had too much. Steadying herself, she went and sat on the sofa, as Luke crossed the room and put on some music and she was surprised to hear Shania Twain coming out of the speakers.

"Oh, I love this song..." she murmured, leaning back into the sofa.

Luke got their wine glasses and brought them through, before going back for another bottle of wine.

"I can't have anymore...", she said, looking up at him, "I have to drive home..."

"Well, technically, you don't have to."

"What?" she replied, feeling fear, excitement, and hope all at the same time.

He moved across the room and sat down next to her.

"Look, I'm going to be honest...I really, really like you. I know you're married, but he sounds like a right idiot who doesn't deserve you."

Katy looked at him and couldn't quite believe her ears...he fancied her! And she realised she fancied him!

"You can stay here the night. I'm not in tomorrow."

"Neither am I," said Katy at once, the alcohol speaking, "But what will I tell John?"

Luke smiled the confident smile of someone who knows

they can get what they want. He moved his arm along the back of the sofa round Katy's shoulders. It felt so natural to Katy that she moved into him, feeling his warmth through his shirt and relishing it; it felt so good to be wanted, to be close to him.

"Tell him anything you like.... just please stay with me."

He drew towards her and she kissed him, releasing the pent-up feelings that had bugged her all evening. He quickly undressed, still kissing her and although she couldn't believe it was happening, it also felt like the most natural thing to do. Lying in his arms hours later, the euphoria was being replaced by anxiety, gnawing at her chest; what was she going to say to John?

Chapter 8
The Bitterness of the Grains

John sat looking at his prawn sandwich, thinking how strange a prawn looked when it was naked, unclothed from its hard shell and dangly legs. He bit into the sandwich, enjoying the creamy taste of the mayonnaise, forbidden fruit as Katy wouldn't buy it, regardless of whether he liked it or not. His thoughts turned to her and he had a sense of something not quite right, a change in her, a subtle shift that he couldn't quite put his finger on. He took another bite and was cross to feel a prawn, in a bid for freedom, fall out of the sandwich and into his lap, which had a serviette on it, so at least his trousers were protected. From being a little boy, his mum had always encouraged him to put something over his legs and it was a habit that had stuck. Taking hold of the escapee, he popped it into his mouth, wiping his fingers on another serviette still on the table, the thought of his mum and the countless trips out for lunch in the local café making him feel strangely nostalgic. John quickly put his focus back on to Katy and the difference in her, trying to work out when he had first noticed it. He thought back and managed to pinpoint it; the day he had played golf and she had to work late. Initially he thought she was just tired, or working too hard but the feeling she exuded wasn't really a negative one. She almost seemed happier since the awful phone call where they had shouted and sworn at each other. Having wiped his mouth again, he picked up his cup, the coffee now lukewarm. Maybe she needed to get it off her chest and now she was okay. She certainly seemed happier and he put it down to the fact that she now went to yoga twice a week. It was to his advantage as she had certainly been nicer to him.

John finished the sandwich and sat chewing, deciding not to keep thinking about Katy having persuaded himself that she was ok. His focus had to be on work, the endless meetings, working late, even his meals spent networking. He sighed, knowing that this was the cost of being an MP, the long hours and being challenged at every turn. Having been in the position of Head of Family Values for a year, he had already helped to bring in changes. Free school meals for more children, child tax credits for families in the lower bracket of working class and free nursery places for the children of single mums. This particular policy galled him and he swallowed the last of his coffee, the bitterness of the grains at the bottom of the cup causing him to grimace. He had met too many young girls in his constituency that saw a life of living alone with a baby as a career choice, everything paid for by others and complaining when they didn't always get what they wanted. He had visited estates and set up meetings with the residents on the playing field and seen the disgruntled faces of young women, bloated with junk food and alcohol, puffing on cigarettes and moaning about everything. One of them had shouted at him about the state of the local park, how the swings had been out of action for months and every surface was covered in obscene graffiti and what was he going to do about it? He had forced a smile and in true Walter Mitty style, told her to stop blowing smoke in his face, stop spending money on takeaways and get some exercise and reminded her how it wasn't so long ago that it was her trashing the park and writing graffiti on everything and finally how her baby in the buggy who was already obese, drinking a bottle of sweetened tea, face covered in grime, would grow up to do exactly the same, if not worse things.

In reality, he spoke soothingly, saying that children's play equipment was of the utmost importance to him, that children deserved to have time out in the fresh air, playing and running around and that he would do everything in his power to get things like this fixed. She eyed him with the usual look of scepticism that accompanied many of his meetings within his constituency and stalked off, no doubt to discuss his plans with her so-called friends, the type who said one thing to her face and then talked about her in the unkindest way behind her back. Jeremy Kyle had a lot to answer for. John suddenly became aware of the woman behind the counter staring at him and he hastily collected up his stuff, papers and notes that he had to look through before going to the House of Commons the next day. He hadn't even opened them up, and chastised himself for thinking about things that he couldn't change and in truth, didn't want to change...these things didn't affect him, childless as he was and he couldn't help but feel that a lot of these problems were due to poor life choices, people not wanting to stop the rot and get out of the poverty cycle. Glancing back, he saw again that the woman was staring at him and this time she smiled. John smiled back and went to leave.

"Excuse me," she asked, smiling almost apologetically "But are you the MP of Heningford?"

He smiled back, trying to be positive externally and yet

inside bracing himself.

"Yes, that's my constituency."

She looked relieved and carried on.

"I just wanted to thank you. My sister came to speak to you recently about the state of the park."

John groaned inwardly at what he thought was coming next, but then remembered she had started by thanking him.

"And because of your new policy about nursery places, she has put Brandon into nursery three days a week and volunteered at the council to keep the park tidy. Because of her determination, they have offered to fix the swings and she has used the graffiti removing machine to clean it up."

Swallowing, his words came out as a rush of relief.

"Oh, that's wonderful, I am so glad she has had a chance to do something worthwhile."

John smiled as he left, clutching his briefcase. Maybe he was doing some good after all.

Chapter 9
Disappointing-Looking Cheesecake

The day they were caught had started as ordinarily as the wedding days often did. The sun was bright, Ivy had the usual flutter of excitement in her chest and a new outfit was laid out on the bed. The only difference was the day of the week. It was a Friday, which from their point of view, was a strange day for a wedding. Bill was looking at the map to work out where he had to go and where to park. That way he wouldn't need to talk to too many people, he would just look like he knew where he was meant to be. Ivy changed into the new outfit, bought with the money they had saved on food and heating and was quite relaxed about the whole thing. She could never understand why Bill got so stressed about it, they were having a wonderful time. She particularly enjoyed listening to the real-life situations of other families and saw herself as a bit of an agony aunt, giving advice to a variety of people; women who were unhappy in their marriage, men who hated their jobs and even children who were trying to make sense of their parents' separation. This she found particularly hard as she had no experience and had to rely on what she had read in magazines and heard on Radio 4 documentaries. Generally, she tried to make the child feel good about themselves and explain that it wasn't their fault, these things just happened. She finished getting ready and came down the stairs, taking care not to stumble in her new shoes. It felt wonderful to be able to afford nice things again and she smiled at Bill, sitting at the table studying the map, feeling that at last, things were going well for them.

"Right, I've worked out the route...shouldn't take more than forty minutes along the back roads and then we can park in the pub car park opposite the church."

"That's good, not too far and a very nice place to go. I've heard golf club receptions are really swanky. I wonder if the food will be a sit-down meal again like last time...that minted lamb was so good, wasn't it?"

Bill closed the map abruptly and got up from the table.

"Alright, don't get too carried away, we haven't even got there yet!"

She noticed the strangled tone and looked at him sharply; he was very pale and his forehead was beaded with sweat.

"What's the matter? You don't look too bright."

Looking out of the kitchen window, Bill pulled his tie out and undid the top button of his shirt.

"I don't feel too clever." he said, staring out and then turned to look at her, "I have a bad feeling about today."

Ivy couldn't keep the annoyance from out of her voice.

"What do you mean 'a bad feeling'? You always feel twitchy beforehand and are fine when you get there."

"I know, but...it just feels wrong, like we are lying all the time."

She crossed over to him and took the tie from his trembling hands.

"Look...we're not lying, it's just a game, you know that really. I know you worry about getting caught. I did wonder whether we could really do it but you have to admit, it is such good fun, meeting people and eating lovely food. We are really living again, instead of just surviving. I don't want to go back to scrimping and saving."

Bill still looked dubious as she started to put his tie on again. She knew what she needed to say to get him on board.

"Let's just go for the drive then," she suggested, finishing his tie and brushing off his shoulders, "We could head over that way and see how you feel when we get there. If you don't feel great, we could pop in the pub for a drink and come home, whereas if you feel better, we can go in the church...okay?"

"Alright, as long as you listen to me. If I say I'm not feeling too good, we leave, no questions asked."

She smiled as he went through to the lounge to close the curtains, a sure sign that he thought they would be out until it was late. Little did she know how much she would appreciate the curtains being closed when they came back hours later...

* * * * *

John had been sat at his desk for most of the morning trying to decide which of the new policies would get his backing. He had been given them to look at yesterday, but had managed to avoid reading them through by tidying up his drawers and having a long lunch. Scanning the papers quickly, he felt lukewarm about them; food bank vouchers being allocated to the neediest families, more youth workers wanting financial support and the rights of fathers in custody battles. His people had talked to the policy makers people and meeting after bloody meeting had been set up, each one headed up by a person passionate for their cause. He had learned to move his head and murmur in a non-committal way, with a serious look on his face as if he was listening intently when actually, he was thinking about all sorts of things. In the midst of conversations, his mind would wander off...what was for dinner tonight, what day was it, was Katy out at yoga this evening, why did vegetarians all look the same, weedy and almost apologetic for having to breathe the same air as everyone else, wearing grey clothes that matched their complexion. When things became tense, as they often did when people got passionate about their cause, he imagined himself reacting like Basil Fawlty and having a complete meltdown, ranting at them, and being witty and sarcastic. Outwardly, he just resorted to asking for a written report of all he had just listened to so that he could make an informed choice, the meeting a complete waste of time, but one that he was well paid for and therefore happy to attend.

He got up and walked round the desk to his window. Looking out over London still gave him a sense of pride, as if he was responsible for the way the city kept moving... he noted the sky, a troubled grey, threatening rain...typical. Peering down, noting the taxis and buses, the busy roads of London full of people rushing to God knows where. He wished he was in one of those taxis, being driven away, anywhere but here, then thought of his parents and checked himself...maybe not just anywhere. John couldn't think about them without feeling a mixture of anger, sadness, guilt and hard-heartedness, in equal measure. When was it that you stopped enjoying spending time with your parents? Had he really laughed and joked with them as a teenager, played squash with his dad, washed up with his Mum? When had his middle-aged father become a stuffy, overbearing bore, who only asked about how well his car was running? Or his mother become the anxious, shallow mouse of a woman, who didn't dare say anything that might upset him? John knew it all coincided with Katy marrying him and the realisation for everyone that children were not an option. He hadn't realised how much his parents wanted, no, actually expected them to appear and how difficult it would be to continue seeing them and having such shallow interactions, his mother-

"Excuse me, sir?"

John almost bumped his head on the window, as he was so deep in thought and unaware of anyone coming into the room. He spun round and saw another new intern standing by his open door, looking nervous.

"Yes? What is it?" he snapped sharply, his throat tight and strangulated.

"It's just that the guys are here to discuss the new policies, the meeting starts in half an hour...?"

The policies, of course. He walked back to his desk and sat down, taking up the papers again, ignoring her. She stood, awkwardly, unsure of what she should do or say next and could feel her face going red at the thought of him suddenly looking up and seeing her there. In the end, she just quietly closed the door. John passed his hands wearily across his eyes knowing that there was at least a two-hour meeting to be dealt with. Thinking of the policies, he decided to settle on the foodbank vouchers, feeling that people must be pretty desperate to need to go to a foodbank and at least it wasn't money that could be spent on cigarettes or alcohol.

* * * * *

Ivy smiled smugly as the bride and groom walked out of the church. The wedding had gone by without a hitch. She wondered why people said that they were 'getting hitched' regarding marriage - was there a link to everything going without a hitch? She should look it up when she got home, give it a googley, or something like that. Bill understood computers and would help her look things up. She had heard an interesting programme on Radio 4 about the importance of keeping up with technology, using your brain to stay young and focused, even mentioning a certain type of fish oil that helped your brain work better...maybe there was a link to evolution or something. Ivy was suddenly aware that the church had emptied and Bill had also disappeared. She hurriedly got to her feet and went to the doors of the church. They were locked. Panic stricken, she turned to go to the side door; this too was locked. She could feel a prickle of sweat make its way down her back, causing a shudder across her shoulders. Where did everybody go? Who locks a church at a wedding? And where the flipping heck was Bill? She looked up at the crucifix, at Jesus looking down on her and she felt guilt and fear. Serves you right, her inner voice told her, you shouldn't even be here and now you are trapped! The panic began to rise again and she moved towards the main door. Perhaps it was just stiff, she reasoned and tried to open it.

It didn't budge.

In despair, she turned away and was about to sit on a pew when a familiar voice the other side of the door said, "I'm dreadfully sorry, Father, I can only assume she is still in there..."

Bill! The relief washed over her as the key was turned in the lock and bright sunshine flooded in as the door was pushed open. Bill looked sheepish and the vicar looked bemused as Ivy rushed out as fast as her wobbly legs would allow her to.

"There you are! I was looking everywhere for you!" chortled Bill and put out his arm for Ivy to link up. She gratefully took it and turned to the vicar.

"I am sorry for the trouble I caused." she said contritely.

The vicar gave a tight smile.

"No harm done." he muttered in a voice that sounded like he would have liked to do some harm.

Just then, the chief bridesmaid came marching around the corner and, seeing the vicar, stopped abruptly.

"What is the hold up? The bride wants a photo with you, Vicar and if we don't take one soon, we will be late for the reception!"

"We had a slight mishap with one of the guests." he informed her, looking at Ivy, who blushed. "I just need to lock up the church again and then I'll be over."

The irate young woman regarded Ivy with distaste and then turned and flounced off, the beauty of the claret dress lost in the shadow of her face, clouded with a scowl. They went to stroll off, but then Ivy stopped and turned suddenly.

"Ooh, can I ask...why do you lock the doors of the church?"

The vicar's face darkened.

"Because there has been a spate of burglaries in the local area and other churches have had metal and ornaments stolen...even the candlesticks have to be locked up."

He turned to lock the doors again and grumbled "Thieving bastards!"

Stifling a giggle, Ivy and Bill made it to their car before she collapsed into the front seat, laughing to the point of tears, Bill using his handkerchief to wipe his brow, chuckling away to himself. As he drove to the reception, he explained that after the service, he had needed the loo and as everyone seemed to be outside on the grass taking photos, he assumed she had gone too... after ten minutes of looking, he realised she wasn't there and tried to go back in the church and found it locked. It took him a while to persuade the vicar that there really was somebody in the church and that he wasn't an old man who had an imaginary wife. The laughter had relaxed them and they both began to look forward to the next part. Ivy hoped it would be a sit-down meal as she was feeling very hungry. As they pulled into the golf course, the sheer size of it amazed her. Grass as far as the eye could see and the golf club, a vast, new building which the owner had obviously known would get used for weddings. It was very ornate, with stone steps leading up to the front entrance and a privet hedge lining the walkway. The windows were tall and she could see that the guests were already sitting down at the tables. Bill parked the car and started to go to open her door, but she beat him to it, even forgetting to swing her legs around in her haste to get out quickly. She took his arm as they walked up the stone steps, and he received it, all the while muttering to her the details of their deceit.

"I am an old friend of the bride's father. His name is George, calls himself Georgie, started out as a window cleaner and is now a self-made millionaire."

"Where did you get all that info from?"

Bill smiled and patted her hand.

"I found him on LinkedIn. It's all there, bio of his life and he has so many contacts and clients, we can tell his daughter that's how we know him."

Ivy stopped and looked at him just before they went in.

"What about my connection? If his wife..."

"Debbie" cut in Bill.

"Right, so if Debbie asks how I know her daughter...what do I say?"

"You are her old English teacher from uni ...you made a big impression on her...it amazes me what people put on Facebook."

"Let's get in there then."

She smiled and went through the doors. A table with champagne laid out on it was set up outside the main hall and a waitress smiled and offered them one.

"Thank you." gushed Ivy, taking a swallow and feeling refreshed and cosy at the same time. There was a seating plan attached to a flip chart to the left of the door into the great hall. Ivy felt a stab of fear but only because it was going to be a little bit more difficult than a free-for-all sit where you like. She looked at Bill who took control by taking their champagne glasses and putting them back on the table.

"Do you need help finding your place?" suggested the waitress brightly.

Mild irritation flicked across Bills face, but he smiled as he took Ivy's arm.

"No, thank you...could you tell us where the toilets are, please?"

"Oh, of course, just down the corridor and on the left."

Bill thanked her and they followed her directions. When she was out of earshot, Bill leant and spoke quietly to Ivy.

"Go in there for ten minutes. I will pop out after five and see if there are any spare seats. If not, we will have to leave."

"Oh." Ivy couldn't help being disappointed.

"I'm sure there will be, there's always some that don't turn up on the day..."

She wandered into the toilet, no longer amazed at the beauty of the architecture, not stopping to look in the abundance of mirrors and found an empty stall. Locking the door, she put the seat down and sat on it, feeling despondent, hungry and a little queasy...she wished she hadn't drunk the champagne so quickly. She heard the door go and the sound of two women coming in, laughing before they went into the other empty stalls. Ivy decided to stay in until they had gone. She couldn't help but hear their conversation.

"At least it was sunny for them."

"Oh yes, nothing worse than rain on your wedding day."

Ivy tutted under her breath; there were plenty more things that were worse than this, she thought and then flushed the toilet, meaning she only just caught the end of the conversation.

"But they won't be coming to the meal, I mean, fancy not coming to a wedding when it's as posh as this!"

"How daft...what was their problem?"

"Oh, they thought their precious daughter should have been invited too, but numbers were tight so it was meant to just be them."

The toilet flushed and Ivy heard both the women come out and go to wash their hands.

"People are so fickle, aren't they? And expect too much, I mean they were only neighbours, it's not like they were relatives or anything."

"The worst thing is, they didn't tell them, they just haven't turned up."

The women left and Ivy opened her door, and found herself looking in the mirror. She smiled at herself and then went out to find Bill. He came forward and met her.

"I said ten minutes!"

"Listen! Some old neighbours haven't turned up, something to do with a misunderstanding. Quick, check the seating while the waitress isn't nosing about."

They crossed over to the seating plan and found the two seats without a tick by the names written next to them and Ivy memorised them both; Julian and Sandra Holmes, the stroppy neighbours who had provided them with a chance to join the party. Ivy went to go in, but Bill pulled her sleeve back towards him.

"You need to remember your name...Sandra, not Debbie anymore. Let me go first," he warned, "I want to make sure we won't be noticed after the kerfuffle back at the church."

He went in, pleased that the meal had already started as everybody was too busy eating and chatting to one another to notice an elderly couple walk in. He scanned the room and spotted the two spaces tucked away in the corner. They made their way over and sat down, Ivy taking off her jacket and putting it on the back of the chair. She was pleased to see that there was a young woman sitting next to her and Bill had a little boy next to him, so chatting about themselves wouldn't be too much of a problem. The waitress came over to them, with a clipboard, smiling.

"Oh, Mr and. Mrs Holmes, isn't it?"

Bill nodded and Ivy smiled.

"Can you remember what you ordered?"

Bill suddenly looked panicked and began to splutter, but Ivy jumped in.

"Oooh, no, it was so long ago," she exclaimed brightly, glancing down at the plates around her and spotted a red coulis and a half-eaten pâté and toast.

"I think I went for the melon and, did you go for pâté, dear?"

Bill had recovered his voice and said "Yes, I believe I did."

The waitress wrote something down and said, "I'll get those for you now," before heading back to the kitchen. Ivy smiled at Bill, who was too busy eating his roll to notice. She was glad that he had relaxed enough to eat. The young woman next to her caught her eye and smiled shyly. Ivy thought she could discern a sadness about her, even that she had been crying recently, but before she could say anything, the woman spoke to her in a gentle voice.

"Did you get stuck in the traffic?"

Ivy remembered just in time that they had turned up late and began her story.

"Oh yes, well it's quite a distance from Wales...we left at five o'clock this morning and had to stop. My husband has to take his blood pressure tablets, so we had to eat something."

The woman looked uncertainly at Bill who was stuffing his face and Ivy patted her arm "He does like to eat...it's linked to his health."

The waitress was back with the starters and Ivy tucked in to her melon. The table was laid out beautifully, the colours of the wedding, white, claret and gold reflected in the flowers, napkins and table decor. With all the weddings she had been to, she was surprised at how no two weddings had been the same. The room had a high ceiling with what looked like crystal chandeliers hanging down, the magnolia walls providing a lovely backdrop for any colour. Ivy looked across at Bill who was telling the little boy a joke. He seemed pleased to have the old man's attention and Ivy felt a little stab of sadness that there were no grandchildren in their lives to tell jokes to. The last piece of melon got caught on the lump in her throat and she coughed it back up to chew some more. The woman looked alarmed and then relieved as Ivy smiled at her. Finishing, she pushed the plate away and picked up the cloth napkin and wiped her mouth and hands.

"The service was lovely, wasn't it?"

The woman spoke again, haltingly and unsure of herself and Ivy noticed she was twisting her napkin on her lap as she spoke.

"Yes, weddings are such fun, aren't they...unless you are a child, I suppose and then they are dull."

The woman smiled, her teeth yellow against the paleness of

her skin, her eye makeup, more noticeable now that Ivy was looking at her squarely, poorly put on as if she had been in a hurry. The hair was thin and lank, hanging down the side of her elfin face and the word poverty hung over her, like a dark cloud.

"Is he your little boy?" asked Ivy gently, motioning to where Bill was blowing a tiny pot of bubbles across the face of the lad next to him, making him laugh and clap his hands.

An array of emotions passed over the woman's face as she glanced across at him...love, pride, fear and anger.

"Yes, Dylan is my boy...he is a good lad, never any trouble to me...plays football and with his cars...he is a good little soul, really."

The sadness came back again and she looked defeated. Ivy was dying to ask what was wrong, but the waitress chose that moment to clear the plates away and it seemed impolite to keep talking. When she had gone, the woman opened her handbag and took out her phone. Frowning at it, she flicked her finger on the screen and became absorbed in her virtual world. Ivy reached for the water jug and poured herself a glass. Taking a swig, she was pleased to see the waitress come back with what looked like two plates of lamb shank.

"Aaah, this is for you two." she stated, setting them down in front of the woman and reaching across to Bill.

Turning to Dylan, she asked "And did you order the chicken?"

He looked at his mother, who nodded and he nodded too.

"I'll get that for you and bring your vegetarian dish."

She directed this statement to Ivy who had to cover her indignation with a look of concentration, as if she was remembering choosing this option. The woman looked uncomfortable again.

"I hope you don't mind me sitting next to you."

"What?" snapped Ivy, forgetting the fragility of the woman in her irritation.

The woman looked wary.

"Because I'm eating meat, what with you being a vegetarian and everything."

Ivy recovered herself and managed a little smile.

"Oh, no, don't worry, it's not about the animals. I just fancied a change, that was all."

The waitress came back with the little boy's chicken and a jacket potato with salad for Ivy. The woman was still looking at Ivy, who was fed up by now and took her plate less than graciously and tried to catch Bill's eye. But Bill was absorbed with cutting up the chicken for his little companion and didn't notice her glaring at him until he was halfway through his meal, by which time, it was too late to swap. Ivy ate her potato miserably, and picked at her salad. She had been so hungry and the weeks of eating rich meals had an effect on her that she wasn't even aware of - becoming selfish, picky, only wanting the best, justifying her thinking and behaviour with the reasoning that they were taking a risk every time they turned up at a wedding, so the food, wine and company better be good and make up for it. The woman picked at her meal and Ivy couldn't help wishing she would just eat it and not waste such a sumptuous meal. She decided to make conversation again.

"Are you not feeling hungry?"

The woman was startled and looked up suddenly and then back down at her plate.

"Oh...not really. I've got a lot on my mind."

Ivy wiped her mouth on the serviette and went into agony aunt mode. Leaning forward, she spoke in a low voice.

"What's going on that makes you feel so sad?"

The woman looked surprised.

"How do you know?"

Ivy couldn't help feeling the pride creep through her at getting it right.

"I can sense it, dear...you wear your sadness like a cloak." Was that a line from Mrs Doubtfire she thought before continuing, "Can I help in any way?"

The woman looked uncertain and Ivy went on.

"Sometimes it's good to get it off your chest."

The woman sighed and fiddled with her meat again.

"It's Dylan's dad...we split up when he was a baby. I'd just been diagnosed with post-natal depression and he didn't think I was giving him enough time."

Ivy settled back in her seat, tutting at the appropriate moment and getting more annoyed with Dylan's dad as she went on.

"Well, anyway, I hadn't heard anything from him for years, not a card for his birthday or Christmas, nothing. Dylan turned five in January this year and a card came...it was from Lewis, his dad, and said that one day, he could come and live with him."

Ivy interjected "Maybe when he is older, yes, he can choose to, but do you really think he would choose a stranger over his mother?"

She was shaking her head and tears appeared in her eyes.

"You don't understand...he isn't talking about in the future, he wants him now. I got a letter from a solicitor, telling me that Lewis is taking me to court... he wants custody of his son, because I am an unfit mother!"

The desperation spilled out of her mouth and she started to sob, using the serviette to mop her tears.

Ivy was aghast. "He can't do that, he left you and when you were poorly too, so mean!"

The wretched woman dried her face and her despair became evident.

"That's just it though - his case is based on the fact I had to go on medication to help me through my post-natal depression. A mentally-ill mother isn't a good basis for looking after a child, there's still so much stigma."

"But surely a judge will see that you have worked hard to bring him up" Ivy said, looking over to Dylan, who was now playing with a toy car, driving it on the table, while Bill made a road out of knives.

"Look out for the fork in the road!" chortled Bill, guffawing at his own joke, while Dylan just grinned, unsure of the joke but liking the old man's attention.

The woman put her hands in her lap and smiled sadly.

"It doesn't work like that; the judge doesn't know me or Dylan and will go on the evidence on the day and I can't afford to defend myself - it costs thousands. I just don't know what to do, I can't lose him, it would break my heart!"

Ivy was surprised at her depth of feeling for this woman. She wished she could solve the problem, fix it, do something, anything to make it right. They sat in silence as the dessert was brought out, a disappointing-looking cheesecake, but Ivy was past feeling excited about anything. She looked again as Dylan, who had tired of playing, got down and climbed onto his mummy's lap, wrapping his arms around her neck and snuggling in. Ivy felt helpless as she put the first mouthful of cheesecake into her mouth, the bland dense filling sticking to her palate, making her feel queasy. She pushed the plate away and took a swig of water, all the while watching Dylan and his mother, talking to each other, whispering in ears and cuddling. An idea was forming in her mind and at first, she disregarded it, knowing that she couldn't get too involved with people at weddings where she wasn't technically meant to be, but her humanity and compassion were stronger and, in the end, she spoke out.

"Listen...is there some way that I can help? Could I support you by coming to the court, showing that there are others on your side?"

The woman looked flummoxed.

"But...you don't even know me...would you really do that for me?"

Ivy smiled. "Of course, I can't stand it when things are not fair and this is definitely not fair!"

Ivy took her handbag from the floor and having abandoned the cheesecake, rooted around for a scrap of paper and a pen. She put her name and phone number on the paper and handed it to the woman, who gratefully received it. Dylan had gone back to sit with Bill again and Ivy smiled again at the picture of him with a young boy, reminding her of Johnny and the close bond they had shared throughout his childhood.

She suddenly became aware of some movement in the corner of her eye, not a commotion, more a sense that something was wrong. Ivy glanced over and her stomach lurched; a policeman, standing by the door was looking over at her table, the chief bridesmaid in animated conversation with him, pointing at her, the malice visible even with the distance. The waitress who had served them was at his other side nodding in agreement. Ivy felt the cold fear of exposure creep across her back and she quickly looked at Bill. He was making a boat out of the serviette, oblivious to the impending doom.

"BILL!" she hissed, making him jump. He looked up sharply and saw the fear and anger on her face just before the policeman appeared at their table. He looked shocked to see him and just stared as the policeman reeled off his patter.

"Hello there, I've had a call from a member of the public regarding your presence here...is there somewhere we can go to have a chat?"

Dylan looked up in awe, having never seen a real policeman before. His mother found her tongue before Ivy could reply.

"What's the problem? What have they done wrong?" asked Dylan's mum, surprised at this intrusion.

Ivy felt sick and tried to stand, her jelly legs causing her to flop back down again. Bill had beads of sweat appearing on his forehead and took out his cravat to mop it. The policeman smiled firmly "Nothing to worry about."

"They're impostors!" shouted the chief bridesmaid, appearing from behind him, relishing her moment in the spotlight, "They don't even know the bride or groom. I checked with them, they've just turned up! That's fraud!"

The mania of being right gleamed in her eyes and she looked in triumph at the guests around the table. The room had fallen silent and all eyes were on the old couple, trying desperately to get up and out. Bill managed to stand but Ivy was having trouble breathing now as well as her legs giving way and she felt like crying.

"There's nothing wrong with you" spat the bridesmaid, "You were walking fine when you came in here."

The policeman, who was used to dealing with situations of this nature, intervened.

"Look, let's get you into another room, we don't want to disturb the wedding any more than we have to."

"But –"

"That's enough, thank you Gemma." interrupted the best man who had slipped up to the table. He regarded the old frightened couple with pity and put out an arm for Ivy to take.

"They are criminals, you know!" threw Gemma over her shoulder as she stalked off, to discuss her role in the capture of such dangerous criminals with the other bridesmaids. After helping her to her feet, the best man turned to walk her out into the foyer. Dylan's mum gripped her arm again and Ivy looked down at her.

"Were you telling the truth about supporting me? Is this even a real phone number?"

Ivy looked shocked and then patted her arm. "I meant every word. Call me."

Reassured, the woman smiled and turned back to her son, giving him a book to read from her bag. Bill and Ivy left the room with all eyes on them, the policeman leading the way, the best man supporting Ivy until they went into a small lounge area. He then left them to discuss everything, annoyed with Gemma for making such a fuss and for getting involved instead of informing him. By rights, he as best man should have dealt with it and he would have been far more discreet on such a special day, probably wouldn't even have called the police; it was obvious they were harmless. He would have had a quiet word with them, done a deal and then asked them to leave. Now he had no idea what would happen and he really needed to go back into the main hall to get the wedding back on track, ready for the speeches. As he left, two more policemen appeared and closed the door on him. Ivy had sat down on a wing backed chair, but Bill stood, regiment straight, ready to receive his punishment.

"Right, let's get down to business." commanded the first young policeman, standing in front of them both.

"A complaint has been made against you saying that you are here under false pretences and pretending to be somebody else. This amounts to fraud by false representation, section two of the Fraud Act 2006…it's a criminal offence."

He looked at them both seriously. "We will need to discuss this further at the station."

Ivy looked terrified and shot a glance at Bill, who was still standing upright and looking straight ahead. He cleared his throat and took out his handkerchief to mop his brow and top lip.

"I have nothing to say."

Ivy gasped and began to stammer "But – I – we didn't know any…"

"Don't say anything, dear…not until we have a solicitor."

"Surely it won't come to that?" cried Ivy, looking at the other policemen in the room for reassurance. They didn't provide any, just exchanged glances.

"Well, we need to take you in, to discuss this further."

Ivy looked horrified and turned to Bill, who was now staring at the floor.

"Take us in? You don't mean to arrest us…can't we talk here?"

The desperation had crept into her voice and the tears sprung to her eyes as the reality of the situation finally hit her.

"Do what you need to do." sighed Bill, resignedly, offering up his wrists.

The policeman shook his head and smiled a tight smile.

"It shouldn't come to that, assuming you will come without any trouble?"

Bill nodded and he went on. "I need to caution you. I am arresting you on suspicion of fraud, by false representation. You do not have to say anything, but it may harm your defence if you do not mention when questioned something that you will later rely on in court. Anything you do say may be given in evidence. Anything you say from now on will be written down. Do you understand?"

"Perfectly." stated Bill.

"Let's go then. Mrs Ashton, you can go with my colleague Jason and I'll take you." He nodded at Bill, who followed him to the door.

"Can't we go together?" gasped Ivy, her voice quavering as she stood up.

"Sorry, we have to keep you separate until after your interviews." explained the policeman feeling sorry for them both.

They left the room and Ivy kept her eyes down, not wanting to get eye contact with anyone. She could hear the wedding speeches in full swing, with laughter interspersed with speaking and she wished to be back in there, with Dylan and his mum, in fact, she wished she had never come today. Bill had been right to have a funny feeling, although this was anything but funny.

Chapter 10
Dealing With Muppets

The cold air of the evening hit her and Ivy shivered and pulled her shawl around her shoulders before the police car door was opened for her. She smiled weakly at the policeman, who gave her a sympathetic smile back as she sat in the car, straining to see Bill through the front window as he was taken by Jason to get into the back of the other car. She couldn't quite believe what was happening. As the policeman turned on the ignition and made his way to the local police station, Ivy watched as she passed fields and trees, shrouded in darkness. She checked her watch, peering at the face and screwing up her eyes to see the hands… twenty past nine. Ivy wondered what would happen once they were at the station and whether Bill would be okay. She dreaded having to face him alone back at the house later, assuming they would be sent home tonight. She felt confident that this would be the case and tried to keep calm. She was feeling a bit queasy, the young man driving was obviously used to zooming along winding roads, but she was not and hoped that they would be there soon. She kept her eyes facing forwards and heard the crackle of the radio, loud enough to be heard but too low to understand what they were saying; jargon mainly. It wasn't long before they were pulling into the station carpark on the edge of a town unfamiliar to her. The gates opened as the car pulled forward and the policeman expertly parked the car in a tiny bay next to the main door. He jumped out quickly and went around to let her out. Ivy breathed the night air in deeply, hoping to catch sight of Bill before going in, but his car wasn't back yet. She made her way with the young man steering her arm through the door of the police station and found herself in the foyer. A high desk with another police man standing behind it was in front of her and she wondered why it was like that. Within seconds she found out, as the door behind her was barged open and a youngish man threw himself up and at the desk, shouting profanities and trying to head-butt the man on the other side. His hands were handcuffed behind his back and Ivy marvelled that he had been able to get so high without hurting himself.

"Watch yourself, Coleman!" shouted the desk sergeant. PC Coleman shielded her from the abusive man and moved her further away as another policeman came in to deal with the troublemaker.

"I'm sorry, but I'm going to have to take you down to the cells," he explained and seeing the horror on her face, quickly added "For your own safety…you haven't done anything wrong. Just until I get this one sorted out, then we can interview you - okay?"

Ivy was feeling panicky again, but tried not to show it, wishing that Bill was there. The handcuffed man had managed to cut his eye and was now moaning about the pain and how he wanted a bacon sandwich, the policeman dealing with him speaking with the right mixture of respect and empathy, trying to get him to calm down. Ivy was led along to the next desk where she was asked by the duty officer to remove her shoes, belt and glasses. The troublemaker had started to shout again and Coleman ran back to assist his colleague.

"But I can't see without them." Ivy quavered, anxiously peering at the hardened woman in front of her.

"That's the rules, I'm afraid." the woman stated in a patronising voice "We can't have you hurting yourself now, can we duck?"

Ivy was feeling very sick and panicky and struggled to take off her shoes. The room swam as she stood and she reached forward to steady herself on the desk. Coleman came back and looked concerned.

"You alright?" he enquired gently, at which point, Ivy burst into tears.

The woman behind the desk raised her eyebrows at him and he put his arm around the sobbing woman.

"It's ok, don't get yourself in a state…just breathe… breathe! Quick, pass me a bag!" he yelled at the desk sergeant who grabbed one from behind the desk and handed it to him. "Breathe into this" he commanded Ivy, who was doubled over, hiccoughing and struggling to breathe, the panic attack reaching its peak and causing her to wheeze. Once she had breathed into the bag, which even in her agitated state she noticed stank of tobacco, she was able to calm herself enough to speak.

"Oooh…I am sorry. I just couldn't cope…I haven't felt this bad for so long."

"Don't worry about talking, just get your breathing right again." he smiled kindly, patting her arm before taking a pen out of his pocket. "Are you on any medication?"

She shook her head "Not anymore. I used to take Citalopram, but I've been so much better, I haven't used it for over a year."

He wrote this down on the form that he had been filling in since she arrived. She heard Bill's voice, asking if his wife was alright and started to cry again.

"I'm sorry, but you need to go and sit in the cell."

PC Coleman was being as nice as he could, walking her down the corridor, metal doors on either side. She shuddered at the thought of going in and he stopped outside the furthest one and took his keys out. The door swung open; it was worse than she had expected.

A single bed attached to the wall, a sink and an open toilet. At the sight, she realised she was going to need to use the facilities.

"I know it looks awful but you have to remember we are usually dealing with muppets like that one at reception, not respectable people like yourselves. You won't be in here for too long. I'll get my colleague to interview you first."

Ivy stopped in the centre of the room turning sharply to look at him.

"But does that mean Bill will have to go into a cell?"

"Yes, only while we speak to you…"

"NO!" shouted Ivy emphatically, "Interview my husband first, please. I don't care how long it takes, just deal with him quickly."

He looked unsure. "Your husband will still have to go to the cells while we interview you."

"It doesn't matter, just let him go first…please." she added before sinking down onto the bed.

"Okay, I'll let them know." Coleman reassured her, before leaving and locking the door.

Ivy felt sick and exhausted, the panic having been alleviated, just left her feeling ill. The urgency to pee pushed against her insides and she went across to the toilet. Not daring to sit on it and using her shawl as a cover round her, she squatted down, relief and fear flitting across her chest in equal measures. She flushed and turned back to the bed. Deciding to lie on it, the tiredness of the afternoons events finally caught up with her and she closed her eyes, to think through what she would say in the interview. Seemingly seconds later, she was woken by the bang of the cell door as Coleman appeared, looking concerned.

"Are you feeling ok? It's just we are ready for interview now, if you feel up to it."

"Oh yes, I'm ready," replied Ivy, struggling to sit herself back upright.

Ivy felt thirsty and hoped that there would be an offer of a cup of tea. She could certainly do with one, she thought as he led her down the corridor again. Stopping at a door marked Interview Room, he opened it, revealing a windowless room, lit by an overhead strip light. There was a large desk, with a policeman already seated at it on the side nearest to her, with his back to them. He turned his head as they came in. There was a chair opposite for her to sit down in and she hurried around the desk to take her seat.

"Hello, Mrs Ashton, sorry to keep you waiting. My name is PC Wigmore and this is my colleague PC Coleman."

He motioned towards Coleman before forcing a tight-lipped smile that didn't quite reach his eyes. These were hooded, giving him a suspicious, unfriendly look. She looked at Coleman seated next to him and was heartened that at least he was smiling sympathetically. Wigmore cleared his throat and glanced down at his sheet.

"We need to interview you, but before we do, I need to record what is being said, so if you don't mind, just speak as you normally would."

Clicking the button on the recorder, he proceeded "For the

purpose of the recording, it's the fourteenth of September two thousand and thirteen, the time is twenty-two thirty-four hours and in the interview room are PC Sam Coleman and PC Rodney Wigmore. We have just been joined by the accused. Can you confirm your full name?"

"Ivy Mabel Ashton." Ivy's voice quavered as she spoke, trying to think about what she should say.

PC Wigmore sat back in his chair and folded his arms.

"So, in your own words, can you tell us what happened today."

Ivy looked uncertainly from his face to Coleman's who smiled at her encouragingly.

"Take your time." Coleman said kindly as Wigmore looked at him sharply.

Ivy hesitated before plunging in with her question. "Shouldn't I have a solicitor, or something?"

"I don't think that's necessary."

"Well, what did Bill do? Did he have someone to represent him?"

Wigmore passed his hand over his eyes and Coleman couldn't help but smirk at him.

"We can't discuss your husband's response. We need to hear from you, to get your side of it all." Wigmore said firmly.

He tried to get on the right side of her and smiled tightly. "Just tell us your version of events today."

Ivy hesitated, straining through her thoughts, trying to remember what Bill had said. She glanced again at Coleman, who surreptitiously shook his head at her. She suddenly remembered what Bill had said in the room back at the wedding.

"No comment."

She murmured it quietly, catching sight of Coleman's smile

as Wigmore looked at her sharply. "You what?"

Ivy looked more confident and spoke louder. "No comment."

Wigmore turned to Coleman, who stared straight ahead, not wanting to get into a conversation with him. Wigmore sighed and tried again.

"Look, it's not worth giving me the 'No comment' treatment, you'd be better off telling me things from your side of the argument, get the facts straight, paint you in the right light."

Again, Coleman glanced at her and she knew she was doing the right thing.

"No comment."

"Oh, for goodness sake, you're not on TV you know, this is serious! You'd be better off telling us the truth instead of saying nothing! What happened today?" he shouted, really riled by her.

She sat back in her chair and folded her arms.

"No comment." she stated again and looked around, bored.

The furious man stood up suddenly and left the room. Coleman raised his eyebrows at her, winked and then left too. She could hear them outside the door, Wigmore trying to keep his voice down and failing, hissing that the whole thing was ridiculous and he wanted to go home. Coleman spoke calmly and she heard him say that bail would be the best thing, let them go home and sort out the court date at a later time. Wigmore reluctantly agreed and they came back in the room together.

"Right," began Wigmore, "As you haven't been able to provide us with any answers, we will need to make more enquiries. I'm going to suggest that we let you out on bail so that we can investigate further. We'll be interviewing witnesses over the next few weeks and taking statements from the bride's parents. I still need to take your fingerprints and your photograph."

Ivy looked shocked but resigned herself to getting it done. "Has Bill already had his done?"

Wigmore ignored her, filling in the paperwork in front of him and again, Coleman nodded without him seeing. Ivy relaxed a bit, glad that she would soon be leaving. She felt tired and drained and desperately wanted a drink, but didn't dare ask. Having finally got her fingerprints done and a photo of her looking like a startled rabbit, she was led out to the front desk, where Bill was waiting for her. He looked so serious, she didn't speak to him, just stood meekly next to him as the policeman on the desk finished their paperwork and got them to sign out. PC Coleman drove them back to the wedding venue, to pick up their car. After saying 'Goodnight' he left them to make their way home, in silence.

* * * * *

Ivy crept down the stairs in her fluffy dressing gown, her woollen slippers catching on the worn carpet. It was still dark outside and her headache and slightly queasy feeling told her that she hadn't slept for long; the sense of doom settled on her chest and she groaned inwardly at the thought of having to face Bill while feeling so fragile. As she got to the front door she paused, wondering if flicking the kettle on would wake him...just thinking about a cup of tea caused a wave of nausea to pass over her and she decided just to go and sit in the lounge, in the darkened room, glad the curtains were closed. She sat in her favourite chair and hugged her dressing gown around her. It was such a big room and had never seemed warm even with the heating on. After yesterday's events, she knew the dream of going to weddings was over, money would get tight again and they would struggle, tears pricked her eyes and caused an ache in her chest. She wished she had listened to Bill yesterday, he obviously picked up that something was going to happen, a sixth sense? Is that what they called it? She couldn't remember, but what did it matter? If only they had just gone to the pub and had a drink and come home, then this mess could have been avoided and they could have carried on with their fun days out...

"It's the shame of it, that I cannot bear."

Ivy jumped at the sound of another human voice and turned sharply to where it had come from. She leant forward, past the supporting pillar to see Bill sitting at the dining table, very still and upright, hands in his lap, his glasses in front of him, open. She could see that he had taken them off to rub his eyes. He didn't look at her, just stared straight ahead, the stillness of him in the cold room unnerved her.

"Oh, I didn't realise you were there...thought you were still in bed." she twittered shrilly, trying to make light of it all. But Bill was past being jollied along.

"I didn't sleep well, not surprisingly." he grumbled, rubbing his eyes again. "I think I must still be in shock - being arrested is bad enough, but a court case? How did it come to this?"

Ivy felt the dread not only from having to go to court, but the disappointment from Bill added to her upset.

"Hopefully, it will all blow over and be forgotten about." she ventured feebly, as he got up and left the room.

And it probably would have done, if it hadn't been for Max, the charming best man at the wedding, who was so kind to them both. He worked as a reporter for the local paper and wanted to tell their side of the story, portraying them as a modern-day tragedy. When the paper was delivered a few days later, Ivy felt a spike of excitement that was doused down immediately with regret...there was no point looking at the forthcoming wedding section and as she bent to pick it up, decided to bin it straight away. She went through to the kitchen and opened the recycling bag and as she tossed the paper in, something familiar caught her eye...a little photo of a young man, smiling made her think she knew him...where had she seen him before...of course, it was Max, the lovely man at the...oh no. Ivy's legs threatened to buckle and she snatched the paper up and launched herself into the chair at the kitchen table, slamming the paper down, fear making her hands shake as she spread the page out.

'MODERN DAY TRAGEDY' shouted the headline and she read in horror about the 'elderly couple' so lonely they had been going to 'strangers' weddings to feel loved and cared for...she quickly scanned for names and her heart sank to her fluffy slippers as she found them, halfway down, along with the story of their arrest and impending court case and then, horror of horrors, the article ended with the question 'Where is their family?'

* * * * *

John felt exhausted. This meeting was proving harder to chair than he had thought. There were several important people sitting round the table waiting for him to explain how they could work together to make their relevant policy work; a Police Inspector, a Community Safety Officer, a Social Worker, an MP in charge of Community Finance and a Youth Pastor. He had just covered the community values of his party and the importance of families looking out for each other. His bug bear that he believed as a team they could begin to deal with was unsupervised children who were the bane of society, showing no respect for elders. The Youth Pastor was just about to explain how his street mentoring project would help this situation when there was a knock at the door. Not wanting to seem rude when there was a man of the cloth in his midst, John sighed and said, 'Come in.'

The door opened and John was surprised to see that it wasn't the unfortunate new girl being sent to interrupt the meeting, but Simon, one of his colleagues.

"I'm sorry to interrupt, John, but I think you need to see this..."

John looked irritated but tried to smile.

"Surely it can wait..."

"Not this time."

He handed John the paper, pointing to the paragraph that showed that his parents had been arrested, the impending court case and the question of their family. John stared unbelievingly at the paper, and then put his head in his hands. Simon stood behind John and smiled.

"I suggest you go, John and I can carry on chairing the meeting..."

"Fuck my parents!"

John suddenly exploded, standing up so fast, that Simon had to jump back to avoid being chinned. He snatched the paper up and stormed out. Simon sat down in his chair, trying to regain some composure.

"So, what were we talking about?"

The Youth Pastor, clearly shocked, referred to the notepad in front of him.

"Erm...respect for elders."

Chapter 11
Third Bombshell Of The Afternoon

John had never felt so angry in his life and this was saying something. Having left the room in some kind of shock, he had grabbed his things out from his office, noting that none of his colleagues would look at him as he swept through, apart from the new girl, who seemed to be looking at him with, what, was that pity in those eyes. She even managed a tight smile at him and he rudely turned his back on her as he stalked across to the lift, eyes down, his mind in overdrive. He had to think about what to do and how to limit the damage. He re-read the paper, trying to make sense of what he was seeing; his stuffy parents, the moral fibre of society, the type who always drove at 30mph, even on the motorway, or pointed out if they hadn't paid enough for something, his parents had been fraudulent. It just didn't make sense. As he walked out of the lift, he noticed again that the lobby staff were not looking at him, at least not until he had passed them and then a sly sideways glance was thrown his way. He suddenly felt fearful, it hadn't occurred to him until that moment that this might affect his position, that his parents' foolishness could cost him more than the respect of his fellow workers. He dumped the paper and his bag on the back seat, sliding into the front seat and paused, trying to decide what to do next. He wasn't one for sentiment, but it did occur to him that this could be the last time he would be here. He glanced up at his office and caught sight of the new girl, staring down at him, still smiling. She looked like the penguin in 'The Wrong Trousers', all smug, on the inside, with him outside of it. He had watched it that last Christmas with his parents and the thought of them made him angry again. Setting his face grimly, he decided on what course of action to take, to go home, collect a few things and then drive to see them, to try and sort it out, maybe wait until Katy was back from work and see if she would come too, she had always got on with them.

The security guard waved him through and again, smiled as he left. He was getting paranoid now, he knew it, and began to wish he hadn't had such a big lunch, feeling queasy at the thought of seeing his parents again.

As he pulled onto his drive, he was surprised to see Katy's car already there. Perhaps she'd had today off, he couldn't remember her saying so, but then he couldn't remember her saying anything recently. He decided to try and be nice so that there was more chance of her agreeing to help him. Opening the front door and putting his things down on the hall table, he stopped suddenly. He could hear Katy up in their bedroom, the sound of her opening the drawers travelling down the stairs as he went up.

"Katy?"

The noise stopped as he stood outside the door.

He pushed it open and Katy stood, looking guilty and defiant at the same time. The suitcase was open on the bed, with piles of her clothes ready to be packed and for one confusing moment, he thought she must know, but how?

"How did you know...?" he began, but she cut him short.

"I didn't think you would be back yet, otherwise I would have sorted this out earlier."

"Sorted what out?"

She took a deep breath and tried to keep the drama out of her voice.

"I'm leaving you, John."

"What?"

"I'm leaving you."

John looked flummoxed and then started to open the drawers and pulled out the clothes he needed. Katy stared incredulously at him, unsure what to do.

"Did you hear me? It's over, John, you and me, us, we are over, finished...I am packing my things and leaving you."

John straightened up and looked at her, taking in the new haircut, make up, had she even lost a bit of weight? Mid-life finally catching up with her, the need to change things. He weighed up his options and couldn't help being pragmatic.

"Okay...but I need the suitcase."

"What the hell is that supposed to mean?"

She was furious now, and beginning to shake, "I tell you it's over, that our marriage is finished and all you can say is you need the suitcase!"

The anger that had been contained jumped to attention in John's chest.

"What do you expect me to do? Plead with you, demand that you stay, knowing full well that you will do what you want anyway, like you always do!"

"Huh, that's rich coming from you!"

Her eyes bulged as she spat the words and started throwing her clothes in the suitcase. John stood helplessly as she shoved her things in, feeling the stress rise up in his chest and threatening to close his throat. He suddenly felt old and defeated and the shock of the afternoon's events began to catch up. John staggered to the bed and sat down, watching her pack.

"I didn't want to argue…" she stated shortly.

"Yes, you did." he shot back and Katy looked at him sharply.

"I didn't even think you would be back yet, so no I didn't. I had a note written and everything, it would have been a lot easier."

He laughed drily and the anger flashed in her eyes again.

"It's not funny! This is the hardest thing I've ever had to deal with and you're not making it any easier."

"Am I meant to feel sorry for you? Is that what you want? Because I am all out of pity today…you have no idea."

The defeated tone surprised her and she thought about how oddly he was behaving; she had run through several scenarios in her mind and none of them prepared her for the bizarreness of this one. She thought back to his initial comment, that had seemed out of context…how did you know? Know what?

"Why are you back early? What's happened?"

"My parents have been arrested…"

The shock knocked the defiance off her face for a moment. "WHAT?!"

John sighed.

"I know, unbelievable. I was coming to take some clothes and go and stay with them for a couple of days, hence the suitcase."

He swallowed, knowing it was futile but hearing the words come out of his mouth,

"I hoped we could both go…"

The defiance was straight back.

"Well, that's just not possible, not now, it's too late."

"Obviously, I didn't know that."

Katy swallowed as she dropped the third bombshell of the afternoon.

"There is a lot that you don't know."

Catching the seriousness in her voice, John looked at her.

"I've been seeing someone else."

Now it was John's turn to look shocked and he was glad he was already seated. The power of speech had left him momentarily which was a good thing as his thoughts were so extreme, he knew he would say something he would regret. She looked at him carefully, taking in the sagging shoulders, the hurt and shock clearly etched on his face, making him seem older and just sad looking and she was annoyed to feel a stab of pity for him. This wasn't how it was meant to be and she knew she had to get out to keep her resolve.

"Do I know him?" he managed to say hoarsely, looking directly at her.

Katy looked down a bit abashed and fiddled with the zip before doing the suitcase up.

"Just somebody from work." she said lightly and then, as if it mattered "You don't know him."

John felt jealousy and anger claw his chest and was frightened by the strength of the pain.

"Is it serious?"

She did the zip up and straightened.

"What do you think?" she snapped and then seeing how broken he looked, took a deep breath.

"Yes. I think so… he treats me really well and- well, we love each other."

It all made sense to him now, the weight-loss, the make-up, new hair, not talking, being out to yoga so many times a week; he realised how foolish he had been and the anger inside grew.

"I thought it was only men that behaved like this." he said bitterly.

Angrily she retorted "No I think you'll find it's often the man who ignores his wife and takes her for granted that gets left!"

Wearily, she went to the door and turned to speak. John still sat, unsure what he was meant to do.

"I'm sorry about your parents John. They don't deserve any of this and they certainly don't deserve you as a son, in the same way I don't deserve to be treated like this. I have to go."

She pulled the suitcase off the bed and then turned back.

"And I'm taking the suitcase with me, it's mine anyway. Everything else that is mine has already been taken...but then I suppose you haven't noticed that either."

Katy carried the suitcase down the stairs and with a final look round the hall, opened the front door. Luke was waiting by the car across the road and as he saw her, smiled and came to take the case. Opening the boot, he put it in and she gave him a little smile as they both got into her car, having agreed not to talk until they were back at his flat. She couldn't help but give him a hug, so pleased that this time in her life was really now over. She was finally moving on.

Chapter 12
Turned To Liquid

The sun was low as John drove through the town to where his parents lived; the three-hour journey had felt a lot longer. Turning into the familiar estate, the memories of former visits threatened to overwhelm him and he regretted not ringing his parents to warn them that he was coming, hoping that the shock wouldn't kill them, he could just imagine the headlines. They were probably in bed, knowing them, 8.00pm was late for the retired. The house was still the same, the frosted glass of the front door looked dated, the render was starting to come off. Probably because of the tree still being there, he mused, having told them it would cause problems but would his father listen? He reversed onto their drive, boxing his father's car in and turned the engine off. Rubbing his eyes, the sheer madness of the last six hours caused an involuntary sigh; so many feelings were buzzing through his mind, he couldn't decide which one to use first. In the end, it was decided for him. As he got out and went to the boot to get his bags, a large group of people suddenly appeared around the corner, all eager to speak to him.

"Mr Ashton, is it true your parents have been arrested?"

"Do you realise that as MP in charge of Family Values, this is embarrassing for the government?"

"Have you got anything to say?"

"Is it true that you will resign from your post?"

"Mr Ashton? Mr Ashton?"

Microphones were thrust in his direction as photo after photo was taken and he put his hand up, to get their attention.

"I have no idea where you have got your information from." As John stated this, images of his work colleagues replayed through his mind. "I haven't even spoken to my family yet, so have nothing further to say."

"Mr Ashton, is it true that you haven't seen your parents for over three years?"

"Mr Ashton, can you confirm that there has been a climate of bullying in your office, reflected by your treatment of your parents?"

John looked taken aback, but only for a moment, the new girl had obviously given her biased side of the story.

"No further comments." he retorted and headed for the front door, using his bag as a deflecting weapon. He was surprised as the front door was opened before he rang the bell. His father stood in the doorway, looking grey and much older than his sixty-five years, feeling more surprise at seeing John than the dozen journalists at his front door.

"Hello Dad." he said softly, aware of the watching media and hoping they would not get a show.

His father cleared his throat.

"You'd better come in." Bill replied as he stepped back to make room.

John swiftly moved through the door jamb and closed it behind him as the furore of questions began again. He dropped his bag at the foot of the stairs and went through into the lounge. His father sat in the wing backed chair nearest the window, the curtains still drawn from the day before. John crossed over to the mantelpiece, too agitated to sit down, unsure of how to proceed.

"Did I hear the door go?"

His mother had come in through the back door and was bending down to remove her boots, her hands stiff from the cold. She made her way to the kitchen sink, and washed them with warm water, causing them to tingle. Somewhere in her mind she could hear her mother telling her off: 'You'll get chilblains!' Whatever they were. She dried them on the tea towel and then filled the kettle up, taking care not to overfill it, not wanting to waste any more electricity than was necessary and still conscious of Bill's scrutiny when it came to using anything.

"Did you fancy a cuppa?"

She turned and went to go through the archway into the lounge and stopped dead in her tracks. John was standing awkwardly in front of the empty fireplace, his face displaying an array of emotions.

"Oh...John...I didn't know.... when did...oh Johnny!"

Ivy's emotions got the better of her and she hurried across the room and flung her arms around him, tears of grief, relief and maternal devotion running down her face.

"I can't believe you are here...I just can't believe it."

John felt foolish, knowing he should be able to hug her back but feeling unable to bring himself to feel anything. He just stood there, dumbly as his mother continued to hold onto him, weeping.

Bill cleared his throat and took his glasses off and began to polish them.

"Well, he isn't here for a social call, dear."

Ivy stepped back, confused, the tears stopped in their

tracks. She fumbled for the tissue up her sleeve.

"Why are you here then....is Katy ok? Are you ill? Has something happened?"

She wiped her face and nose, trying to focus on his reply. John stepped back and ran his hand through his hair, trying to pull himself together enough to speak, but the emotional trauma of the afternoon had finally caught up with him and being in his parents' house had caught him off guard. He felt drained again as if his insides had turned to liquid and were seeping out through his heels. Slumping down onto the sofa, he put his head in his hands.

"He is here because of us...because of our, sorry, your stupid, hare-brained fraudulent idea of turning up at stranger's weddings as some kind of fun day out!"

Ivy looked crestfallen "But it was a good idea, you agreed."

"More fool me, then," replied Bill " Because now, it's splashed all over the papers and our son will have to pay the price."

Ivy looked confused.

"What do you mean, pay the price? We are the ones that did it, it's nothing to do with Johnny, why, we haven't even seen him..."

She tailed off, not wanting to say how long it had been and Bill sighed as his son looked up suddenly and stared at his mother as if she had two heads.

"Don't you understand anything? Your actions have probably cost me my job! Everything I have worked for, for over God knows how many years, all for nothing!"

Ivy was shocked that he had raised his voice to her and tried to soothe him.

"Don't upset yourself, Johnny, you can easily get another job in the Civil Service."

"I am a bloody MP!" he exploded, making her jump and

scuttle over to the relative safety of Bill.

He stood and began to pace towards the fireplace and back.

"Not just any MP ...I am in charge of family values!" He laughed mirthlessly, "Now that is a joke, what do I know about that? No wonder the press are all over it."

"Press?" Ivy said sharply.

Bill patted her hand "Look out of the window, dear."

Ivy leant over him to peek through the curtain. At the movement, the remaining five journalists jogged over to see if they could catch a glimpse of the fugitives. Ivy gasped and pulled the curtains closed.

"When did they get there?"

"Just before I got here, I expect. My work colleagues obviously let them know everything and added a load more rubbish just to make sure I am really finished."

He stopped and stared at the floor. "I expect Katy will do her bit, too."

Ivy misunderstood what he was saying and latched onto something familiar and what she saw as safer ground.

"How is Katy? Is she coming over once she has finished work? I have missed chatting to her." she added wistfully, leaning back to sit on the arm of the sofa. Again, it was like touching a flame to paper and John exploded, the anger spilling out as he stopped pacing and turned abruptly.

"Katy is a bitch!" he spat, pointing his finger at her. "In my hour of need, when everyone else completely let me down, she chose that as the perfect moment to tell me she is leaving me...can you believe that? She even took my suitcase so I only had a poncy holdall."

He had started to pace up and down and kept running his hand through his hair. Again, Ivy tried to reason with him.

"Surely you can work it out with her? She always seemed

so easy going."

John stopped and smiled wickedly.

"Oh, she is easy alright. She's been shagging a bloke in the office for months, so I think it's safe to say it's over between us."

His parents looked dumbfounded at this news, but he was too angry to care.

"Apparently, I'm as bad at being a husband as I am at being a son. It's a bloody good job we never had kids; I would have ruined them as well."

All the angst had left him and again he slumped down onto the sofa, the material feeling cold through his shirt and he shivered.

"Why is it so bloody cold in here? Is the heating on?"

Ivy looked sharply at Bill, who cleared his throat and stood up, put his hands behind his back and walked over to where John was sitting.

"No, the heating isn't on," he began, before his shoulders sagged, "The truth is I can't afford the gas."

He fumbled over the words and Ivy moved to where he was standing. She looked at John, saw the confusion on his face and cut in.

"That's why we had been going to the weddings...it wasn't just the fact that we were lonely, it saved us money being out all day; eating food and being warm. The chats with the guests were a perk of the whole scheme."

John's face changed from confusion to annoyance.

"Can't you hear how ridiculous you sound?" he stated incredulously "This isn't just a walk in the park, a bit of fun."

He stood up, to make his point.

"This is fraud. That food you ate, that was stealing, Mum."

"Oh, it wasn't like that..."

John's face hardened as he grew more agitated, running his

hands through his hair.

"Yes, it was, that is exactly what you did; stole food and drink, it was their wedding day for crying out loud, you should never have been there in the first place!"

"Well, now you put it like that, you make us sound like petty thieves!"

Ivy's pleasure at seeing John after so long was quickly replaced with the irritation that had peppered their conversations in the past.

"This isn't really getting us anywhere, is it?" suggested Bill quietly. "We know we have done wrong and will have to face the consequences of our actions."

John tried to gather his thoughts into one tidy pile and sifted through, putting the one that needed addressing on the top.

"What have the police said to you?"

Bill looked sheepish and cleared his throat again.

"They were nice enough. After the initial arrest, they let us go on the same day. We had to provide a statement each and your mother spent some time in the cells."

"That was very stressful." cut in Ivy, folding her arms.

"And the chief bridesmaid persuaded the bride's parents to press charges."

"I didn't like her from the start, far too up herself and the way she swanned about, talking about us as if we were criminals!"

John looked at her without sympathy and she stopped abruptly.

"Anyway, it looks as if there will be a court case, where we will have to explain our actions." finished Bill pragmatically.

"So that explains why the press are all over this," remarked John grimly, "The parents of an MP who preaches family values and yet never see him."

He wearily stood up, and went to the holdall in the hall.

"I need to write my letter of resignation. I'll have to charge my laptop up…and the heating needs to go on, my hands are seizing up."

Ivy looked again to Bill, who in turn looked at John. Seeing their faces, John looked puzzled and then the realisation of why they looked so worried dawned on him.

"I can pay for the electricity if that's what you are thinking about."

"I can't let you do that." demanded Bill, knowing it was futile to protest, but being too proud to just take the handout.

"It sounds like you will have to, whether you like it or not."

John spoke firmly and then softened. "I might need to stay here for a few days until I have worked out what to do…is that okay?"

Ivy clutched at the straw offered to her.

"Of course, stay as long as you need to," she gabbled, "I'll go and make up the spare room."

She scuttled off, glad to be able to do something useful and John picked up the holdall and set it down on the sofa. Bill went through to the kitchen and flicked the kettle on.

"Do you want a cuppa?" he called through as if it was the most natural thing in the world to do.

"I'll have coffee, black, no sugar." answered John.

He realised how hungry he was and not wanting to put any more on his parents, made the decision for dinner that night.

"I'll get fish and chips in for tea. Let me know what you want and I'll go and get it from Carters…assuming the press have gone home for the night?"

Bill looked through their kitchen window.

"It looks quiet enough out there."

John plugged in his laptop and took out his work diary, trying to decide what would need to go first. He knew there were appointments for the next day that needed cancelling and decided to call in the morning, citing stress as an excuse, the effort required to explain was too great. Rubbing his hand across his eyes, he sat back in to the sofa, still in a state of disbelief at the events of the last twenty-four hours and stared off into the distance, not wanting to think of Katy, but finding himself picturing her over the last few weeks. He knew he had been a fool not to notice the change... well, to be fair he had noticed the change, but just assumed that it was down to him, down to the fact that they had, in his mind, cleared the air. The reality that she was happier because she had been with another man galled him. Ivy watched him from the stairwell, saddened by the change she could see in him and yet so happy he was in her home again. He glanced quickly at her and she guiltily came into the room, feeling nervous.

"Did you want me to make some food? I've got some tinned mackerel in the cupboard."

Bill came through, carrying the drinks.

"It's alright, love, Johnny's going to get some fish and chips for our dinner."

Ivy went to protest, but John raised his hand.

"It's fine, Mum, I'm happy to get it, in fact, I'll go and get it now."

After taking their order, John left the house to walk to the chip shop, relieved to see that the streets were empty. He wondered if they would be back in the morning and whether they would have fresh information from Katy.

He hoped not.

* * * * *

Katy was running a bath at Luke's flat, the stress from the day finally subsiding so that all she now felt was exhilarated. She had done it, actually done what she had imagined doing for years. Part of her wished she had done it well before now, but she knew she couldn't have done it on her own; the thought of growing old alone filled her with utter terror. No, she needed a reason to leave and Luke had come along at just the right time. She put her hand under the hot tap, feeling the warmth and pressure run across her palm and looked around for some bubble bath. The only one was a manly-looking bottle of Radox, so she tipped a good glug of it into the water and swirled it around, the smell reminding her of her father and she had to force herself to think of Luke, to renew the smell, so that it was all about him. She felt hot in her toweling robe and stood up, looking around the bathroom, planning the changes she would make, assuming they would stay here. On their combined wage, they could afford to rent a much bigger flat...or they could buy a place, as she would have half the money from the sale of the house. She thought about John and wondered what would happen to him now, without his job to fill his time.

Removing her robe, she stepped into the bath, the water seemed near scalding as she inched her way down, exhaling as she got her shoulders under. As she soaped her legs, she marveled at the fact his parents had broken the law, especially his mother, having always seemed such a sweet, slightly scatty woman – how could she be involved with fraud? And his dad! He was such a typical old gentleman and all her dealings with him had been positive. She would never in a million years have ever thought he would do wrong.

"Can I come in?"

Luke's voice, the other side of the door, sounded playful and she grinned and replied, "You may enter."

He opened the door and came to sit on the side of the bath, the steam rising from the water, curling tendrils around his hands as he swirled the water.

"Cor, that's hot!" he exclaimed, taking his hand and wiping it on the towel hanging above her head.

She smiled luxuriously and settled down even further, pleased that the bubbles covered her up. Although they had now been seeing each other for six months, she still felt a little coy in front of him.

"What are we having for dinner?" she asked, enjoying the freedom of asking such a thing of the man in her life.

Luke reached forward and tucked her hair behind her ear.

"I thought we could go out for dinner, celebrate your freedom."

Katy looked perturbed and played with the bubbles.

"We only went out last Friday night, plus we need the money this weekend to pay for the train tickets."

Luke stopped fiddling with her hair and stood up, crossing to the mirror to draw smiley faces in the steam.

"Ok, I can make Marmite Spaghetti if you would rather stay in. I just thought it would be nice to celebrate your first evening officially as my lady."

Katy felt touched that he felt so strongly about it and sat up a bit, in earnest.

"Oh, that's a lovely idea. I suppose it should be marked as a special occasion. Call the Greek restaurant, they will give us a table."

Luke smiled and rubbed off the smiley faces, drying his hand on the towel.

"You won't have to pay for a train ticket this weekend, I'll see Mum on her own, as usual."

Seeing Katy about to protest, he quickly carried on. "She isn't feeling too good anyway and I think we should leave it a bit before I introduce you. Mum is quite old-fashioned and might struggle with the fact I have caused a marriage to break up."

Katy immediately jumped to his defence.

"You haven't done anything of the sort, my marriage was over long before I met you."

Luke stood over her again, smiling.

"I know that, but my mum will take convincing and I think we should leave it for now."

Katy sank back down under the water, her shoulders feeling re-scalded again, causing her to breathe out quickly.

"Let me go and book the table. We can chat over calamari and a bottle of champagne, my treat."

He kissed her lips and she reveled in the moment, feeling special and loved. He left the room, whistling and she closed her eyes, the image of John and his parents looking faded and old and decided to look forward to the evening ahead with Luke, without feeling guilty.

Chapter 13
Medicine Box

It had started to rain as John left the fish and chip shop so by the time he got back to the house, he was wet and fed up. Exhaustion made his bones ache and he was glad to get inside. Ivy, watching from the kitchen window, hurried to open the front door, calling to Bill that the food had arrived.

"Oh, is it raining out?" she commented and John fought the urge to reply sarcastically.

"Yes, just a bit." he replied, glancing in to the lounge where the dining table was. With a sinking heart, he saw the table set for the three of them, his hope of working while eating faded as he carried the food in. Taking the paper package out of the flimsy plastic bag, the back of his hand became wet and he quickly took it out before tearing off some kitchen roll to dry it.

"Do you want anything to drink? Another coffee, perhaps, or water?"

Ivy fussed around the table and he quickly sat down to stop feeling irritated.

"No, I'm fine, I just want to eat."

"You need to drink, Johnny, it's better for your digestion."

He gritted his teeth as Bill came to join them at the table. "I don't want a drink...and my name is John."

Ivy looked hurt and scurried off to get a jug of water and glasses for her and Bill, who had sat down at the table. As they ate in silence, John was reminded of a film he had once watched with Katy when they had first met...was it Route 66? A story about a guy visiting his parents who haven't seen him for years and the awkwardness that followed...the camera shots showing each of them looking at each other, not speaking...Buffalo 66, that was it. Katy had loved it, discussing in great detail the psychological damage each character suffered, whereas he just thought it was weird. The girl in it was pretty enough to make it bearable.

"Can you pass the salt, please?"

His father broke the silence and John reached out to pass him the little white pot. He noticed the ketchup then, having been so consumed with eating, his knife and fork working their way through the fish at colossal speed. He took it and having shaken the bottle, whacked the end of it to get a suitable amount out, unable to remember the last time he had used a glass bottle. He didn't even think they still made them anymore. He stared at the bottle label and was aware that his parents were watching him.

"What?" he snapped abruptly.

Ivy smiled weakly. "It's just so lovely to have you here, after all this time."

Bill cleared his throat. "I just wanted the ketchup." he countered dryly.

John cracked a tight smile and passed him the bottle, taking his fork in his right hand and stabbing the chips one at a time, immersing them in the visual bloodbath and carefully chewing before taking another. His mother was still staring and so he felt the need to speak.

"I know it's been a long time - I certainly didn't expect us to be meeting up like this."

Bill looked uncomfortable and took a swig of his water while Ivy went back to eating her chips.

"But circumstances as they are have forced my hand and I need some time to sort out my next step."

John knew that he sounded like an MP, but felt unable to say anything else. He wiped his hands and mouth with more of the kitchen roll and sat back in his seat, feeling bloated.

"I have to write my letter of resignation ready for tomorrow and then work out what I need to do about Katy."

Ivy leant forward. "Is it really too late for you and Katy? It seems such a shame, you were so close."

John felt the tang of bitterness in his throat and a sense of grief which surprised him and he had to keep the tremor out of his voice as he replied.

"We were, but not anymore. I mean, she's with someone else. You can't get more 'over' than that."

He stood and crossed to where his laptop was charging and sat on the sofa, setting it on his lap. Ivy sighed and feeling full, even though there was half a fish and lots of chips left, took the plates through to the kitchen, the familiar ache of anxiety scrabbled about in her chest. It had been too much today and she knew she would need an early night, to try and build the reserves back up. Her head felt fuzzy and she wished she hadn't eaten such a heavy, oily meal. She couldn't bear to throw so much food away and so covered the plate with clingfilm and left it on the side to cool a bit. Going to the cupboard near the back door, she took the medicine box out and sought out the Rennies that she knew would help settle her stomach and poured herself a mug of warm water from the kettle. She went back into the lounge, where John was busy, his hands flying over the keyboard as he typed, hitting the keys with unnecessary force. Bill was still sitting at the table, reading the paper. He looked up as she stood in the doorway.

"Alright, pet?" he said, concern etching his face.

Ivy smiled weakly. "Yes, fine. I think I will go to bed, though, as I'm quite tired."

Bill stood and folded the paper over.

"I'll join you." he replied and turned to John who was too absorbed in his work to notice.

"Are you ok to turn everything off, John?"

John looked up, irritated and stopped typing.

"What?" he spoke sharply.

"Your mother and I are going up, so can you turn all the plugs off? I'll lock up."

"Yes, fine, I'll do it in a minute." John muttered, going back to typing manically.

Bill patted Ivy's shoulder as she went upstairs, knowing she was feeling wobbly. He took the keys from the hook and locked the front door and pulled the curtain across it, finishing by locking the back door and turning off the plugs to the kettle and toaster. Satisfied, he went to the bottom of the stairs and turned to call into the lounge.

"Goodnight."

No reply, just loud tapping greeted him and bemused, he made his way upstairs.

Chapter 14
Medicine Box

Ivy woke to the sound of a car door being slammed shut and opened her eyes to see the ceiling bathed in sunlight. She lay there for a few minutes, trying to think why she was feeling a mixture of deep joy and untold sadness at the same time. The memory of the last forty-eight hours came through her mind slowly, the newspaper, the reporters, John turning up, the impending court case, the news that Katy had left John and the late-night supper of fish and chips added to the slightly queasy sensation she had while thinking of all these things. Bill wasn't next to her and she heard him moving around in the en-suite, the occasional splosh of water giving away the fact that he was shaving. She turned awkwardly and sat up, waiting for her eyes to catch up, blurry and sore from yesterday's tears. Her head felt fuzzy and she felt full even though it had been hours ago that she last ate... 'heavy meals take longer to digest, especially if you are stressed.' Where on earth had she picked that little fact up from? Honestly, she marveled again at how she did so badly at school with a memory that was like a sponge. The trouble was that, like a sponge, she couldn't differentiate between good stuff to absorb, or bad; like the dripping from the roast she had as a kid, the unsuspecting washing up sponge would be used to suck it all up and would be doomed to the bin, the viscous liquid clogging every pore, making it redundant. Her thoughts too often kept this daft information and left her looking like a dithering old woman.

"Which is what you are," she muttered out loud, getting up and reaching across for her dressing gown. Having wrapped it around her, she went out onto the landing and noticed that John's door was open. Stepping inside, she noted the bed was made and the curtains drawn. She felt a sense of pride that John had grown into such a neat, organised man and liked to think it had been her influence on him, even though really, she knew it must be Bill's genes.

"Are you alright, dear?" called Bill from their bedroom.

Ivy smiled as she went downstairs.

"Yes, dear, just popping down to put the kettle on."

Gripping the handrail, she made her way carefully down the stairs, still not really with it.

She went through to the kitchen, filled the kettle and flicked it on, before making her way through the arch, into the darkened lounge and automatically opened the curtains. A barrage of shouts, faces and cameras greeted her and she 'Ooohed!' loudly and stumbled back into her chair. Ivy saw that John hadn't made it to bed as she had assumed as he was just stirring, slouched on the sofa with his laptop in his lap. I wonder if that's why they are called laptops, she mused as he came to, leapt up, the laptop clattering to the floor and closed the curtains, snatching the material across, instantly irritated.

"What did you do that for?" he yelled accusingly.

Ivy was too surprised by everything to reply as Bill appeared in the doorway.

"There's quite a crowd out there today. Anybody want a tea?"

"Well, thanks to mother, they have now had a show! Couldn't you have at least got dressed?"

Ivy had recovered enough to reply.

"I'm sorry...I didn't think, I forgot...I thought they would have gone..."

"Your mother didn't do it deliberately, Johnny - John." Bill quickly added, "I was surprised to see so many of them."

John was angry again.

"Why is it so hard for you to understand? I am RUINED! Of course they are going to be here, to hear me announce my resignation!"

The outburst was halted momentarily by a loud knock at the door. Ivy jumped, fear gripping her heart and Bill turned to the sound.

"Don't you touch that door!" hissed John, as he bent down to pick up the laptop. "They can wait for their story."

The knock came again, louder this time. John crossed over to where Bill was, took a deep breath and called out.

"What do you want?"

"Mr Ashton? Is that you? We have some news for you." came the muffled reply through the door.

Another voice, female this time, spoke.

"We want to be first to interview you, Mr Ashton....and your wife, if possible."

John started to say, "That's not possible..." when his father put up his hand, to silence him. Ivy hurried over from the sofa, straining to hear. Bill called through the door "Can you repeat what you just said, please?"

The woman started to talk again.

"The BBC are very interested in interviewing you for the Radio 4 programme The World at One..."

A man cut in;

"But first, the local rag would like to interview you both about the positive impact you have had on so many of the wedding guests."

Looking puzzled, John reached forward and opened the door quickly. Ivy peered round, her eyes like saucers as she looked at the sea of faces that were all vaguely familiar, smiling back at her and a cheer went up as she stepped forward. There were about sixty of them, some clutching bunches of flowers, others holding A3 card with the words 'Justice for Bill and Ivy' written on them in big marker pen. A couple of them were being interviewed by the local TV station, the words carried up to where she was standing.

"...and Ivy was just lovely, she gave me such brilliant advice and I am now speaking to my Mum again..."

The man standing with her then spoke up.

"When we read about the story in the paper, how they would be going to face a court case, we wanted to do something to help. It was Julia's idea to go on Twitter to highlight the case, under the hashtags: #happycouple #justicebill #notpoisonivy and so many people contacted us and said they wanted to help."

Julia beamed "Which is why we are all here today, outside this very special couple's house."

The interviewer smiled and turned to the camera.

"Well, that's a lovely story and I think we can now go and speak to the couple in question...Ivy and Bill, can we get a quick interview with you both..."

Ivy had always imagined that she would one day be in this position, well, maybe not with all the details, but to be given a chance to speak publicly to the nations, her few minutes of fame and thought it would be a dream come true...
but like so many things, the reality had come at the wrong

time, she wasn't prepared and worst of all, she was in her tatty old dressing gown. All she could do as the man with the microphone made his way towards her was look panic stricken at Bill, who stepped forwards, shielding Ivy with his body, which was smartly dressed in slacks and a tweed jacket, usual attire for his morning stroll. He cleared his throat and leant forwards towards the microphone. Every other reporter held up their recorders as the cameras clicked.

"First of all, I would like to thank you all for taking the time to come here today. My wife and I are overwhelmed by the support and need a bit of time to come to terms with the situation. As you can imagine, the last few days have been very difficult and we both need time to sort out our next step."

Ivy smiled at the ease in which he delivered this address as if he had been practicing for weeks. John stood awkwardly in the background, unsure as to what to do. The woman from the BBC started to talk again, moving forward into position, the sound crew with her surging forward too.

"Would you be willing to do an interview for the World at One?"

Bill looked at Ivy, who leant forwards and spoke.

"I would love to do an interview for such a prestigious radio station," Ivy gushed, "But although it's only radio, I would rather like to get dressed first."

Laughter rippled across the crowd at this and she beamed round at them. A few pushed forward, offering their flowers to her, but Bill put up a restraining hand.

"If Ivy is able to go and get ready, we will reconvene out here for photographs for the press and get a chance to thank you all personally. Normally, I would offer you all a cup of tea, but the sheer scale would be difficult. However, the corner shop does a lovely hot chocolate, so I can recommend you pop there. Thank you all again."

At this, the crowd gave another cheer as he and Ivy waved at them, king and queen for a day and closed the front door. John stared at them in disbelief, the dreamlike quality of the morning leaving him at a loss as to how to proceed.

"I can't believe it!" squeaked Ivy "I'm going to be on Radio 4! You wait until Gladys hears about this...this is on a par with her visit to Buckingham Palace, how she went on about it. Well now it's my turn. I wonder who will be in today... Martha Kearney does it normally...I do hope it's her, such a nice girl."

Bill laughed and put a hand on her arm

"Now Ivy, one thing at a time. Get yourself dressed first and then we will decide what we are doing."

"You won't get to go to the studios, Mum." John ventured.

Ivy stopped smiling and confusion clouded her face.

"But you heard them...they said they want to interview me."

John put on his best patient voice and smiled.

"They can interview you here, with all the equipment and then play it in the studio."

Bill looked at him sharply as her face fell and John immediately wished he hadn't said anything.

"Oh...well...I had better get changed anyway."

John looked guilty as Bill tried to bring back the joy of the moment. "At least you will still be heard on Radio 4...that's something to tell Gladys."

Ivy smiled weakly. "Yes, I suppose so."

She made her way upstairs as Bill went through to re-boil the kettle. An awkward silence fell on the two men and John flicked through his thoughts to find something to say that took him away from feeling bad.

"I wonder what I should do then." he mused, leaning

against the counter.

Bill squeezed the tea bags between two teaspoons and threw them into the bin under the sink. He turned to give a cup to John and then stood facing him.

"What do you mean, what you should do?"

John surveyed the tea, unable to recall the last time he had drunk it but not wanting to seem ungrateful, so took a sip.

"Well, I thought I was going to have to resign and suddenly, everything has turned around and I'm flavour of the month again. This is the problem with working in politics, things turn around in a heartbeat...maybe I should go into the office to sort out some stuff...what?"

John stopped talking as he caught sight of his father, looking at him incredulously. Bill stirred his drink, went to say something, paused and then resumed his usual closed face look before he spoke.

"Those people out there are not here for you...this isn't about you. It's because your mother is so lovely and made people feel special. That's all. Nobody even mentioned you."

Bill took a sip of his tea, put it on the side, folded his arms and continued. "What is your actual job title?"

John was feeling like a little boy and struggled to reply without being petulant.

"MP for Heningford, in charge of family values."

Bill snorted and picked up his mug again. "Family values."

He faced John and looked him directly in the eye. "What are your family values, John? You haven't seen your mother for over three years and your wife has left you...what does that say?"

John thought for a minute

"That women expect too much of me?" he ventured and jumped as his father slammed the cup down, tea sloshing onto the work surface.

"No, it says that you have lived your own selfish way for too long and are as far removed to teach others about family values as anybody else I know. You must know you have to resign, not because you got caught out, or because your parents have been foolish, but because you cannot do the job properly!"

Bill had turned puce and reached into his pocket for his handkerchief, wiping his top lip and coughing a little. John was aghast. He had never seen his father react in this way and for the second time that morning, couldn't believe what he was hearing and seeing. Putting his handkerchief away, Bill picked up his drink again and drank it all, finishing by putting it in the sink. He pulled off a piece of kitchen roll and mopped the side.

"I think you have got some growing up to do, to start behaving like a man is meant to and do the right thing, the first being to resign from a job that you are in no way qualified for."

John knew he wasn't going to win this one and, as is so often the case, the truth was only just beginning to dawn on him.

"You're right," John found himself saying "I know you are right. I'll finish my letter and send it."

Bill had got himself back together and was able to see that for the first time in a long time, his son had listened and appeared to be taking the advice given. John slouched, looking defeated and Bill decided to tackle a conversation that he didn't want to, but felt John needed to hear.

"Now I'm not into all this touchy feely mumbo jumbo stuff..." he began and John looked at him in alarm.

"But do you think you might need a bit of help?"

John was confused and jumped to the wrong conclusion.

"Dad, I've been writing for a long time, I'm sure I can

manage to write a letter of resignation."

"I'm not talking about the letter." The old man cleared his throat, "I mean help with your mind...a therapy session... you know...to help."

John went from 0 to 60 in a flash of indignation, as his mother made her way down the stairs.

"Why would I need that type of help? I'm not mad, it's the rest of the world that has gone cuckoo! It's not my fault these things have happened."

He folded his arms across his chest and muttered "I can't believe you even suggested it."

Ivy stood in the doorway, dressed in a blue twin set, looking like Margaret Thatcher in her later years. Bill looked at her sheepishly and John was still too cross to realise the impact his words had had on his mother. She decided not to be offended and made her way towards the cupboard where her cereal lurked.

"Well, having had a psychiatrist ever since you left, I can vouch for the benefit of one." she garbled, in a voice that betrayed her, crackling over the words. She coughed and opened a second cupboard to get her cereal bowl out. Having poured herself a bowlful, she put the pack back and turned to face the now visibly embarrassed John.

"You have had several difficult situations happen in a very short time...one of them would be enough to send someone to the edge." Ivy stated, quoting her therapist's words.

John continued to look uncomfortable as she went to the fridge to get the milk. Pouring it on and taking a teaspoon, she turned to go out and then looked at him again.

"Obviously, it's up to you, but I think you will struggle to get through a day in your current condition, let alone weeks, months and years. I know I would have."

Ivy went through to the lounge and sat at the dining table,

to eat. John stood, unsure again as to what to do and Bill again came to the rescue.

"She's right...it helped her a great deal. At least think about it." he suggested as he went to put his shoes back on.

"Okay." reasoned John, letting out a sigh and followed him, going to sit back at his laptop. Ivy was reading a magazine and turned the page to show John.

"Look, all these celebrities have a therapist, it's quite trendy now."

John smiled weakly at her and said, "I'll think about it."

Chapter 15
Celebrity Couple

John sat at the breakfast table, eating toast and marmalade and drinking tea. He had forgotten how much he liked tea, having drunk coffee for so long. Three weeks had passed since he had turned up on their doorstep and yet it felt like a life time away, so quick was the slotting back into place that occupied his role of son. After the initial difficulty of living back with his parents and all the changes the last few weeks had brought him, John began to feel more settled. His resignation had been accepted without hesitation and although there was a pang of hurt that they hadn't tried to keep him, he knew it was for the best. He looked out of the window as the neighbour went past with her dog, striding purposefully, muffled up against the biting cold of a November morning and he stared at her. She stopped suddenly as the dog decided something needed sniffing and glanced in and saw John staring and after an initial look of surprise, she smiled at him. John, embarrassed that he had been caught looking at her, quickly looked down at his cup, turning it around in his hands and not looking back until he had seen her move on from the corner of his eye and then watched her carry on down the road. Feeling foolish, he thought of Katy, wondering what she was doing and the ache that had settled into his stomach since she had left him, was stoked up, leaving him feeling even more depressed than ever.

Wearily, he took the plate and mug through to the kitchen and put them next to the sink. He washed his hands and dried them on the towel, trying to decide what to do today. He didn't want to stay in for another Saturday and knew that his parents would be in for most of the day. He could go into town and buy a new suit for interviews that he knew he would have to go to soon...financially he was more than ok as his final pay packet had included a healthy bonus as part of severance pay...even though he had resigned, they had wanted to thank him for his work. A lot of his policies had come to fruition and were working; just a shame he wasn't, he thought ruefully. But he needed to work again, to keep his mind active and to earn money. His dad came around the corner and stood, getting his keys out of his trouser pocket. John went to the door to let him in and opened it. Surprised, Bill put the keys back in his pocket.

"Oh, I didn't think you would be up yet." remarked Bill as he put his hat on the hook.

The last few days, John had been unable to sleep until the early hours of the morning and then slept in until eleven, waking up feeling groggy. Last night, he had deliberately put his laptop away and taken a mindless novel off the shelf to read, to take his mind away from everything. It had worked as he was asleep by eleven and found he woke at eight feeling less sluggish.

"I slept better." he replied, putting the marmalade back in the fridge.

Bill smiled and took a cup out of the cupboard to make

a cup of tea. "Well, that's good...you must be feeling a bit better then."

John gave a tight smile, but knew there was no truth in the statement. If anything, he was feeling worse. It was the main reason he wanted to work...all the while he just had his own thoughts to examine and overanalyze, he became more irate and bitter and just wanted a break from it all. Ivy came down slowly, holding onto the banister and carrying the glass she took up at night. Bill put some bread in the toaster and got another cup out for Ivy.

"Oooh, could you put me a piece on, please? I just fancy a bit with marmalade."

"Will do. I'll make the tea too."

John found the way they spoke to each other cloying in its sickliness and he felt the urge to get out. He put his plate and knife in the sink and took his phone out of his pocket. There were no messages. He knew there wouldn't be, but just to look at something else seemed to stop conversations...it was a technique he had learned from Katy.

Ivy crossed to the cupboard where she kept the marmalade. After moving a few things, she realised it wasn't there.

"Where's the marmalade?"

John was reading the news and didn't hear her. Bill turned to him.

"You had it earlier John, didn't you?"

"Mmmm?"

He looked up from his phone to see both parents staring at him.

"The marmalade...I need it for my toast." said Ivy, pleasantly.

John opened the fridge and took it out.

"Here." he remarked, setting it on the worktop and going back to his phone.

"Well, what's it doing in the fridge?"

"It keeps it fresh," murmured John, "It will go off in the cupboard."

Ivy looked at Bill, who shrugged as the toast popped up.

"But I've always kept it in the cupboard and I've never had any problems with it going off!" cried Ivy, feeling annoyed.

John ignored her and carried on reading. She spread her marmalade and muttered "I've never heard that it's supposed to be kept in the fridge."

John decided in that moment that he was getting out... discussing the storage of marmalade was beyond him and putting his phone into his pocket, he crossed to the coat pegs. Taking his jacket and putting it on, he stood in the doorway to address them.

"I think you will find its written on the side of the jar, Mum." he countered, and seeing Bill open his mouth, put up a hand to stop him "And before you ask, yes, I am going out...see you later!"

As he opened the door, the postman appeared with a bundle of envelopes, all different coloured. Bill saw him from the window and reached past John to take them.

"Morning Bill. Got quite a number for you today."

John wasn't interested in their post and so smiled and went quickly to his car. He unlocked the door and slid into the front seat. Feeling in his pocket to check his wallet was there, he put the key in the ignition and turned the engine on. The diesel was low so he decided to get some before he went shopping. Pulling off the drive, he glanced back to the house to see his Mum and Dad talking and laughing with the postman and he was glad to be out of there.

Bill had taken the stack of letters and, thinking that it might relate to the court case, chatted briefly with the postman about their five minutes of fame weeks ago and how Ivy had been to the Radio 4 studios to discuss her infamous son and the weddings. Having laughed about the absurdity of the situation, he had let the postman continue his round and closed the front door. Going into the lounge to sit at the dining table, Bill put his glasses on and opened the first envelope, his hands shaking, his mouth feeling dry.

"I don't believe it." he croaked and slowly got up to show Ivy. She took the letter and read it quickly, her mouth agape.

"What does it mean?"

Bill looked at the letter again and said, "Well, they obviously want us to go…but can we if we have the court case?"

Ivy took a pink envelope and opened it quickly. The wedding invitation sparkled as she drew it out and again, she was astounded to read that the pleasure of their company was required at the wedding of an unknown couple, who had heard about them and wanted them to attend. The first had been a letter of the same theme, explaining that their story had touched the young couple and they had a few tricky relatives that could be very difficult and a couple as lovely as Bill and Ivy would be perfect to redress the balance. Another envelope revealed a powder blue invitation, asking if Bill would give the bride away as she had never known her father and wanted the 'celebrity couple' to come to her wedding. The three remaining envelopes contained wedding invitations and Ivy's eyes grew wide as she read them. Having thought that everything had blown over, she realised it was all about to blow up again.

"What do we do?" Ivy queried, turning to Bill, who was still reading them.

"Well, we can't go…not with the court case coming up."

Ivy jumped in "But we've been invited! We wouldn't be breaking any laws now."

Bill put the cards into a pile and took his glasses off. He reached across to put them into their case and Ivy marveled again at their differences. She wouldn't even know where her glasses were, let alone the case and yet there he was, everything to hand, neat and ordered. Out of the corner of her eye she saw a bright flash of colour and turned to see a police car coming to a stop outside their window. She recognised the young constable from the wedding and fear gripped her heart.

"Bill, the police, it's him, the policeman's here, get the door, quick!"

"Ivy, calm yourself, I'm here, I'll deal with him, you just sit there." soothed Bill and crossed to the front door as the young man got there and opened it, a smile in place for their new-found friend.

"Good morning!" exclaimed Bill brightly, extending a hand.

Jason smiled back. "Good morning…bit of a chilly one, mind. Is it a good time for me to pop in? I just need to update you."

"Of course, come in," replied Bill as Ivy hurried back into the kitchen.

"I'll pop the kettle on." she cried shrilly, but Jason lifted a hand to stop her.

"No need, I won't be here that long and I need you in on the conversation too."

"Oh…okay."

Ivy crossed to where she had been sitting and took her seat. Bill as always, remained standing. Jason took his place in front of the fireplace, hands clasped behind his back.

"Well at least I am the bringer of good news this time," he stated, looking from one to the other. "Mr and Mrs Wolverton have dropped the charges."

Ivy gaped as Bill continued his steady gaze. "Does that mean we will be found not guilty?"

Jason laughed "It means more than that. There is no court case to answer, no judgement required, you are completely free of any charges of wrongdoing."

Ivy began to feel the relief wash over her as she reached for a tissue. "How did that happen?" she sniffed as the tears filled her eyes.

"Well, it seemed there was a bit of publicity over the case and they felt that they would be portrayed in a bad light… plus I'm not sure the CPS would have said there was a case to answer…it's hardly in the public interest."

"Ah, that is brilliant news." remarked Bill, rubbing his hands together.

"I like this part of my job, bringing good news to lovely people like yourselves."

He looked from one to the other. "If that's all well and good, I'll be on my way."

Ivy got up to see him off and as they got to the door, caught sight of the envelopes on the hall table; she suddenly remembered what she needed to ask him.

"Oh, I meant to say…we have been invited to a few weddings, by complete strangers…are we allowed to go?"

Jason considered this, looking at the envelopes she now had in her hands.

"Yeah, I don't see why not…you've been invited, they know who you are, so yeah, go for it."

With this cheery commendation, the young policeman left, whistling as he went up their path. Ivy was overjoyed, hoping that this was the last time she would see a marked police car at her home.

Chapter 16
Staccato Rhythm

The roads were so well known to John that it felt like he was in a favourite film, seeing the familiar outlines that studded the landscape of his youth…the tree he sheltered under, having stormed out of the house in the middle of a teenage dispute, returning home soaked through tears mingled with the deluge of the sky. 'God's crying too' his mum used to say whenever it rained…he doubted God even looked in his direction, let alone cried about him and his miserable existence. The park, nothing like how it was when he was a child, still evoked the 'King of the castle' element. Standing at the top of a twenty-foot slide that was now banned, due to health and safety poxy laws, the metal from it melted down and made into a garden ornament, no doubt, he thought ruefully, rubbing at his chin, the stubble feeling itchy in the heat from the sun through the car window. Although it was nearly December, the weather still seemed to be having an inferiority complex, with downpours of rain interspersed with bright sunshine, none of the bitterly cold days of his childhood. John quite liked the crispness of a winter morning, with frost on the ground and smoke from his mouth. He had his duffle coat on and could feel the sweat slide down his back, uncomfortable and yet unable to do anything about it. He pulled into the forecourt of the garage and stopped by the diesel pump. Getting out, the cold initially a relief, turned into being uncomfortable as the damp from his back connected with the damp of the air and chilled him. He went around to the side of the car and then had to go back as he had forgotten to push the button to release the cap. Annoyed, he went back to the cap and removed the nozzle from the cradle. The numbers didn't change to zero and he looked into the shop, hoping they would notice him. An older woman was in the kiosk, with a guy talking animatedly to her. He looked again at the numbers, but there was no change. He looked back at the woman and raised his hand to try and get her attention. At this, the guy having seen him out of the corner of his eye, gestured to him and the woman turned and quickly pressed what was required to set the pump back to zero.

John felt the irritation in his chest and throat, gripping the pump and putting it roughly into the opening. The diesel flowed through and then cut out abruptly; John pressed again and it did the same, over and over, catching the skin on his palm, making him wince and all the while he could feel the anger bubbling under the surface, hot molten lava on the move. He managed £13.76 before he had had enough of the staccato rhythm, yanking it out and slamming it into the cradle again, the diesel that had been so difficult to get out, now seemingly inspired to spurt all over his hand, trouser leg and shoes. John cursed, the liquid greasy on his hand and snatched at the paper towel, wiping his trousers knowing it was futile, the stain would remain, the smell would follow him for days. He glanced into the shop, but the guy was still at the till, unaware of John's annoyance. He went in and soon realised why the guy was still there. He was shouting at the woman behind her screen, aggrieved by the injustice of being asked to pay before he moved his car, his voice dripping with sarcasm.

"So, you can just stick your stupid policies up your arse! I had to move it cos there's no air in my tyre, I told you that!"

The woman was visibly upset and tried to speak "But I'm not allowed to let anyone leave without paying…"

"I wasn't leaving without paying! I'm here now, aren't I? You've got your money!"

"But I didn't know…"

"No, you didn't know, and you didn't wait and see, instead of announcing it over the tannoy…daft bitch."

John sighed, feeling more and more angry…could this day get any more ridiculous? He just wanted to get in, pay and then get on with his day and instead, he was feeling more than angry, there was the crush again around his heart that kept troubling him. He realised that there was a new feeling creeping in, a sense of impending doom, a need to get away and lie down for a few hours. John looked at the sweets, trying to distract himself, and grabbed a Snickers.

"Well, thanks for your help, it's been a pleasure, really it has."

The sarcastic parting shot as the young man left, a grim smirk on his face, gave John a flicker of hope; at least he would be served now. But the woman was ringing up her manager, relaying all that had happened, reiterating that she was on her own and had felt threatened; the glass screen offering little protection of the hurtful words flung through them. John began to seethe again and felt a wave of dread pass through him. He checked himself, confused as to what it was. It subsided and then another wave hit him, causing him to catch his breath as the room swam slightly…he felt the urge to go back to the safety of his parents. The woman was off the phone, picked up her banana, went red and then burst into tears.

"Oh, for crying out loud, I need to pay for my fuel!" The fear of another wave engulfing him caused him to react angrily and he slammed down the Snickers and took out his wallet. The woman was surprised enough to stop crying momentarily, gulping down before asking "What number?"

John looked at her incredulously and then turned slowly to look at the only car on the forecourt. She hastily tapped the button to release the amount and then continued to weep as he put his card in to pay. He went to punch in his pin and then realised there was nothing in his mind, no numbers in the depths of his subconscious to unlock the finance in his bank and he felt a stab of panic again. He couldn't fathom what his pin was and rather than risk getting the card locked, he pushed the cancel button and opened the flap in his wallet. Receipts waved at him, but alas, no notes.

"I don't bloody believe this." he growled through gritted teeth and the woman stopped her tears and looked at him suspiciously.

"Oh, you're not another one, are you?"

"Of course not, I just can't remember my pin, that's all," he snapped, "Is there a cash machine here?"

"Yes, round the side, near the toilet." she stammered, relieved that there wasn't going to be another incident.

John strode out and went around to the machine. It only dawned on him when he went to punch in the pin that he couldn't remember it and that this was a futile exercise. Another wave came over him and his knees felt weak, he must have a virus or something, he felt like death. He realised what he was going to have to do, much as he didn't want to. He took out his mobile and rang his parent's landline, all the while conscious of the woman behind the screen staring at him as she ate her banana. It rang a few times and John was beginning to lose the will to live when at last, his father informed him of the number he had just rung.

"Dad it's me…yes, I'm fine…well, actually, no, I don't feel great…but….no, it's not an emergency, I just need some money…I know I have, but I can't remember my pin…look, I'll discuss it later, can you come and meet me at the petrol station on Court Road? About £20…No, I don't need to speak…no…Dad? Oh, right, Mum, I can't really talk…no, I'm okay, just feeling a bit ill…no, really, I'm fine. Okay, I'll maybe get a bottle, now I must go…bye."

The grass on the roadside verge swam as John finished the call and he thought he was going to faint. Leaning forward, he felt shivery, trying to get his head low and hoping that when he stood up, he would feel better.

He didn't.

The woman was on the phone again when he came back into the shop and he quickly went to the drinks section. Finding a bottle of Lucozade, he picked it up and took it to the counter, the woman put the phone down and looked at him nervously.

"It's okay…my dad's on his way with the cash…so I will be able to pay for this then."

"You can't open it until you have paid for it…it's not allowed."

The woman had recovered from her earlier upset and was back into full 'abiding by the rules' mode. John felt too weak to argue and so he just nodded, wanting to go and sit in his car but having no energy to ask, knowing his request would be denied. Relief washed over him as he saw his father's familiar car pull in, with Ivy in the front, looking concerned. It brought a lump to his throat and he knew he must be feeling unwell to get so emotional. He coughed and went to the counter as they came into the shop.

"Thanks Dad." he said gratefully as his father took out his wallet and gave him a twenty-pound note. He handed it to the woman, who obviously still felt the world was out to get her; she held it up to the light and then put it through the till, giving him his change, without saying a word.

"How are you feeling?" enquired Ivy, going to put her hand to his forehead.

"Mum, not here...I'm okay, I just felt...a bit weird." John started to speak and then realised that he felt fine; his head had cleared and the sense of doom had left him, he didn't even feel cold as they left the shop.

"Well, maybe you have a virus, or something, you need to take it easy...drink your Lucozade."

"I'll have it when I get home. I need to pop to the bank now, to reset my pin...see you when I get back."

Chapter 17
That Was Enough

Linda was just finishing her hoovering when the lift opened in front of her, causing her to visibly jump. She watched as Katy strode out, looking immaculate and smiled knowingly, the years of observing others telling her that this was a woman who had landed well and truly on her feet. Obviously, she had heard the rumours, the young girls in the office had made it very clear what they thought of an older woman pushing in and taking Luke captive; the fact she had been married only added to their indignation, the critical judgements stemming from jealousy, no doubt. She might only be a cleaner, but she had observed enough about human behaviour to know what was behind it. Katy normally liked to see Linda, always willing to stop for a chat, but she didn't like the look on her face this morning and decided to keep it brief.

"Good morning, Linda…is anyone else in?"

Linda licked her top lip and smiled cunningly.

"No, only me and you are daft enough to come in at this time. You are looking very well…have you lost weight?"

Normally, this type of comment would have pleased Katy

and she would have revelled in the attention, but she knew that Linda was going to want more information. She smiled tightly and went over to her desk.

"Not that I'm aware of, but I have been eating well."

Katy turned her computer on and bent down to open her bottom drawer.

"I expect you have been getting more exercise too." rasped Linda slyly.

Katy sat up sharply and looked at her, knowing that she was having a dig yet her face was a picture of innocence as she wound the Dyson lead round the machine.

"Again, not that I'm aware of. I really need to get on, so if that's everything?"

"Oh yes, that's everything." sniggered Linda, pushing the machine from the room and grinning to herself.

Katy pushed the drawer shut and put her stapler on the desk, the irritation of Linda's insinuation sitting heavily on her chest. She had expected the girls in the office to gossip about her relationship with Luke, having listened in enough times to the in-depth conversations they had discussed in the past. She often felt sorry for the person being flayed publicly. These young girls, immaculate makeup, all smiles and innocence to your face and yet so malicious when it came to the backstabbing judgement of others. The number of times in the past when they had been mid-flow in their venomous musings and then remembered that she was there and would catch her eye. Katy would smile politely, the distance in generations keeping her out of the frame, unable to comment and not willing to do so anyway. Since she had moved in with Luke, the office atmosphere had changed from hard-working, with humorous banter to tense moments of interaction and awkwardness, especially from Sophie, the confident young secretary who thought that

Luke was really into her and had discussed their non-existent relationship regularly to the other girls, even when Katy had first been seeing him. She took the stapler and began stapling some paperwork together, pressing down harder than she needed to, wanting to release the tension. She clicked on her emails and saw there were thirty-five, eleven of which were marked high priority. They would need dealing with today, so she was glad that she had made the effort to come in early. She looked out of the window and could see the dawn beginning to appear on the horizon, the darkness of the winter months usually depressed her but it all seemed different now. In the past, she would have been bothered about the young girl's chatter, the way they looked at her with sneers and stopped talking when she came into the room. That was another reason she came in early...it meant she was already there so they couldn't bitch about her. She smiled as she piled up the now stapled paperwork and put it into her outbox and thought about Luke and how happy she was and that was enough.

Katy went through to the coffee making area and filled the kettle up. She noticed her name on the whiteboard, next to Martin, her Managing Director's name, which meant she had a meeting with him in the afternoon. Flicking the kettle on, she felt annoyed as she hadn't arranged the meeting with him, knowing that it must have been planned when she wasn't there. She took her soya milk out of the fridge and put it in her cup, surprised as the carton didn't feel very full. Katy was sure she had only opened it a couple of days before. She took her drink back to her desk and clicked on to open her emails. She began to reply and had got through most of them before the first member of staff arrived, one of the quieter girls in the office. Katy smiled at her and she was rewarded with a furtive smile that left as quickly as it had come, as the girl put her bag down and then took out her phone. Finishing her typing, Katy bent down to take her bag as she went out of the office, down the side corridor to use the toilet. Being a woman was crap at times, she thought as she sat on the loo, quickly changing the soiled towel for a fresh one. She flushed the toilet twice after the initial flush left the water a tell-tale pink. Once satisfied, she went to the sink and washed her hands thoroughly, rubbing the soap all over before rinsing it off. Katy looked at herself in the mirror and smiled. She could see the weight loss even around her face, her cheekbones were defined and the puffiness had gone. She knew she looked visibly happier and better and she felt the warm rush again of wonder that Luke had brought to her life. She was looking forward to meeting his mum soon, to become a part of that world and imagined the happiness she would bring to the old lady, knowing that her son was so happy. Katy shook off her hands and as she didn't like the hand drier because it made her hands feel so rough afterwards, she used some more toilet paper to dry them. She opened the door, and could hear laughter and loud voices. As she walked stealthily along the corridor, she could hear Sophie speaking above the laughter:

"Honestly, who does she think she is? I saw that outfit in New Look, I mean, can you imagine? At her age…think if you wore the same stuff! The horror!"

Much laughter again as Katy glanced down at her skinny black jeans and pastel floral top, purchased in a recent shopping spree, indignation flaming her cheeks and she took a deep breath and stood a little taller as she came to stand in the doorway of the office. Sophie had her back to her, but the others saw her and their laughter froze on their lips, but oblivious, Sophie carried on.

"I think she needs to impress him, that's why she has to

dress so young…you do know that she is seven years older than him…I mean, talk about a cougar, stalking her prey… what a slag…. what?" The question hung in the air as the other girls looked away and walked to their chairs and Sophie turned to see Katy in the doorway.

"Oh, morning…I didn't realise you were here." Sophie said brightly, no trace of shame on her perfectly made-up face.

"Obviously." countered Katy stalking over to her desk and sitting down. Sophie carried on.

"I was just talking about an old school friend of mine," explained Sophie but stopped as Katy held up her hand.

"Please, don't insult me any further, Sophie." she replied firmly and turned her back on her.

Sophie puffed herself up. "There's no need to be rude!" she snapped haughtily and stomped off to her work area, leaving Katy astounded.

Chapter 18
Idea of Weddings

"On the programme, today…as the mother of the disgraced MP for Family Values, Ivy Ashton has had her fair share of upset recently…from the breakdown of her son's marriage to her being arrested for fraud and the fear of an impending court case, life has certainly been difficult. But a campaign on Twitter, led by a number of wedding guests, has seen Ivy and her husband Bill catapulted into the limelight and suddenly everyone wants them at their wedding. Now, Ivy, can you take us back to the beginning…what caused you to want to turn up at complete strangers' weddings?"

Ivy looked at Bill, who nodded at her and she leant forward towards the microphone.

"Well, it was after Bill's retirement meal. We had lots of exciting things planned now that we would both be at home together with time on our hands. When we got back to the house, there was a letter on the mat from the…erm…who was it from again?"

She turned to Bill, who again, sat forward in his seat to get nearer to the mic.

"From the Inland Revenue, telling us that our pension

would be halved due to cuts."

Ivy carried on "So suddenly, we were not as well off as I had thought and we had to cut back on everything."

Jenny sat back in her chair. "But how did you get the idea of weddings?"

Ivy smiled as she remembered. "We had been invited to a wedding by a good friend of ours, whose son was getting married. The whole day we ate well, were warm and it meant we could turn off the heating in the house while we were not there."

Jenny leaned towards her sympathetically. "It was more than that, though, wasn't it? The chance to spend time with other people…how long had it been since you had seen your son?"

Bill coughed and answered, "About three years…it had been difficult to meet up, he was so busy."

Ivy butted in "He didn't want to see us, not really. Lots goes on in families, doesn't it?"

"Well, yes, give me a dog over a human being any day," snorted Jenny, "But the fact is your son was the MP for Family Values, I mean how?!"

Ivy smiled "The thing is, he was good at sorting out other people's families. He got a lot of support from his constituency and was good at arguing a case…still is, for that matter."

Jenny looked down at her notes and back at Ivy.

"So, you started going to the weddings, until inevitably you got caught and arrested…and then the public came to your help?"

"Yes," responded Bill, "The first we knew of it was when we opened the door to the reporters on the Saturday morning. We assumed it was because John was having to resign."

"Was he staying with you then?" questioned Jenny, suddenly.

Bill coloured and Ivy jumped in "Yes, he came around after he found out about our arrest. We were overwhelmed with the support we received and we believe this had a direct effect on the fact the case for fraud against us was dropped. I think the parents of the bride felt a bit petty about it all… they got a lot of flak on social media over it."

"So now you are invited to weddings by strangers who want you there…why do you think that is?"

Ivy looked up and reflected on the question. Bill was about to say something when she raised her hand and spoke.

"Personally, I think it has to do with a couple of things… the people that we had helped at the different weddings spoke up for us and vouched for our innocence and kindness…we may have started out going to the weddings for our own gain but actually gave out quite a lot in terms of advice, sympathy and in one particular case, time. Also, the world is celebrity mad and our story became a popular 'trend', is that the word?"

"Well, yes, you were certainly trending on Twitter," Jenny interjected and again consulted her notes "You have 20,000 followers on your joint account."

Bill looked shocked.

"Do we?" he exclaimed "I know John said there were a lot, but that many?"

"Well, to some people, we are celebrities that they want at their wedding…some have needed peacemakers to help with difficult guests, some like the celebrity tag and others… and this gets me every time." said Ivy, as tears filled her eyes. "Some have never known their father and ask Bill to give them away…what a privilege…and yet so sad."

Ivy wiped her eyes with her hankie and Bill looked at

Jenny.

"I'm sure you bring something special to those weddings," she soothed, taking the top paper off her pile and putting it at the bottom. "How is John in all of this?"

"He is fine." stated Ivy firmly, wiping her tears. "He is living with us until the house can be sold and then will get a nice place for himself. Some good has come out of all our difficulties. We have our son back in our lives."

"And there, I'm afraid is where we will have to leave it, it's been a pleasure having you both here and I wish you all the best for your future."

Ivy stood as Jenny continued on to the next piece, the engineer who had shown them in now directed them to leave through the side door. Bill quietly lifted his jacket from the back of the chair before following her out. They passed a young woman, striking in her beauty coming up the stairs with an entourage of people around her. She strode towards them and smiled faintly, as if she recognised them.

"Oh…it's Ivy, isn't it?" She spoke softly in her American accent, "I love what you guys have done for marriage… you're a great example to us all."

Ivy went pink with delight and Bill tipped his hat and put his hand out.

"Thanks very much, Miss…er…"

"Jolie." The beautiful young woman replied, her cat like eyes crinkling up as she smiled, "But you can call me Angelina."

She took his hand and shook it and Ivy's eyes widened in delight as she turned and shook Ivy's too, her cool hand soft in hers. She went through to where Jenny was introducing her and put on the headphones that Ivy had just been wearing.

Ivy watched her as she spoke and as Angelina caught her

gaze, she smiled and nodded before the engineer showed them out.

* * * * *

John stood in the queue, waiting behind the line for his turn to register with the receptionist, a tall, formidable looking woman, grey bobbed hair, glasses on a chain and a permanent frown line who was dealing with an Eastern European demanding treatment.

"You no understand, I am seek! I need Dorktor!" demanded the man, raising his voice and jabbing his paperwork.

In the calmest voice imaginable from somebody who looked so fierce, the receptionist replied.

"I understand that, sir, but you don't have the necessary documents for me to register you at this practice."

"I have papers HERE!" he shouted, pointing at the sheaf in his hand.

"There's no need for you to raise your voice at me, Sir, I understand what you are saying. These are not the correct papers to register here."

"You are stupid woman! I go and come back now! You wait!"

With this, he turned abruptly and stormed out, catching John's shoulder as he went past.

"Look where you bloody going, idiot!" he threw over his shoulder, before hitting the door hard with his hand.

John stepped forward as the receptionist wrote something down on her pad.

"Well, he was rude, wasn't he? Did you see him push past me, flipping cheek. I don't know how you put up with it."

The woman glanced up and smiled grimly, before putting

the note into an envelope and taking hold of her mouse again.

"How can I help you?"

"I need to register here as I've just moved back into the area."

He didn't want her knowing he was living with his parents and fiddled with his wedding ring, scratching underneath where it itched, contact dermatitis apparently, or so Google had confirmed. He supposed he should take it off now, maybe sell it, but he quite liked it, had chosen the thick gold band himself. Maybe I could put it on my other hand, he thought, watching as the receptionist bent down to open a drawer. She put her glasses on, the purple beads on the chain winked under the spotlights sporadically set in the ceiling and then took a pen from the desk tidy.

"What's your name?"

"John Ashton."

"And the address?"

"Oh – erm - it's 25 Lowgate, Peterborough, Cambridgeshire. PE...oh...I'm sorry, I'm not sure of the postcode."

She used her mouse and typed in the details onto the system.

"I've got an Ivy and Bill Ashton registered here at that address...are they your parents?"

Although she displayed an innocent enough face to him, he still felt as if he had been rumbled and said resignedly "Yes, they are...sorry, I should have said."

With a look that confirmed he should have said, she gave her tight smile and said "No problem, I shall just sort that out. If you can fill in this form for me."

She gave him the form and a pen just as the Eastern European flung the door open and came marching up to the desk, with another younger man following.

"I have come back!"

"So you have." murmured the receptionist, still typing.

"You need to see me NOW!" he shouted, as his friend tried to pull him back.

"You need to wait; I'm dealing with this gentleman now."

"NO, I was first, I go first, I seek!"

She took her glasses off and stood up, all six foot of her. The man looked a little uncertain, thrown by her sheer size and she took the opportunity to speak.

"Go and sit down over there and I will deal with you after I have finished with this gentleman." Although she was still polite, there was definitely a hint of steel in her voice and the younger man began to reason with him. Another receptionist then appeared through the door behind her and at this, she smiled and turned to her colleague.

"Aaah, Mollie, would you mind dealing with this gentleman?" She gestured to the Polish man, who was straining to get to the desk.

"Okay," agreed Mollie, a little uncertainly before sitting at the desk and working on the other computer.

He moved forward eagerly, keen to get his precious paperwork under the nose of somebody who could get him the help he needed and the other receptionist sat back down. John was really irritated by the two men and turned his back towards them as he filled in the form. It seemed so wrong to him, not that people came here from different countries, that he could understand - but that some of them were so demanding and rude seemed to him just a step too far. You'd think they would be grateful for any help they were given, he thought. As he finished filling in the form, he realised that Mollie was saying the same as her colleague, that the man's paperwork was not going to help him get registered. He felt pleased about this and turned to see what would happen.

"But I am seek!"

The man sounded desperate now, less angry and John felt a bit guilty for being mean.

"I know that. Your papers are for your country - we need to give you a new form for you to register here."

At this, she bent down to get a form out of the drawer and, after clipping it to a clipboard, handed it to him. He looked blankly at her, before turning to his friend and speaking in Polish.

"Perhaps your friend can help you fill it out?" she said, passing him a pen.

His friend smiled and nodded and took the pen and clipboard and sat in the waiting area. The man followed him and they discussed it as they filled it in. John finished his form and handed it back to the receptionist, who he noticed had two spots of colour on her cheek. She said nothing, but looked furious as Mollie typed away on her computer.

"Is my form okay?" he ventured.

"Yes, fine," she confirmed quickly, "I'll just get you on our system and then you can make an appointment with your GP…Dr Aldridge."

The two men were back at the counter, laughing and talking fast. Mollie took the form and having scanned it, looked back at them enquiringly.

"It says you have been registered in this country already… at the Munroe surgery and Warders…why are you trying to register here?

They looked at her blankly and the receptionist dealing with John spoke.

"Probably because they want to get some more medicine. I was hoping you would realise they were already registered and therefore not our problem."

Mollie went red at these comments and looked cross. She ripped up the forms and the men immediately stopped laughing.

"Hey, you can't do this, it's not possible…"

"You cannot be registered here, you are already registered elsewhere, I'm afraid I'm going to have to ask you to leave." Mollie rattled off, holding their gaze. They began to protest, getting louder and Mollie picked up the phone and pressed a number. Within seconds, a man appeared from the back of the building, looking mean and the men hastily made their way out before he could remove them.

"Right, that's you registered, Mr Ashton and you can have an appointment with your doctor in three months."

John gaped at her.

"Is there nothing sooner?"

She smiled wryly "I'm afraid not…as you can see, we are rather oversubscribed."

* * * * *

The waiter smiled as Katy walked through the door of the Greek restaurant and she knew that they were now regulars in here. When the waiter gets to know you, it's a sign, she thought, but really couldn't care less. She was so happy, nothing seemed to bother her anymore. As he led her to her usual table by the window, she allowed him to pull out the chair as she went to sit down and took the menu from him.

"Your husband will be joining you?" he enquired and she had to stop herself saying 'God, no!' before realising he meant Luke.

"Oh, yes, my partner will be here soon. He got caught up at work." she chattered happily.

"Would you like a drink while you wait?"

"Oooh yes, a large glass of Zinfandel, please," she stated, relaxing back into her seat.

The waiter gave a little bow and went to get the wine. She glanced around the restaurant, almost full of couples. She liked to people watch, to suss out what was going on in a relationship, wondering how on earth a gorgeous guy had ended up with a plain Jane and vice versa. There was a young couple, even more regulars to the restaurant than her and Luke, in fact they were over in the corner she realised as she took her drink from the waiter. Late twenties at the most, they seemed very ill-matched in her opinion, the woman was stunning, with a great figure, whose presence turned heads, always dressed to impress. Her husband was a bespectacled older guy, with thinning hair and a weak looking body and yet she appeared smitten with him, always touching his face and being coy. Katy couldn't understand it. She took a sip of the wine, just sweet enough to enjoy, just dry enough to feel grown up and recognised an elderly couple that were eating their meal near her. They always ate the same and hardly spoke, comfortable in their own company. Katy watched them wistfully; she hoped that her and Luke would be like that, so comfortable with each other that they didn't need to speak. Much as she loved his chatter and energy, she knew it would have to settle down soon, for them to get into a routine that was sustainable. Her teeth felt squeaky as the liquid passed them and her stomach rumbled. Putting the glass down, not wanting to drink too much on an empty stomach, she picked up the menu. She heard the door open and turned to see Luke coming in, looking windswept and still gorgeous. Katy smiled at him, thrilled that he was hers; her heart swelled as he smiled at her and strode across to join her.

"Hallo darling," he said planting a kiss on top of her head

before taking a seat opposite her, "Sorry I'm late, the traffic was awful!"

"Well, if you will leave the office late." she teased him and glanced at the table next to her where a young couple had just been seated. She caught the eye of the woman who had been staring at Luke and who guiltily looked away, pretending to read the menu. Katy initially felt pleased that Luke had caused such a reaction until she realised that the look was not someone who was guilty of checking out a handsome man; she recognised it as the same look that must have been on her face when she surveyed all the unsuitable partners around her and she suddenly felt indignant.
Bitch, she thought, turning her attention back to Luke and determining not to let anything spoil their evening.

"I'm starving…shall we have a starter?"

"Why not?" decided Katy, "Let's push the boat out. Do you want the calamari again?"

Luke, who had been sorting his napkin, made a face.

"Nah, too much like chewing rubber bands."

Katy giggled, taking another mouthful of the wine.

"You're so uncouth. I suppose you would rather have the bread and cheese?"

Luke feigned a hurt look and pretended to study the menu, until she reached across and stroked his hand, causing him to look above over the top, quizzically at her.

"I'm only kidding," she said softly, "I quite like the bread and cheese myself. Let's get some olives too."

The waiter came and took their order before scuttling away to clear the table next to them.

"How has it been this week?" she asked him before taking the menu again.

He looked thoughtfully at her as she picked up her glass, which was already nearly empty.

"Okay…a bit boring… but nothing a week away won't sort out."

She swallowed quickly, coughing a little as the liquid burned the inside of her throat.

"Oh, I didn't realise you had to go away?"

She felt foolish, as if she was the last to know about a great surprise. The waiter appeared with a basket of bread and a tray of oils, before asking what Luke would like to drink. He ordered a lager and tore off a piece of bread and passed it to her, before taking a piece and sniffing it.

"Aaaah, heaven," he quipped, breathing it in and biting into it. The waiter came back with olives and the open bottle and glass for Luke to pour. He chewed before answering, pouring the drink into his glass before washing the mouthful down.

"Yeah, it's in a couple of weeks' time, the office in York wants to train us up to use a new computer program and so a few of us have been chosen to go."

He took another bite and settled back in his chair.

"York? That's handy, you can pop in and see your mum!" she exclaimed, spearing an olive with a cocktail stick before biting into it, the sour smooth taste exploding across her tongue.

"I'll probably stay at Mum's, to be honest, save on expenses," he murmured, still looking at the menu.

"I could always come with you?" she ventured, using the cocktail stick to poke into his hand. He surveyed her, considering this proposal before taking a swig of his beer.

"You could do," he said at last, before taking his own cocktail stick and attacking an olive. "But who would look after the cat?"

She laughed at the absurdity of the question and he smiled easily. He fiddled with the olive, chasing it across his plate as he spoke.

"I won't have much time for anything, the hours are as long there as they are here and I'd rather we have some time away together when we can spend lots of time…. together… in bed."

He popped the olive in as he finished speaking, a twinkle in his eye and she blushed, thrilled to be the object of such attention.

"Okay…I'll look at booking some time off then…soon." she countered, picking up the menu and watching as the couple next to them got up to leave. She felt triumphant as the woman, who earlier had implied with a look that they were ill-matched, stared as she left, no doubt, in Katy's mind, feeling foolish for judging so wrongly.

Chapter 19
It's A Wonderful Life

The meal at their local pub had been nice enough, usual pub fayre of frozen veg and processed meat. Lisa and Mike had been in at the same time and even John, caught up in his own little world, noticed how awful Mike behaved towards her. He had obviously been drinking most of the morning and although he could be excused for it being Christmas Day, his behaviour could not; his voice could be heard over the carols being played, derogatory comments about everyone and everything. John got the impression he was like it all the time, drunk and obnoxious. Lisa seemed to ignore it, intent on eating and only smiling at Ivy and Bill as they passed her table. She avoided looking at John and he was concerned that he had made an idiot of himself before and that now she didn't want to know him. Bill coughed and spoke as they went to leave.

"Merry Christmas to you both."

Lisa smiled and went to reply as Mike leant forward menacingly.

"Merry, is it? For you, maybe, but not for all of us."

Lisa looked annoyed, but said nothing. The awkwardness

hung in the air and then Ivy spoke.

"Well, it was a lovely meal anyway."

"Mine wasn't hot and there wasn't enough, such piffly portions." slurred Mike, "Waste of money, if you ask me."

Lisa drew in a breath and looked down, visibly embarrassed. John tried to catch her eye, but she wasn't looking at him and so he smiled at Mike and left, his parents trailing behind him. He allowed Ivy to link arms with him as they walked back to the house, the pint of beer that he had drunk with his meal making him feel relaxed.

"Shall we watch the Queen's speech together?"

John groaned inwardly but replied cheerfully enough.

"Yes…and then I think I will go for a walk to the park."

"Don't you want to sit and watch the telly with us? I'm sure there will be a film or two on."

"Maybe later…I need some fresh air first."

After the Queen's speech, which seemed to get more and more religious every year, he pulled on his work shoes and went out the front door quietly, having noticed that both his parents had fallen asleep in their chairs.

It was cold out and he was glad he had flicked up the thermostat so that the house would be toasty and warm for when he got back. Walking up the road, he reflected on the last few weeks, feeling a range of emotions. He knew he had enough money to keep afloat for a couple of months, but wanted to work soon, to keep his mind working. He hadn't been back to the house; just the thought of it made his chest ache. He hadn't realised how hard it would be without Katy, the thought of them not being together had never crossed his mind. When he had married her, he decided it would be for life, just like his parents. But then, he hadn't expected a world to exist when he didn't speak to his parents. Those three years had whizzed by and looking back, he could see how neglected they must have felt; even though he shared a house with Katy, he knew she had been badly neglected too. He crossed the road and made his way to the play park, knowing there would be a bench to sit on. He was disheartened to see the graffiti marring the colourful climbing frame and slide, the male genitalia looking like a cartoon cactus, the fact that Shane loved Ellie marked for all the world to see. It was all so predictable, he thought, have we not moved on as a society, that the same stuff was graffitied on every park in every town exactly as it had been years ago? How many times had the council had to clean it off, only for it to reappear again days later…so much money wasted…what was the point?

Normally, he would have felt angry about it, would have ranted with his work colleagues, or at the beginning of their marriage, Katy. But today he felt nothing, dead to everything. He went through the little gate that creaked as he pulled it open and clanged shut behind him, the springs so strong, he marveled that any child could get in to play. He sat down on the bench, an old style wooden one, that numbed his legs within minutes of sitting, the jeans he wore no match for the damp, old wood. He pulled his coat around him, folded his arms and looked up at the sky, the grey, bleak light already beginning to fade. Lonely didn't even begin to cut it and the cold of the night creeping in made more than his bones ache. The emptiness in his life filled him with a dread he had never experienced before and he didn't know what to do. He often found himself staring into space, not sure what he was meant to be doing, or he would drum his fingers on the table constantly, until his mother would call out for him to stop, irritated by the constant noise. He was doing it now, tapping against the bench and took his hands and laced them behind his head.

He could hear a dog barking and looked in the direction where it was coming from and could see a figure, walking a dog that he recognised as Zippy, Lisa's Staffordshire bull terrier that had an annoying habit of waking him at six in the morning. He sat, watching as Lisa was pulled along, the dog manic in its pursuit of a good bit of grass, nose down to the floor, the leash straining under the power. Such a little dog with all that strength, thought John, keeping still, a silly notion that he didn't want to be seen, but he needn't have worried, because Lisa kept her head down, marching past and would have missed him completely, if he hadn't stood up suddenly and called her name.

"Lisa."

"Fuck!"

Lisa snapped her head in his direction and then relaxed when she saw who it was.

"Oh, sorry, John, I thought…oh never mind."

She stopped to let the desperate dog off his lead and to give her face a quick wipe with the back of her hand. John had realised as she spoke that she was crying and now felt awkward, wishing he hadn't called out. He stood inside the play area, leaning against the red metal fence and watched the dog run away, almost out of sight.

"He's lively, isn't he?" ventured John awkwardly, keeping his eyes on the distance, to give Lisa a chance to regain her composure, but instead, he could see her shaking as she sobbed into her gloved hands, the scarf up around her face providing a barrier for the tears. John turned to look at her and was at a loss what to do - she had covered her face and didn't appear to be stopping, even when Zippy careened back, knocking into her knees. She stumbled back and he instinctively went to catch her. Lisa grabbed the fence and flinched back, away from him.

"I'll just come through…" he mumbled as he went to the gate and walked back to join her. She had a tissue now and was blowing her nose, the sobbing over as quickly as it had started and she seemed to be calmer. John tried again to converse with her.

"Did you not get what you wanted from Santa?" he joked, trying to lighten the mood. She looked at him and at first, he thought he had overstepped a mark or offended her, but she laughed, a gentle giggle and as the dog came bombing back again, she clipped the lead back on him and continued walking around the field. John walked next to her and as his eyes grew used to the now darkened field, he could just about make out the path.

"Something like that," she murmured as she ruffled Zippy's ears, "It's just a bit crap, isn't it? Christmas…when everything is meant to be all family and lovely, making memories, watching 'It's a Wonderful Life' and eating entire tins of chocolates."

John looked down at the ground, hoping that there was no dog poo on the path and that the soft mounds were leaves cluttered together.

"Well…Christmas is a tricky time, yes…I certainly didn't envisage being back here even visiting my parents, let alone living with them." he replied ruefully, putting his hands in his pocket as the cold bit into them. His cheeks were beginning to ache and he wished he was wearing a scarf, but hadn't expected to stay out this long. She kept her head down while walking and turned to follow the path back to the main road.

"I know, it must be weird for them too, having not seen you and everything."

He was glad of the darkness as he could feel his cheeks colouring, but she carried on regardless.

"Is it really over between you and Katy?"

The question, though asked gently, still hit him in the solar plexus and he felt the wave of despair pass over him as they carried on walking.

"I guess so," he answered sadly, feeling that he didn't want to say too much to her about it, "I mean, she is with someone else."

She stopped suddenly and looked at him. John could just make out the outline of her face, although something didn't look quite right and before he could think what it was, she spoke.

"Oh, sorry - I didn't know. That's pretty crap...you'll have to divorce her then."

He considered this as they approached the main road, the street light shining the way back to the village where his parents still snoozed on their sofa, the dog pulling her forward and as she turned her head sharply away from him, it suddenly hit him what was wrong with the picture earlier, the outline of her face. Sensing his realisation, she started to walk a bit faster, tugging Zippy away from the grass, keeping her head down and as he struggled to keep up with her, they eventually stood under the streetlight. John stopped to face her, Zippy still tugging to go on and so he grabbed the lead. She looked at him in surprise and he saw the ugly welt across her cheekbone, the bruising around her eye that had caused the swelling which had distorted her features. He was shocked, but not surprised. The way Mike had spoken to her had given him a bad feeling and so this was only to be expected.

"He only does it when he's had a drink." she explained softly. "Most of the time, we just live our own lives. It's only when we are forced together that it happens."

She wiped her eyes, careful of her damaged side and sniffed

loudly.

"Holidays are rubbish for a bad relationship …I can't wait to get back to work, although I'm not sure they are going to buy my 'walked into a cupboard' story. He's never hit my face before…usually my arm, or back, something that can be hidden, but he was really angry."

John still had hold of the dog's lead and realised that her gloved hand was under his. She carried on. "That's why I didn't look at you in the pub…he's so jealous and I didn't want to argue but he saw you looking at me and that was enough. It started as soon as we got back."

John let go of her as if she had burned him and pushed his hands into his pockets, feeling impotent with rage, a queasiness rising in his throat at the injustice of her situation.

"I'm sorry," he muttered and she put up her hand, but he carried on "No, I am…sorry that this is happening to you."

She smiled sadly and continued walking up the road to their estate. John walked in silence next to her, feeling weary and cold - he would be glad to be back in the warmth of the house and away from this horrible situation. They got to his house and she stopped, turning to look at him again. He bent down to stroke Zippy, who seemed calmer now, almost as if he understood that his mistress was calmer too. John felt awkward again and guessed what the answer would be, but knew he had to offer.

"Did you want to come in for a Christmas drink and a mince pie? I think Mum has made some."

Lisa smiled her quick, bitter smile again and shook her head.

"Thanks, but I'd rather your parents didn't see me like this. Please don't mention it to them. I'd better be getting back, he will wonder where I am."

John looked concerned at the mention of Mike and felt a stab of fear.

"Will you be alright? I mean...with him?"

Lisa stroked where John had ruffled Zippy's fur and used the dog as a go between

"Yeah, we'll be alright, won't we boy? You look after me, don't you sunshine?"

The dog wagged his tail and started to get excited again as she went to go up her path.

"Well...Merry Christmas," called out John, feeling glib and yet not knowing what else to say.

She laughed and called back "Yeah...very merry Christmas!" before disappearing through her front door. John stood outside, mystified by what he had heard and seen and felt tearful as he came quietly into his parents' home. They were still snoring and he decided to leave them and go up to bed. He bent down to undo his shoes and the tell-tale smell told him that the soft piles he had stepped on were not leaves. Annoyed, he took the offending shoe and put it in the conservatory, leaving it until the morning to clean. He suddenly felt exhausted and it was all he could do to climb the stairs up to his room and flop on the bed. John felt strangely emotional and found himself staring at the ceiling, tears rolling down his face, unsure of what he was so upset about, but crying none the less. His head ached and he felt cold again and so pulled the duvet over him, though he was still fully clothed. His eyes felt heavy and his limbs like lead...he just wanted to sleep.

* * * * *

John was to stay in that bed for six weeks, only going to relieve himself before staggering back to the safety and warmth of his cocoon, his body unwilling to cooperate, his mind seemingly shut down. His father thought he must have a virus and called his GP to discuss it and was told if he could get his son to the clinic, they would look at him, but they didn't do house visits now, so there wasn't much they could do. Ivy knew what was wrong, but went along with the virus plot, bringing his meals up and giving him Lucozade to drink. He barely spoke, seeming to just want to stare and Ivy began to sit with him, talking about what she had done that day and about the next wedding she was going to. He would sit and smile, almost childlike, occasionally falling asleep as she talked. In the end, she rang her psychiatrist, to ask her advice and offered to pay her to come and assess him. Dr Atwood came to see him, bringing her books and pens to make notes on the man that had caused her client so much anguish over the years - she was quite interested in him. She was surprised to see him looking so vulnerable. All her dealings with his character were that he was a harsh, cold-hearted individual with no empathy for others. His photos in the press showed him looking immaculate, hair brill creamed into place, wearing sharp business power suits and so to see him reduced to a t-shirt and jeans that were stained, hair unkempt and weight loss that made him look almost frail, well, she knew things must be bad. She smiled as she walked forward to introduce herself.

"Good morning, John. I'm Dr Atwood. I'm here to see how you are doing."

She spoke brightly and John looked at her, unsure of what he was meant to say.

"Do you understand what I'm saying? I'm a doctor and I'm here to help."

John still just stared at her and so she took out her notebook from her bag and found a pen and wrote his name at the top.

"John, I'm going to speak about a few things and as you listen, if there is anything you think might help you, then you can tell me, ok? You are safe to tell me and I will do what I can to help you. Do you understand?"

He nodded, glancing at Ivy, who was hovering by the door, and then staring back at Dr Atwood. Ivy couldn't believe he just sat, not saying anything and she almost wished she hadn't asked her to come, maybe it was just a viral thing that would go away on its own. But then the doctor began to speak and the reaction it caused in John reassured her that she had done the right thing.

"Now John, you have been feeling unwell for quite some time, haven't you? Before Christmas, I know your wife left you and then you lost your job and had to come and live here. That was a lot of change, wasn't it?"

She was speaking kindly, as if speaking to a child and Ivy willed him to tell her to stop patronising him, or to make some sarcastic quip, but instead he just stared mutely at her.

"The thing is, that's a lot to cope with and I'm guessing you started to feel overwhelmed, maybe a bit panicky. Did you find yourself in situations where you wanted to get out, that you couldn't cope, a feeling of doom perhaps?"

She looked at him and noticed the widening of his eyes, a flicker of recognition that what she was saying was triggering a memory.

"Can you remember something? Tell me what you can see, John."

"Banana." whispered John, his voice hoarse. Ivy moved forward.

"Are you hungry again?"

But Dr Atwood put her hand up to stop Ivy talking and carried on.

"What was that, John?"

He licked his lips and frowned in concentration.

"She was eating a banana - the man was rude to her…I was angry…I couldn't remember the number."

He seemed worn out by the effort of remembering and slumped back onto the pillow, but Ivy was so pleased that he had spoken that she took up the story.

"Oh yes, the day we had to come and rescue you. He had forgotten his pin and so Bill and I had come to pay for the petrol…"

"Diesel" croaked John, making her stop and look at him.

"Oh yes, so it was, diesel. And he said he didn't feel well then, but was fine when we got there."

The doctor nodded and wrote down in her book.

"Had you forgotten your PIN number before?"

She directed the question at John, who was looking more interested in her.

"No…I have an excellent memory… are these my grapes?" he croaked, suddenly noticing the plate next to him.

"Yes, I bought them from the market." stated Ivy pointlessly and watched as John began to tear them off and eat them, slowly chewing them as Dr Atwood continued.

"But the memory loss had been preceded by feeling anxious, panicky, a sense of doom?"

John sat up, and seemed to be trying to shake himself out of his dazed state.

"I thought I was ill…but when they turned up, I felt better."

She wrote again and then looked at him, eating his grapes.

"How long have you been like this?" She spread her arm across the bed and he looked up at the ceiling.

"A couple of days, I suppose."

"Oh John, don't be daft…you've been like this since

Christmas!" exclaimed Ivy, amazed at his not realising.

John looked at her and for a moment, she could see the old John about to explode out, correcting her and telling her she was the daft one. But then he took a moment, glanced down at his clothes, looked at Ivy and then at the doctor, who was still writing notes and he said, "How long have I been in here?"

Ivy swallowed, not sure how he would take the answer, but knowing she would have to come clean.

"Just over six weeks."

"Six weeks!? But what about New Year…and my job interview? The house, my God, the house!"

At this, he tried to spring out of bed, but weak from lying down and barely eating, he only managed a stumble to the floor, ending up looking up at the doctor, who observed him with a bemused look.

"It's not bloody funny." he muttered, sitting up and wrapping the duvet around him and Ivy began to cry - he was beginning to sound like his old self at last, she thought.

Dr Atwood looked serious.

"Oh, I'm not laughing at you, honestly. It's just all very interesting for me."

"Well, I'm glad I can be of assistance." said John in his best mocking voice and Ivy's heart was thrilled. He looked at her suddenly.

"Mum, I'm starving…can you get me some toast?"

Ivy looked at the doctor, who nodded.

"Yes, dear, of course," she replied and trotted out of the room, looking back in as she closed the door. Dr Atwood continued writing and for a moment, John sat, feeling strange, trying to remember why he wanted his mum out of the way…what did he need to ask her?

"So, what's the diagnosis then?" he finally managed, trying

to appear dignified, wrapped in a grubby duvet and smelling like a toilet.

She looked at him in a quizzing manner.

"You know," he said waving his arm, "How have I lost six weeks of my life and not known it?"

She looked resigned and put her pen down.

"It seems you have had a breakdown, brought on by several traumatic events" she started slowly. "A breakup that was unexpected, moving in with your parents, losing your job… any one of these could have triggered it. Although it seems odd it was Christmas Day it caught up with you."

John had an image of a dog with its eye hanging out, a gruesome-looking thing, but couldn't remember anything else, apart from the Queen's speech. He assumed he had gone to bed and slept for a couple of days, not six weeks! He must be losing the plot.

"So, what's the cure then? Have you got some pills or something I can take to help get me back to normal, here?" he waved his hand, "Whatever that is?"

She took up her pen and began to chew on the end. She tapped the end against her teeth and then replied, looking back down at her pad.

"John, there is no quick fix with a breakdown. It takes time, rest, pacing yourself. Sometimes medication can help, but I am not in favour of it and certainly not in this case. I would recommend that you have some counselling sessions to help you, to work through these traumas and get you back to your normal."

John sagged under the duvet as Ivy came back in with buttered toast and a cup of tea.

"Here we are, dear," cooed Ivy setting the plate down on the bedside table. John had his head in his hands.

"Do I have to have therapy?" he growled.

The doctor smiled before replying "Do you want to get better?"

As John ate his toast, thoughtfully chewing, the doctor stood up and Ivy saw her to the door. Outside, Ivy asked her what would happen next.

"I'll get my friend to call to arrange some counselling sessions for him. It seems he has shut down, judging by his response to everything, around the teenage years. During the therapy sessions, he will be able to work through the emotions that are causing him the high anxiety. It will take time, Ivy."

"But he will get better?" suggested Ivy anxiously.

Dr Atwood smiled and patted her arm.

"Of course, he will go back to being his usual, obnoxious self."

Seeing Ivy smile, she continued "You never know, he may even come through a nicer person."

"That would be good, although I would settle for my obnoxious boy back."

As Ivy opened the front door, John shouted down the stairs.

"Mum, I need a shower, I stink!"

Dr Atwood smiled again.

"Look like he's making progress already." she mused as she left the house.

"I'd better get him a towel," volunteered Ivy, "See you next week."

Chapter 20
Sloshy Indifference

The rain was falling heavily as John made his way to the adult education centre in town, the water seeping through his trainers, feeling icy before the warmth of his feet reduced them to a sloshy indifference. Bill had dropped him off before going on to the supermarket for a few things, trying to be jolly in the car. John had travelled in near silence, only saying that he would text when he had finished. As he approached the door, a car sped past, the water collected in the gutter now cascading over him, like grubby confetti and he sighed as it ran down his face, chilling him. He felt it physically but no more. No emotions reared their ugly heads and so he went to pull the door. It was a push door and he stumbled in, the water causing him to slip. Once in, he wiped his feet on the mat and walked forward to the desk. There were a few chairs in two lines, facing each other; one occupied by an elderly gentleman and two chairs with a middle-aged woman who looked forlorn and next to her, a bored looking teenage girl, her hair scraped back from her face, exposing razor sharp cheekbones. If John had been thinking straight, he would have recognised the personification of anorexia in front of him, taken in the legs that were as thin at the top as they were at the bottom, the upper arms looking as though they could snap at the slightest pressure. But in his unwell state, he noticed nothing and went and stood at the desk, waiting for the receptionist to finish her phone call. She smiled at him and quickly finished the call, looking at her list as she asked for his name.

"John." he stated matter-of-factly.

"And who are you here to see?"

John looked confused, not expecting to be asked this.

"My therapist. I'm here to see my therapist." he managed, before walking over to the waiting room.

The receptionist smiled to herself as she ticked his name off. John sat with his phone in his hand, fiddling with the settings on it. He was glad he hadn't brought his briefcase with him, but still felt a little exposed without it. After turning off his mobile data, God only knows how long that had been on for, he stuffed the phone into his jacket pocket, hoping that this woman was good - the sooner he could get better, the sooner he could sort out stuff.

He was suddenly aware that the elderly gentleman was staring at him. To avoid eye contact, he looked down at his dirty sodden shoes but the feeling persisted and John couldn't help but glance in his direction. He instantly regretted it as the old man's face had turned bright red and he stared at John with utter contempt.

"Are you one of them fuckers?!"

His voice, surprisingly strong for an older man rang out across the waiting room.

"Well?! Are you?" screamed the old man, rage clear in his eyes, spittle clinging to the sunken cheeks like a final spray of squirty cream.

The receptionist had stood up as soon as he had begun to

speak and knocked on one of the doors off the waiting area. A man appeared promptly and moved quickly across the room to where the gentleman was still swearing profusely.

"Ok, Samuel, let's get you in and talk about your options, yeah?"

The voice, like golden honey, dripped into the very place that obviously hurt so much as Samuel allowed himself to be manoeuvred into the room, quietening down as the door was closed after him.

"Sorry, are you okay?" the receptionist enquired as she passed by, looking him full in the face.

Disconcerted, he dropped his gaze; the dryness of his mouth alerted him to the fact that his mouth had been open and he swallowed, moving his tongue over his lips, trying to moisten them.

"Yes, fine," he croaked and coughed to clear his throat, embarrassed.

The woman carried on and sat back at her desk, going back to whatever she had been doing before Samuel's outburst. John swallowed again and looked up at the ceiling, swirled patterns that looked rough to the touch and he was transported back to being a child and staring forlornly at a piece of rubber in his hands. He had been at a neighbour's birthday party, a little girl called Gaynor, who in his and most people's opinion, should have been a boy, boisterous and rough as she was. The children had all been given the most wonderful balloons, marbled dark colours and bigger than he had ever seen. They were a gift to take home after the party and John had stared in amazement and wonder at such a rare balloon. Gaynor, clutching her own, came over to where he was and hit his with such a force, it shot out of his hands and up, onto the roughness of the ceiling and burst, with a disappointing pffft. John had stood, shocked just as his mother had arrived to collect him. Ivy had tried to make light of it, ruffling his hair and promising to get another balloon. He couldn't remember if she had bought him one, but he was never friends with Gaynor again. How weird to be thinking of this, he thought, still looking at the swirls above. Suddenly a door opened and a young woman came out and smiled at him.

"Mr Ashton?"

John glanced at her, observed the tailored dark trousers, cream blouse and maroon cardigan, on what appeared to be a twelve-year-old and sat forward.

"That's me...I've already signed in with the secretary," he said, pointing at the desk.

"Oh, that's good," she continued, "Come through to my office."

The woman indicated that he should join her.

"Oh."

John fumbled with his phone in his pocket and stood awkwardly, before moving to join her in the doorway. She stood back to let him pass and he somehow clashed with her, catching her hip with his elbow and apologised, trying to move quickly in.

"It's okay, don't worry," she reassured him, before closing the door and taking a seat behind her desk.

The room was surprisingly light for such a grey day, a huge window behind her let in enough daylight to not need the lamp stood at the end of a leather couch. He stopped fiddling with the phone in his pocket and looked across at her. She was opening a folder and flicking through some papers. Selecting a piece of A4, she held it in front of her and scanned the words, before smiling and looking at him. She was pretty, in a fresh, girl next door kind of way - no pencilled eyebrows here, just an English rose complexion, framed by dark curls and her eyes, her best feature, were big and blue.

"My name is Lauren Pearson and I am a therapist here. My colleague came and assessed you a couple of weeks ago and thinks that you will benefit from some therapy."

John suddenly felt scared, the bird fluttering in his chest beat against his rib cage, trying to break out.

"I just need a bit of help…some tablets or something." he mumbled, waving his hand around.

Lauren pressed her lips together and referred to the paper.

"I'm afraid it's not as simple as that," she stated gently, "From what I can see in your notes, you have had panic attacks, leading to a breakdown and heavy depression. These are not solved with medication alone. It may help, but the underlying issue needs addressing. Therapy is key to getting you back to your type of normal."

John fiddled with his cuff, desperate to get out and then glared at her.

"You have no idea about my 'normal' what can you know, you're a child!"

He stood up and she observed him with a quizzical look on her face, the unpencilled eyebrows raised, unmoved, even when he turned away and headed for the door. Instead, she spoke in a soft voice, devoid of emotion.

"It's your choice, obviously, I can't make you stay. But this is what you need, to be able to enjoy life again and, to be honest, I think it would be a while before you'd get another appointment." she added ruefully.

John stopped, his hand outstretched for the door handle and sighed, tipping his head back and being met with the same rough, swirly ceiling. He knew that the feeling of anxiety while in the room would be nothing to how he would feel back at home again and he dropped his hand to his side and walked back to the chair.

"Sorry about that," he mumbled before sitting back down. "I just feel so crap."

"I know and I'm here to help. First, we need to agree a contract."

"What for?"

"So that you know what you are going to get out of our sessions and so I can help you to the best of my ability."

"What's your success rate?"

She smiled and looked down as a slight flush crept over her cheeks.

"Well, I'm fairly new to this, but I have had success with past cases."

"Well, that is comforting to know," murmured John, with more than just a hint of sarcasm and he took his pen out of his pocket and removed the lid.

"Where do I need to sign then?"

She pushed the sheet over to him and kept her hand over the signature box.

"You need to read the terms and conditions bit first – to know what you are getting into."

"Really? I can't just take your word for it and be done with it?"

She screwed up her face and shook her head.

"Not really…we need to agree so that neither of us backs out of the contract we have made with each other."

"Shame we can't do the same for my marriage." grumbled John grudgingly and then, taking the piece of paper in his hands, he read it through.

"I'm glad to see it's confidential, I don't like the idea of having to talk to you about everything and worrying you might discuss me to your friends on a night out. What's this bit for?"

He looked puzzled and passed her the piece of paper with his finger against the question concerned.

Again, the faintest flush crept across her face but she kept her reply steady.

"That's just in case either of us start to get feelings for one another."

He couldn't help but chuckle.

"Oh, is that likely? I mean, come on…it's hardly…"

He stopped as he caught sight of her bemused expression and felt flustered.

"I mean, does that happen…often?" he managed before falling silent.

"It does actually. You are sharing intimate details of your life with somebody and they're listening and being really nice, so that's why it's important to agree to be transparent about it."

He signed it and passed it back to her.

"I should have asked for a male therapist!" he joked, sitting back and folding his arms.

She regarded him steadily.

"What difference would that have made?"

Realising he had said the wrong thing again, he started to tap his fingers on the table, wishing that he could be finished already. She signed the bottom of the sheet and began to read through his notes.

"So, what happens now?" he ventured after a few minutes.

Lauren put the notes down and opened a folder on the desk. Taking a pen from the desk tidy, she wrote across the top 'Initial Assessment of John Ashton'.

"We've done the tricky part. You've signed the agreement, so now I just need to get a few things straight and then you can go."

She opened the desk drawer and took a stapler out, putting

it down on the desk before tucking her hair behind her ear.

"Go?"

John was thrown, having just psyched himself up to baring his soul and now she was telling him it was over? What kind of therapy was this?

"First session is getting to know you, making a plan, signing the agreement and booking the next session, so you know what to expect next time…is this okay?"

He realised that he was showing his thoughts on his face and smiled, a little relieved that not too much was expected but a little disappointed too; he was impatient to get started.

"Yeah, that's fine."

She put her pen down and sat back in her chair.

"So, what are you expecting from these sessions?"

It seemed a strange question to John and he looked back at her quizzically.

"What do you mean?"

She moved forward and put her hands together in front of her face, each finger pressed against the opposite one as she studied him.

"What do you think happens in these sessions?"

"Well, I assume I talk about the stuff that bothers me and you listen, take notes and tell me how to deal with it - is that the right answer?"

"Yes, pretty much," she replied, "So in answer to my question of what are you expecting of these sessions, you are expecting to be listened to and learn techniques that will help you to cope on the days you don't feel well…yes?"

John considered this and then nodded before thrusting his hands into his pockets and leaning back in the chair.

"Well, it's good to know we are on the same page. Now, did you fill in a form at the doctors about your mental health?"

Lauren leafed through his papers, her brow furrowed. She looked to the side and then checked in another folder, before looking up at him.

"I haven't seen my doctor yet…there was a bit of trouble when I was being registered and they told me it would be a couple of months before I had a general check over, like an MOT, I suppose."

She looked perturbed and took a form from a file off the shelf above her head.

"You should really have done this assessment before coming to see me, but that's okay. Can you fill it in now? There's still time in your session and I need you to be as honest as you possibly can."

John took a pen from his top pocket and read through the form. Questions that didn't make a lot of sense to him filled it and he ticked the box he thought was appropriate to how he was feeling. When it came to the bottom, he had to describe his current mood in one word. He wrote numb and then handed it back to her. She read through it quickly and wrote something on the top of the sheet, before setting it down and sitting forward in her chair.

"So, did I pass?" John quizzed, head cocked to one side. She smiled faintly.

"No, it seems you did not pass. Your score was too high."

"I thought the point of a test was to score high," he replied, perturbed.

"Usual tests, yes, but for an assessment for your overall mental health, it's different."

Lauren looked him fully in the face until he felt uncomfortable and looked away.

"You have scored high for depression and anxiety and, in my opinion, a little low dose antidepressant will help you on your road to recovery. Hand in hand with the therapy, you should start to feel better within a month, though it can take up to a year to feel better and usually takes longer to get back to your usual self."

John didn't like the sound of any of it, but was aware that he had now committed to her and he knew she was right in her assessment. He had been honest after all.

"So, do I need to see my doctor to get this medication?"

"No, I can sort that out."

She opened her top drawer and pulled out an old-fashioned prescription pad. She scribbled on it and snatched it off, before handing it to him.

"It's a little pill called Citalopram. I've started you on ten milligrams, taken in the morning, just to see how you get on with it and if necessary, we can take you up to twenty."

He went to take it, but she held it there and held his gaze.

"Be warned though, it may make the symptoms worse before they get better," she shrugged. "I don't know why, it just does. But don't stop taking it, persevere and it should settle down. I'll make your next appointment in two weeks to see how you are getting on and to start your therapy."

John took the prescription and popped it into his pocket, making a mental note to stop off at the chemist on the way home as he wanted to get started straight away.

Lauren stood up and came around to his side of the table. He stood too, fumbling with his paperwork and wishing now that he had bought his briefcase. She went to shake his hand and he stuffed the papers into his pocket before shaking her hand vigorously.

"It's good to have met you. See you in a couple of weeks."

She opened the door and he went to go through it.

"Oh, do I make the appointment now?"

"Yes, Sarah will make you one at the desk there."

She smiled as he went and closed the door on him.

John was relieved to see that there was nobody else in the waiting area and hurried to the desk to make his appointment. He glanced through the window and saw his dad's car there and it brought a lump to his throat. He had to clear it to confirm that he could make the appointment being offered and then, with more paperwork in his hand, he left, before Samuel or anyone else could come and accuse him of being something he wasn't.

* * * * *

The phone was ringing when Ivy came in, she could hear it through the window as she opened the front door with her key, fumbling to try and get there in time. She inhaled sharply as her knee gave a twinge as she hurried over to the phone. Snatching it up, she said "Hello?" sharply and a voice she couldn't quite place spoke softly into her ear.

"Oh, hello? Is that Ivy?"

Ivy steadied her breathing and put the keys on the table. "Yes, speaking."

There was a pause and then the woman spoke again.

"You probably won't remember me, but I met you at a wedding…"

"Oh, which one? There's been so many!" Ivy exclaimed smiling, a warm feeling spreading over her as she sat to rub her knee.

There was nervous laughter and then the voice again.

"The one where you got arrested."

Ivy paused and then remembered whose the voice was.

"Of course, I can't forget that one. It's Dylan's mum, isn't it?"

"Maria. Yes. I'm only calling because I am desperate and you did give me your number."

"Yes of course, don't worry," Ivy quickly reassured, remembering how nervy she was, "What can I do for you?"

Maria took in a deep breath and then spoke quickly.

"It's Lewis…the court case is next week…he's going to get Dylan …and I'm going to lose him…Ivy, he's going to take him away from me!"

Maria was crying now and Ivy struggled to hear what she was saying.

"I can't bear it! What if I lose him…I can't…I just…can't!"

The poor woman was hiccoughing and Ivy took the chance to speak.

"Hold on, love, let's just calm down a bit. Now, I said we could help and I'm sure we can."

Ivy wandered through to the kitchen to flick the kettle on and went to the drawer to get a pen. She went back to the table and found her notebook.

"Now, give me the details again…which court is it you have to be at?"

"The Family Court in Grantham…Tuesday morning at ten o'clock. I don't even have the money to get a taxi there."

The despair in her voice caused Ivy to flood with compassion as she wrote down the details.

"Now look, Maria, isn't it? We can get you there, Bill is free to drive and I can come for moral support."

Maria gulped her tears back and tried to show her reluctance to inconvenience them and yet not lose the golden ticket of a lift. "Oh, that's so kind of you…. but are you sure? I don't like to impose…but it's so difficult financially for me." Panic returned to her voice as she had another thought "But hang on…you don't have much money…the papers said!"

Ivy made soothing noises and spoke gently and proudly "Oh, no, we are okay, since John has been back…he pays rent and buys all the food, so we are fine and a promise is a promise...plus it will be lovely to see Dylan again, assuming he will be there?"

Maria's voice opened up with love at the mention of her son. "Yes, he has to come as there's nobody to pick him up from school. Plus, the judge may want to ask him questions too. Oh Ivy, this is such a weight off my mind, I can focus on trying to keep him...thank you so much!"

After Ivy had taken all the details she needed, she finished the call and left the paper on her coffee table. She was worried that Maria would lose Dylan, but at least if she was there to help support her, that would be a help. She went through to the kitchen to make herself a cup of tea. Taking a cup from the cupboard, she went to the back door and looked out. Bill was standing with John, pointing at the fence and touching the bushes. Bill had his duffel coat on and a scarf but John was in a t shirt, unaware of how cold it was. She banged on the window, causing them both to jump and turn around. She smiled and mouthed 'Tea?' at them and they both nodded and turned back. She went back through and took two more cups from the cupboard. Putting a teabag in each one, something she had stopped doing when money was tight, preferring to share a bag with Bill, she bent down to get the milk out of the fridge. Ivy heard their voices as they came in from the garden.

"It all needs to be cut back, really...the apples will grow better if it's all cut back hard." Bill informed John as he removed his wellingtons. John leant against the wall as he kicked off his trainers. "I can help with the cutting back... but I'm not sure about the apple tree...aren't you meant to cut it back in the autumn?"

"I don't think it matters, it's only a few months."

Ivy stirred the drinks and put the milk away. "Did you

want a biscuit, or shall we wait for lunch?"

Bill went to the sink to wash his hands and took the towel off the small radiator in the kitchen to dry them. "I can wait."

"I'll have a biscuit…I quite like those Bourbon ones and we never had them at home." John stopped abruptly, not wanting to think about Katy or the house and so took his tea and went off into the lounge. Ivy took the tin out of the cupboard and brought it through with her. John had sat himself down in her chair and absentmindedly picked up the piece of paper she had been writing on.

"What's this?" he enquired, taking a biscuit from the tin he was offered.

"Oh, a friend in need…I have to speak to your father about it."

"Sounds ominous," countered Bill as he went to sit down in his chair by the window. Ivy explained that Maria had called and needed them to go with her for the court case, not just for a lift but for moral support.

John sat listening, thoughtfully chewing his biscuit and regarding the words written on the page.

"I'm just so worried she will lose custody of him…she was so upset."

"Who has she got representing her?"

Ivy looked confused "Well, nobody as far as I can tell…"

"And the partner…has he got legal aid?"

"Yes, I think so." said Ivy slowly and jumped as John guffawed.

"She will lose him then." confirmed John, getting up to take another biscuit.

"Oh, don't be so mean, John!" cried Ivy "She can't lose him, he is everything to her."

"I'm not being mean, I'm being realistic. The odds are

stacked against her if he has representation and she doesn't. It's a good job you are going there too."

John took a drink from his cup and sat back. Ivy felt helpless and tears of frustration pricked her eyes. She spoke quietly "He is pushing the fact she had post-natal depression after Dylan's birth. It just seems so wrong and unfair!"

Bill regarded the newspaper and glanced at her. "Don't go getting yourself all upset, dear, we can only do our best for her."

John sat and thought about what his mum was saying. He knew this was something that he could get involved with, some way of helping another person and keep his mind active. He didn't want to sit for two weeks waiting for medication to start working; he needed to be doing something. He swallowed some more tea, to wash away the sludge left around his teeth, the cloying sweetness making his tongue work extra hard.

Ivy was still whittling about Maria. "It's so wrong, surely they can't penalise her because she was ill! I thought they had to be more understanding these days."

John made his decision and stood up suddenly. "Well, the courts will decide what's in the best interest of the child. I can speak to James, my old golfing buddy…he's a lawyer."

Ivy looked hopeful and smiled "What, will he represent her, then?"

John who had been about to leave, stopped dead in his tracks and gave her a bemused look.

"Don't be daft, Mother," he scoffed, "I can't afford his rates. She will represent herself, after I've told her what she needs to do, once I've got all the advice I need."

He marched out of the room, picking up his mobile as he went, leaving Ivy open mouthed as she turned to Bill.

"I can't believe he is going to do that, can you? I mean, he doesn't even know her!"

Bill ruffled the paper, appearing to scrutinise the page as he murmured "Well, these things can happen, dear."

Chapter 21
Alone On The Podium

Ivy had just finished making the beds when she heard the doorbell ring. It was a Saturday morning and John was over at the house, sorting things out, Bill had popped into the next town to get some floss for a food trap between his crowns that had been driving him up the wall and she had taken the opportunity to get the house sorted. Even though John was an adult, he seemed to create as much mess as he did as a child, she thought and having cleared the lounge of papers, crisp wrappers and dirty cups, she was now in his room stripping off the bedding. She tutted as she pulled out his bottom sheet and crumbs flew up, scattering across the brown carpet like cheap confetti. That would mean having to hoover too, Bill wouldn't be impressed as he had only done it a few days earlier. She found the culprit under the little table next to the bed, a packet of Oreo cookies he had smuggled up there without her knowledge. She couldn't help but smile at the thought that he was with them now, for however long it took until he found a nice new place, she knew that they would continue to see each other once he had moved out. They had been through the hard times and John was getting better, albeit slowly. She couldn't complain too much, especially now her anxiety seemed to have gone completely. It appeared to have been rooted in not seeing John. Ivy went over to open the window as she was feeling hot and bothered from struggling to get John's duvet cover off and it was then the bell rang. From her vantage point at the window, she could see that Ernie's car had pulled up onto her drive and watched as Gladys got unsteadily out of the front seat. Ivy called down through the open window 'Cooee!' and waved as Gladys looked up, startled.

"I'll just come down," called Ivy, puzzled by her friend's lack of smile.

She picked up the duvet and sheet and went to the top of the stairs. Holding onto the banister, she carefully walked down, taking care not to trip on her cargo. She looked at Ernie's face through the glass and couldn't quite place the look, like someone who has won a prize, but feels bad for the losers. Ivy dropped the pile on the floor of the kitchen and unlocked the door, opening it outwards as Gladys burst into tears. Ernie quickly ushered her in, helping her up the step by holding her elbow as Ivy received the rest of her, letting her lean on her shoulder as they went through the to the lounge.

"Whatever's the matter?" cried Ivy, "Gladys, dear, you're shaking!"

"Oh Ivy, I'm…so…upset!" she sobbed into her friend's shoulder and Ivy patted her on the back, making soothing noises.

Ivy looked to Ernie, who was seated uncomfortably on the arm of the sofa and raised her eyebrows in question. Ernie shrugged before speaking.

"It's Beryl."

Before he could say another word, Gladys broke in

"Oh, she's dying! And I have been so horrible to her!"

She took a tissue from her bag and blew her nose, wiping her eyes with her hand. Ivy was shocked by this revelation and wasn't sure what she should say. After Gladys had stopped sobbing, Ivy took her hand and held it before telling Ernie he could go and put the kettle on. Ernie, pleased to be released, scuttled out through to the kitchen. Ivy took Gladys' other hand and smiled sympathetically.

"Is she really dying?"

Pinching the bridge of her nose, in some way trying to gather herself, Gladys took in a deep breath. Composed, she managed to speak, her voice strong.

"It's cancer. Originally breast, but now lung - they gave her six months at Christmas."

"Oh, I'm so sorry…have you been to see her?"

Gladys started to twist the hankie in her hand and avoided Ivy's gaze. Ernie came through with a cup of tea for them both, setting it down and going back into the kitchen for his own. Ivy couldn't work out why Gladys didn't reply and guessed she's was upset again. But then Gladys quietly said, "She doesn't know I know…"

Ivy was surprised.

"Then how do you know?"

"George told me in confidence. He didn't like the idea that Gladys was so ill and would die alone and knew I would have felt awfully guilty after...well, you know. I wish I hadn't been so mean now at the wedding…going on about her weight loss. Now I know why…oh, it's just all so petty!"

Fresh tears pushed their way down her reddened cheeks glistening in the light from the lamp, necessary for the gloom in the lounge. Ivy felt helpless, unsure as to what the best course of action, if any, they should take. Ernie came back in, stirring his tea and clutching a Bourbon biscuit in his closed hand. Gladys received it gratefully, nibbling at it as she sipped her tea. Ivy sat back on her seat, thinking and saw Bill through the window as he came back, fumbling for his key before opening the door and coming through, his smile broad as he turned to see Ernie walking into the kitchen.

"Cup of tea?" Ernie enquired and Bill looked into the lounge.

"I'd love one, but where are the girls?" he replied, taking in the tear-stained face of his friend's wife and the furrow of annoyance on his own wife's face.

"Ah, I'll leave you to it, love." he stated quickly before joining Ernie in the sanctuary of the kitchen.

"Typical man," murmured Ivy, patting her friend's hand and passing her a fresh tissue, "What do you want to do, then? If she doesn't know, how are you going to meet up with her?"

Gladys stared into her tea, as if the murky water could give her the answer, like a tea leaf from the past and then took a sip, washing away the saltiness of sadness.

"I don't know. I keep thinking if only I had a better relationship with her, I could arrange to pop in and see her, or at least call to chat, but even after the wedding, I had no desire to keep in touch, she annoyed me so much." she reasoned ruefully, giving her nose a good blow, as if the force would remove the issue she now faced.

"What would you do in my situation?"

Ivy had several thoughts that presented themselves behind her eyes and all had their hand up, shouting 'Pick me!' The first and, as is often the case with the first, most unhelpful was to say, 'I wouldn't have let a relationship with my sister get this bad!' She mentally kicked that one off the podium and looked at the next one, a sly little blighter 'Why not lie and pretend you want to meet up, to catch up on time lost?'

She knew that Gladys would not be comfortable with this, unable to keep up the pretence and so again, this one was removed forcefully from the podium. A little boy skipped up next, suggesting that George could act as a go between? But again, he was told nice idea, but it wouldn't be fair to use anybody as a go between. In the end, the last idea was Gladys alone on the podium, phone in hand, explaining that she knew everything and wanted to meet up. Satisfied, Ivy put the winning sash around the mini-Gladys and smiled at her friend.

"If it was me, I would call her, tell her the truth and say you want to visit her."

Gladys looked at her as though Ivy was speaking to somebody behind her, as such an idea seemed preposterous.

"But she won't want to see me…she hates me!"

"Oh, you know that's not true, she's just a very different person, that is all. And I really think this is your only viable option."

Gladys pushed her hair back from her face and sighed, sitting back in the chair and wincing as her back cracked.

"I can ask George for her number, I suppose."

Ivy sat back in her chair, pleased that her advice had been listened to and taken. She drank her tea and, knowing that the men would be deep in conversation about what perennials to plant this year, decided to leave them to their chatter. A thought suddenly occurred to her.

"Where is Beryl living at the moment? Is she renting somewhere nearby?"

Gladys sniffed and looked at her phone.

"She is staying in the hotel where George had his wedding."

Ivy looked amazed at this revelation and Gladys smiled.

"Even in illness, she manages to be grand. Imagine the

cost!"

"I know the hotel was lovely for a wedding, but don't you think it's a bit sad that she is staying in a room on her own? I mean, she must be in pain and lonely."

Gladys considered this for a moment as Ernie and Bill came in through the back door, laughing. Having taken off their shoes, they walked through the kitchen and joined the women in the lounge.

"I hadn't thought about that."

"Hadn't thought about what?" interjected Ernie pleasantly.

"I'm going to call Beryl, tell her I know and go and see her."

Ernie's face fell.

"Is that wise? Remember the wedding?"

"Of course, I remember the wedding, it wasn't that long ago!" snapped Gladys, before putting her head in her hands and instantly regretting her rash words.

"I'm sorry. I know, but I need to do this…she hasn't got long."

Gladys went and stood in the kitchen to make the call. Bill cleared his throat and started to talk about the garden again and Ernie, pleased to discuss something he could understand, enthusiastically chatted about his idea of a vegetable patch. Ivy smiled at them, straining to hear Gladys. It took a while but she eventually tuned in.

"Beryl, yes it really is me…well, I want…I want to…I'm not stammering, I…want to come and see you…you know what for…yes, he has, it's not his fault, he just felt I should know…I am your sister! No, I don't want to argue…I just want to visit you…well, to talk…before…you know…oh, do you have to be so harsh?"

Ivy could imagine Gladys's shocked face and had to remember to nod and smile at Ernie, who insisted on telling her about his cucumbers, to the point that she could no longer hear Gladys. After some more frustrated conversation, it went quiet in the kitchen and Ivy wondered if she should go to her friend. But Gladys at last appeared in the doorway, her eyes bright, with a triumphant look on her face.

"Boy, was she argumentative…insisted I waited until tomorrow morning. Finally, I got what I wanted. I'm going to see her – tonight!"

"Oh, that's good," started Ivy, but Gladys silenced her with her next comment.

"And you are coming with me!"

* * * * *

Lauren smiled as she sat opposite John, aware that he was nervous. This was his fifth session and she knew that he felt uncomfortable about opening up. All the techniques that she had used so far had been met with awkwardness and a sense of nothing to share and she was concerned that she wasn't doing a good job, so much so that she had mentioned as much to her supervisor the night before. He had encouraged her to persevere and try a different tack, maybe to go back even further into childhood, to have some distance for the patient to remove themselves from.

"So, how are you feeling at the moment?"

John swallowed and said "Fine."

Lauren kept her smile in place even though inwardly she was groaning – the F word, the one everyone used to keep people at bay. She probed gently.

"Really? Fine? Nothing to say, no strange feelings, nothing you want to share?"

There was a long pause, one she thought he might suddenly break with interesting speech, but instead he just continued.

"Not that I'm aware of."

She opened her pad, just to have something to do and took a pen from her drawer.

"How is it going with the medication?"

"Good. Ten milligrams seems to help keep me calm, like all my nerve endings are coated with warm fuzz. I don't feel jangly."

She smiled at this description and scribbled down a note, before plunging in with her question.

"So, I'm interested in finding out why you have been so unwell."

"I'm feeling so much better though, can't I just take the tablets and be done with it?"

Aaaah. So, this is the reason we're not getting anywhere, she thought and put her pen down, before leaning her chin on her hand.

"It's a good idea, but it won't work in the long run. Your brain shut down because it couldn't handle any more emotion. We need to establish what that emotion is and then see if we can help you work through it. Medication just provides a bandage over a wound – therapy digs out the infection and cleans it up."

John winced before stating "That sounds painful."

"It is," she carried on gently, "It can be excruciating, but it has to be removed before the healing can take place."

He sighed resignedly before leaning forward in an engaged way.

"Okay, what do I need to do?"

Lauren decided to continue with her original idea for the session.

"I think it would be a good idea to go back to your childhood, to see if there are any memories that stick out?"

John considered this for a while, before looking dejected.

"I had a good childhood. An only child, parents that doted on me, textbook stuff really."

He suddenly looked thoughtful.

"Although I did have a weird flashback type thing when I first came here…because of the ceiling."

Lauren looked at him quizzically, not wanting to speak and yet not sure what he meant. He carried on.

"The patterns on the ceiling took me back to being at a neighbour's house for a party – they had the same ceiling," he said as if this explained everything. "Anyway, I was there with my friend Gaynor and we'd been given these amazing marble coloured balloons, I'd never seen anything like them and I was just standing there, waiting to be picked up and then Gaynor, who was a right thug, whacked the balloon up out of my hands and onto the ceiling and it popped. My mum picked me up and could see that I had been crying and she promised to get me another one."

"And did she?" enquired Lauren, looking up from her notepad where she had been jotting these facts.

"I honestly don't remember, but I don't think so. I never played with Gaynor again."

"So, what was your overriding emotion then? Were you angry?"

John sat back in his chair and crossed his legs. "I don't think it was anger…more an overwhelming sense of disappointment. I'd had something in my hand that I really liked, could hardly believe I had been given it and in an instant, Gaynor had done something stupid that had taken it away."

He swallowed and looked at her fully

"I think that's what I feel now – disappointment with the way things have turned out."

He looked down at his hands.

"I thought I would be this high-flying MP, beautiful wife, adoring kids. I just assumed they would be an option."

His voice cracked and he felt in his pocket for his handkerchief as a tear rolled down his cheek.

Lauren scribbled on her pad as he wiped his face, before looking up and continuing.

"I guess a lot of people assume that," she said kindly, "And it can take a while to process those emotions, to get through to a place of acceptance of the present situation."

"I never dreamed that Katy would leave – I knew things were bad, but I thought we would work them out, you know…later."

He blew his nose and gave her a sad smile and she smiled back.

"I don't blame her though, I mean, I was a selfish pig. Never even asked her how she felt about not having children, just kept her at arm's length. What an idiot."

John leant forward on the table and put his chin on his hand, rubbing the stubble that appeared after three days of not shaving. Lauren glanced at the clock and closed her notepad.

"That sounds painful…a lot of grief at what you have lost."

Seeing his concern, she quickly added "But that's a good thing…it means you're beginning to heal. You will start to change for the better."

She jumped as he groaned loudly, putting his hand over his eyes.

"Don't say I'm going to turn into my dad!" he moaned, looking at her.

She considered this.

"Is your dad a nice person?"

John nodded and she went on.

"In that case, you probably will be a bit like him…the good bits anyway."

As he left the room and headed out to the carpark, he saw his father leaning against the front of his car, waiting for him and it hit him that there were no real bad bits to his father. The tears flowed freely as he stumbled into the arms of the perturbed Bill, who awkwardly patted him on the back and murmured, 'There there, it's okay,' as if soothing a child. After a few minutes of this, John abruptly stopped, blew his nose and got into the passenger side of the car. No more was said, but John knew that something had changed. He had a peace in his heart and mind that had eluded him for years.

Chapter 22
Denying Access

Bill had offered to take Ivy and Gladys to the hotel, while he and Ernie went for a pint at the local pub. John was out doing his usual evening walk and so the ladies were able to meet up without feeling the need to be elsewhere. Ivy was glad that Beryl had been willing to see Gladys so soon as she wasn't sure that Gladys would have coped waiting; she was fairly agitated already. She could feel the tremor of her body as she linked arms with her in the hotel foyer, having manoeuvred through the revolving door.

"It will be alright" Ivy reassured, squeezing her arm and smiling sympathetically.

Gladys smiled weakly and went over to the desk. The young man on reception, looking like something out of a Kay's catalogue, all dark, tousled hair and smiling eyes, looked up at them as they came over.

"Can I help you ladies?" he boomed, in a deep, warm voice.

Gladys perked up immediately.

"I'm here to see my sister - Miss Beryl Montgomery?"

The man's brow furrowed and the smile disappeared.

"I'll just double check which room she is in today." he snapped briskly, while tapping away at the computer to his left.

"Oh, you know her?" exclaimed Ivy, "That's good customer service," she added, addressing Gladys.

The man continued to look at his screen as he replied.

"I should think everyone knows Beryl. She is pretty... unique. Room 77, on the third floor, there is a lift over there."

He trundled out and then got up to leave, before turning back.

"Oh, and good luck!"

He smiled briefly, before going into the adjacent office, leaving Gladys perplexed.

"What was that all about?" she wondered as Ivy pressed the button to call the lift.

"Don't let it bother you, I'm sure she is just being a little – demanding – you know what she is like!"

Gladys laughed as they went into the lift.

"Only a bit?"

Ivy felt the lurch of her stomach as the lift took them up to the third floor, the smell in there reminding her of the time Bill had bought a new car, proudly taking them all out for a spin in it, tissue paper still covering the seats. He really felt like he had made it. A week later, John had spilt a milkshake in it and the car smell had been replaced by something altogether foul. Typical John...and poor Bill. The lift doors opened and the two women made their way along the corridor, checking the numbers on the door until they found Room 77. Gladys looked quite pale now and took hold of Ivy's hand and again, Ivy squeezed and waited for her to knock at the door. She took a deep breath and knocked. They waited a minute and then knocked again.

They waited again and then Gladys, annoyed now, let go of Ivy's hand and pounded the door. A voice called out 'come in' and Gladys tried the door handle. It opened and she went through with Ivy.

The first thing that hit them was the smell, a sickly-sweet odour that was trying, yet failing, to mask the smell of faeces. The second thing they noticed was the heat - it was stifling compared to outside and Ivy began to feel nauseous. The third thing was how dark it was in the room, the curtains were pulled almost together, a thin slit of light the only means for them to see where they were going. As they made their way into the room, they could just make out Beryl. She was seated upright, her back against the cushions around the headboard, the thin sheets betraying her now frail body, the smell stronger as they got closer to her. Gladys was having trouble adjusting, not only to the light, but to the whole situation. There was a chair next to the bed and Ivy sensed that she was hesitating about staying and so quickly took charge.

"Gladys, you have the chair, I am happy standing." suggested Ivy as brightly as she could and Gladys slowly sat down, afraid that something might break.

There was an awkward silence before Beryl broke it.

"If this is all you are going to do, then you can go."

Her voice, rasping and harsh, was surprisingly strong. Gladys immediately jumped in

"What do you mean? We haven't done anything yet!" she remonstrated, her voice harsh against the cloying air.

"There you go again…"

The rasping voice, softer now as the air required to pump through Beryl's lungs had difficulty reaching its destination, the lumps formed in them denying access to the precious oxygen. She coughed a little and Ivy, still struggling to see properly, noticed a little lamp to the side of the bed.

"It would be better if we could see you…" she began and Gladys reached forward and clicked the lamp on.

"NO!" shrieked Beryl, trying to cover her face, but it was too late. The room was bathed in a lemon glow revealing the shock on Gladys and Ivy's faces as they stared at Beryl's emaciated body, the futile clothing that revealed everything, the tell-tale stains on the sheets. Her once beautiful skin that usually radiated health was now pockmarked and translucent, like the eyes of a recently ejected baby bird, tightly stretched over her bones. But it was her face that revealed the terminal nature of her illness, the cheekbones protruding in such a way, it looked as though they would poke through her skin. Her head, only a few months earlier, adorned with a sleek black bob, now had a fine down covering, the image of a baby bird even sharper. Her eyes, usually alight with wicked wit, were now sunken and bloodshot, her forehead jutting out over them, like a protective cover. She reluctantly took her hands down and regarded her sister, balefully.

"Well now you know the depths I have fallen," she murmured, licking her dry, cracked lips, "Bet you wish you'd waited until tomorrow now." she added drily, reaching out for the pot of Vaseline on her bedside table.

Gladys was still struck dumb by her appearance, although had managed to close her mouth. Ivy found her voice as she was curious.

"What difference does it make when we come?"

Beryl's eyes flicked towards her, holding her gaze. Ivy tried to hide her feelings of horror, but failed miserably and had to look away.

"My carer comes in the morning," she explained rubbing a slick of Vaseline over her lips, "Well, I call him my carer, but I think he is the janitor here." she rasped, the effort of speaking causing her to sink down into the bed, only just managing to put the pot back. She struggled to push herself up and Gladys suddenly seeing a way to help, leant forward. One look from Beryl stopped her and she sat back down again.

"He comes in, I demand a different room as this one stinks and he has to move me. I would have been all fresh and dressed. I would even have worn my headscarf."

She gestured over to the other side of the room where the said scarf was in a crumpled heap on the floor.

"I get a bit hot sometimes." muttered Beryl and moved the bed sheets across so that her legs stuck out, two twiglets, the same bluish tinge and tightness to them as the rest of her. The movement caused her to knock over several pill bottles next to the Vaseline and she swore. Gladys sprang up and began to pick them up, looking at the labels as she put them back on the side.

"Well," managed Gladys at last, "I'm not surprised, it's very warm in here."

"I told you to stop."

"Stop what?" exclaimed Gladys.

Beryl sighed.

"Stop pretending to be nice, as if you want to spend time with me."

"But I do!"

"Rubbish!" bit Beryl vehemently, "You couldn't stand me six months ago, so what's changed, darling sister?"

She started to cough again and reached for her glass of water, slowly sipping between breaths, sounding like she might drown.

"Well, you know…you being so ill."

Beryl stopped drinking and rested her glass on her blanket,

the thighs underneath forming a perfect flat surface; she regarded her sister with contempt.

"Ill? Being ill is having a cold, or flu or a tummy upset. I'm dying, Gladys, I'm literally sweating, shivering and shitting myself to the death. And I know that all you care about is not feeling guilty afterwards!"

Gladys sprang up, clenching her hands, her eyes wild.

"Oh, just stop it, will you? It's always about you, every bloody time we meet up! Even when you weren't at home, you were all they ever talked about!"

Beryl sat back and smiled, a trace of cat, albeit a straggly stray one, crossed her features and she stretched her bony shoulders.

"And there she is, back in the room, the sister that I'm so fond of."

Gladys felt cheated and sat back down abruptly. Beryl shifted her gaze back to Ivy and waited. Ivy felt scrutinised by this apparition of contempt, but held her gaze. After a minute like that, Beryl then spoke.

"Nothing to say? Not going to spring to her defence, tell me how awful I am and leave in a huff together?"

In that moment, Ivy realised what was going on and as her insides filled with compassion, she fought hard to remain impassive. Moving over to put her hand on Gladys' shoulder, she allowed herself to smile before addressing the obnoxious woman in front of her.

"You'd like that, wouldn't you?" she suggested gently, "For us to storm off and leave you alone."

Beryl's eyes narrowed and she glanced at Gladys.

"It's how I prefer things, yes," she croaked, trying to push herself back up in the bed and only managing an inch before flopping back.

"Well, that's not how we roll anymore", quipped Ivy,

remembering the phrase from a recent sitcom with James Corden in, such a lovely young man and so funny…really needed to do something about his weight though. She flicked channels in her mind and came back to the one where Gladys was looking at her as if she had just announced she was getting a tattoo.

"How do we roll, then?" queried Gladys, clearly interested in the answer.

"Well, I have spent three years away from my son and these last few months have been wonderful now that he is back in our lives again. I know you haven't seen much of each other over the years, but that's in the past, you can't change that. But you can spend time together now, while there is still time."

There was silence in the room as these words were digested by Beryl, who looked like she was trying to think of a witty retort. Instead, she just got cross.

"Finished your little speech?" she sneered, before turning, with great difficulty onto her side, away from them. "You can see yourselves out."

Gladys looked at Ivy stricken and Ivy put up her hand and nodded slightly, to reassure her.

"Do you really want us to leave? Because we will, if it's really what you want. But I don't think being in a hotel room for your final days is very nice at all."

"You'd be surprised. I get to piss everybody off and they can't do anything about it, because I pay my way and the dying bit, well, seems to make people a bit more tolerant."

These words were directed at the wall she was now facing and only the slight tremor in her voice gave away the tears running down her cheeks and into her pillow.

"Wouldn't you rather be at home?" suggested Gladys gently, matching the same tone as Ivy.

"I don't have a home," replied Beryl curtly, before her shoulders relaxed and she gave in to her emotions.

"I can't afford to cry!" she moaned as Gladys tentatively laid her hand on her back, forcing herself not to recoil as every vertebra jabbed into her palm.

She turned herself back over, wiping her eyes and taking a tissue from the box on the side.

"I end up losing too much fluid and then everything slows down and its…caked in there." Beryl said drily, avoiding eye contact and blowing her nose. "And then it goes the other way, like a fucking dripping tap."

She gestured at the tell-tale marks on the bed.

"It's a bloody living nightmare!" she croaked, throwing the tissue at the bin and missing.

Gladys reached down and picked it up and dropped it in. Ivy couldn't help but feel sorry for her, so obviously miserable and an idea popped into her mind that sounded like a solution to her problem as well as John's.

"Look, let's not be daft here. You are not getting the care you deserve and you need looking after. Even preparing healthy food would help in that department and being in a house, with company has got to be better than this."

Gladys was looking at her perturbed as if she was expected to open her own home to her sister, knowing full well that Ernie would have none of it: their idyllic bungalow wouldn't be able to cope with the spectre of Beryl appearing in every room, soiling the furniture and literally leaving a bad smell. Ivy decided to make the decision for John that she knew he wouldn't agree with, but would eventually have to accept as a solution to his problem.

"You can move into John's old place! He hasn't cleared it yet and he needs a reason to get his stuff out and you living there will be the perfect excuse. Plus, Gladys can be your carer and George and his wife can visit."

"Don't be ridiculous," rasped Beryl, though with less venom, "My sister cannot wipe my arse…she struggles wiping her own!"

As Gladys went to explode, Ivy laid her hand on her arm and shook her head at her.

"Then get a carer in each day. You can more than afford it and Gladys can just keep you company instead. You know this is the best solution until…well, until you have had enough."

Beryl pushed herself up and a brightness had entered her eyes. Ivy recognised a flicker of hope when she saw one and she smiled, pleased that she had helped bring a resolution.

"When can I move in?"

Ivy stood up and observed Beryl from above. She looked so fragile and yet her face had a determined edge to it now, the vulnerability of the initial impression eased by a plan being put in place.

"I'll get John to go over to the house tomorrow and clear it. We can get you in by the weekend."

Beryl smiled a faint smile.

"You will have to bring me a wheel chair. I'm too weak to walk far…and help me dress for the journey. I can't have the masses seeing me looking so rough. I'll even let you do my makeup, sister dear." she mocked, smiling lazily.

Beryl took two tablets off the side and popped them in her mouth, using the remainder of the water to wash them away. Grimacing, she regarded her sister.

"They taste foul, but rather that than stay awake all night. Goodnight, dearest. I shall look forward to you collecting me sharp at eight o'clock Saturday morning."

With this control of the situation firmly taken back, Beryl shuffled down and closed her eyes. Within a minute, she was asleep, her jaw slack although her face was still etched with pain. Gladys, still a little stunned, stood slowly and bent down to kiss her lightly on her forehead, expecting a reaction, but getting none. She straightened out the pill pots and filled the glass back up with water from the jug. With one last look at her sister, she crossed with Ivy to the door and opened it, the sound of the hinge loud in the room. They both turned to look at Beryl, concerned the noise would disturb her, but she was snoring lightly, settled for the night. Once outside, Gladys considered her friend in the light of the hotel hallway.

"Are you mad?" she demanded, staring at her oldest friend, "What will John say?"

Ivy shrugged.

"I've promised a dying woman his home - what can he say?"

Chapter 23
Weaknesses and Strengths

John was getting used to being driven around by his father. Initially, he had thought he would be able to drive himself to his therapy sessions, but often felt so drained afterwards, it was all he could do to walk to the car. He had sat in the driving seat of his car, to start the engine, to keep it ticking over, like his father had suggested but found that his legs shook and he shouldn't imagine his body doing all the things required to drive a car. Changing gear seemed alien to him, how had he done it so automatically before, without even thinking about it. He knew it would be a while before he was driving and so allowed Bill to take him where he needed to be. Today, he was glad of the company, the job interview had left him feeling a bit anxious, but he was determined to get it. He read the job description again as his dad handled the traffic, giving a running commentary on the faults of other drivers, which John managed to tune out as he read. The job was for a Housing Officer with the local council, mainly office based, dealing with the general public. It wasn't particularly well paid, £21,000 compared to £100,000 as an MP, but it was easy, a '9 to 5' and no weekends. He was beginning to understand that his life needed some balance and a job that wasn't demanding was all he could cope with.

"Feeling ok?" asked his father suddenly and John felt a stab of fear. He put the papers back in his briefcase and rubbed his face. The stubble that he had been cultivating while unwell was now gone, revealing freshly shaved skin, but the habit of rubbing his hands across his beard was still with him. It wasn't quite the same without the roughness under his fingertips, but it was something that gave him a bit of comfort. God knows why, he thought wryly and then realised he hadn't said anything to his father, who was now slowing down to park near the council offices.

"Yes, I'm fine," he stated, giving his father a tight smile as he picked up his briefcase. As he swung his legs out to the car door and stood up quickly, his father leant across to call out.

"Good luck...I'm sure you'll be fine."

Again, John smiled, nodded and slammed the door shut. He watched as his father pulled away and then turned, the familiar feeling of anxiety creeping up into his chest. Swallowing, he walked across the car park to the glass doors. Seeing his reflection and feeling less confident, he felt a cold sweat drift across his shoulders. Weight loss didn't suit him, especially without the gym to tone up his atrophied muscles. His arms seemed to float inside his suit jacket and he began to feel foolish, like this was a waste of time and he might as well turn around and text his father to come and get him. But the thought of many more days stuck inside without a purpose propelled him forwards and setting his jaw in a determined way, he pushed the door open and strode over to reception. A young girl was on the desk, in the middle of a phone call and as he came to the desk, she smiled and flicked her black hair back over her shoulder. John stared at her hair, the shine on it something he thought only existed in adverts and wondered what it would smell like. He realised for the second time that morning that somebody had spoken to him and were left waiting for an answer.

She tried again.

"Can I help you, sir?"

He looked her fully in the face, coughing to clear his throat before he spoke.

"Erm, yes…I'm here for a job…I mean interview, a job interview."

He was mesmerised by her eyebrows now, wondering how on earth they were so perfectly shaped, I mean, how? Did she wake up and they were like that? Were there special eyebrow brushes that he knew nothing about, that left young girls looking permanently surprised?

Again, her mouth was moving and he had to tune back into the frequency of everyday life.

"Sorry, sir, I need to know your name?"

John looked at her mouth and registered what was required from him.

"John…my name is John."

The girl looked at the computer screen in front of her and smiled kindly.

"John Ashton, is it?"

John nodded and tried to concentrate enough to appear normal. He gripped the handle of his briefcase, and then relaxed it, a technique his therapist said would help.

"Just take a seat in the waiting area and Mr Wilson will be down to get you," the girl with the immaculate eyebrows informed him, before the phone rang again and she was caught up with another council related matter.

John turned to see three chairs against the wall and assuming this was the waiting area, took a seat. The gripping and relaxing was beginning to work and he felt a bit clearer in his mind. He didn't understand why his mind kept wandering when he was talking to people and hoped that it was something that would stop soon - he kept feeling so foolish in front of others and it wasn't something he wanted to continue. He must mention it to his therapist when he next saw her…when was he next seeing her? As he was staring off into space trying to remember, he didn't hear Mr Wilson speak, the first, second or third time. Eventually, the bemused Mr Wilson went forward and tapped him on the arm and John give a start, suddenly standing up and dropping his briefcase. As he bent down to pick it up, the man put out his hand.

"John, isn't it? Hi, I'm Malcolm, nice to meet you."

"Is it?" asked John, pondering the question and looking at the outstretched hand, knowing he should know what to do with it, but too undecided to react. In the end, he slapped it sideways on, like a gangster rapper welcome and Malcolm looked surprised as John walked away. He stopped to look back at Malcolm, who said "It's this way," and pointed up the staircase.

"Of course, sorry." stammered John, stumbling over his words, willing himself to act like his old self, confident and brash.

At the top of the stairs, Malcolm took him into a small airy office, where a middle-aged woman was seated. She reminded John of Pat Butcher, the televised woman of his youth, short dyed blonde hair and big earrings and John had to press his lips together to stop himself from saying anything daft. Malcolm introduced her as Leslie Crowder, the housing officer who currently worked for them, whose job he was applying for and then seeing John look worried, he quickly reassured him that she was leaving due to a relocation. John relaxed and sat down in the chair offered to him. Malcolm picked up some paperwork in front of him and having read the first few lines, looked up at John and smiled.

"Well, John, this is certainly an interesting CV…Civil Service from school, MP of your local constituency and then head of Family Values…impressive resume. So why do you want this job?"

John swallowed and put his briefcase onto the desk, not sure why he brought it. He sat up in his chair and tried to smile back, his cheeks feeling tight through the lack of use.

"Erm, well I need to be working again…"

"OK, but why this particular job? If anything, you are overqualified."

John tried again.

"I need the money…and this is as good a job as any other."

Lesley looked from John to Malcolm and raised her eyebrows.

Malcolm tried a different tack.

"Well, perhaps Lesley can give us an idea of what the job would entail, to see if this would be an area of work that you would enjoy."

He turned to Lesley, who had been looking at him incredulously, obviously battling within her mind how to respond. She decided to do as she had been asked and sat forward to deliver her information in a monotone reminiscent of a victim of crime during the re-enactment on Crimewatch

"A typical day will see you here in the office during the morning, sat at a desk. You get a list of clients wanting to meet with you to discuss their housing needs and you get given a file on each one. After lunch, which is usually eaten at your desk, checking emails and answering the phone to irate people, you get a chance to go out and assess houses and people, coming back in the late afternoon to write up your reports."

She paused for breath, changing her position and leaning back in her chair, folded her arms. "You're lucky if you get out of here by half six."

Malcolm had been staring at her, getting more and more concerned with what she was saying and quickly interjected once she had finished.

"It's a good job though, isn't it? The sense of achievement you feel when somebody is housed and is grateful to you is…"

Whether the fact she was leaving or just because she felt the truth needed to be told, Malcolm was not to know. But Lesley, looking at him as if he was something offensive on her shoe, leant forward, putting her hands on her thighs in earnest.

"Grateful? Nobody is grateful, they all have a sense of entitlement and as soon as one thing gets sorted, they are on to the next thing to moan at us about. If it's a sense of achievement you are after, go work in Africa."

Malcolm looked horrified and Lesley clarified her comment.

"My sister works out there, I'm not being racist before you get on your high horse, I'm just saying, there's no gratitude in this job."

They both looked at John, who had been turning from one to the other as they spoke, with a weary look on his face,

"Look, let's just cut the formalities," stated John, feeling more relaxed now that somebody else had made themselves look foolish, "I know I am overqualified…and I chose to resign as MP for personal reasons."

At this, Lesley sat forward again, obviously hoping for

more information, but John was not forthcoming, instead carrying on his resolve.

"So, you could argue that I shouldn't be able to do this job. But I need something that is simple to do, that doesn't involve too much effort and that sticks to usual working hours, even if that means staying later."

Malcolm regarded him with interest and John decided in that moment to be honest, even in front of Lesley - she was leaving anyway, he figured.

"I've had a difficult time over the last few months and... well...I have a therapist...it was her idea for me to apply for this particular job."

He rubbed his hands over his eyes as he concluded "And if I have to spend another week in the house with my parents, I may need more than therapy to cope."

Malcolm shuffled his sheaf of papers and smiled.

"Well, that's all we need from you, John, so unless you have any questions?"

John looked at him sharply.

"What, that's it? Shouldn't there be more time, I mean...I haven't been here that long, don't you need to ask more questions? Weaknesses and strengths and all that shit?"

Lesley snorted and failed to conceal her feelings; in her mind, John was an imbecile and John quickly caught on. Malcolm stood and put his hand out again.

"Thanks for your time, we will be in touch."

John shook his hand, feeling like a failure and trying hard to maintain a sense of dignity. This was lost as Malcolm opened the door and John sailed through it, only for Lesley to call out behind him.

"Your briefcase."

Embarrassed, John walked back to the table to pick it up, irritated that she hadn't brought it to him, just sat there, smugly. He could feel the anxiety settle again in his chest and just wanted to get out. Once Malcolm had walked him down to reception, John went straight out of the doors, to a bench he had seen on his way in. He sank down on it, feeling exhausted, the effort of trying to act his usual self had left him empty. John held the briefcase in front of him, feeling foolish for even taking it with him. Taking his phone out, he texted his dad to come and get him, not wanting to speak on the phone, knowing the hopeful chatter of his father would be too much to bear. From the window of his office, Malcolm watched John. If it had been an ordinary manager, in a loving stable relationship that had interviewed John, he would most certainly have not got the job. But Malcolm was no ordinary manager, having only just been promoted, deciding to go for a job where he had to put in more hours. The break up with his long-term girlfriend had been painful and Malcolm knew the difficulty of living with aged parents. He had liked the slightly awkward man presented before him and knew there was more beneath the surface. The therapist had been the final confirmation that he was making the right decision. Anybody who admitted to that in an interview was worth giving a chance to…it showed honesty, was brave and also proved that he wasn't thinking straight.

John sighed and reflected on the situation. Maybe it was the right thing at the moment not to be working, he obviously couldn't cope with everyday life. He hoped that something else would come up soon, as the thought of being with his parents all day filled him with despair. He almost let out a yelp as his phone began to ring. Guessing it was his dad, he went to press the off switch and then realised it was the council number.

"Hello?" he answered warily.

Malcolm's voice crackled through.

"Hi John, just wanted to let you know we have made our decision."

John jumped in, "That's fine, thanks for your time, I'm sure something else will…"

Malcolm cut him off.

"No, John, it's good news. I'd like to offer you the job."

John blinked as the words registered in his mind and a coating of happiness poured over him, drowning out the anxiety.

"Really?" he squawked, feeling the strength return to his legs as relief and wonder washed over them. "Are you sure?"

Malcolm laughed

"I'm sure. You are just what this department needs, plus I'll be managing you. I think we will get along."

John stood up as his father pulled into the parking bay in front of him.

"Well, that's great. Thank you so much."

"Okay, we can work out the detail when I see you. Come in Monday morning and I'll have my PA set you up on the system."

"Thanks again. I need to go now. Bye." replied John, fumbling with the door handle.

He pulled the door open and flopped down into the seat, smiling.

"How did it go, then?" Bill asked, as he pulled out of the space.

"I got it, Dad…I can't believe it. I thought that after making mistakes - I didn't answer his questions and she was quite a tough character, then I swore, accidentally, mind you, and then I had to leave and I was sure I hadn't got it and forgot my briefcase, don't even know why I took it, to be honest. But he just called to tell me I got it!" John blurted out and Bill felt a sense of comfort – his son was sounding so much better.

"Oh, that is good news, your mother will be pleased. I know she has been worried about you spending so much time at home with us."

* * * * *

Ivy had made some lunch so that John and Bill could eat once they got back from the interview. The knot in her stomach kept tightening. It had seemed like the perfect solution, telling Beryl that she should end her days in John's house, but now it came to asking him, she was beginning to regret it. He had every right to tell her no and she would have to go back on a promise, something that seemed obscene considering the circumstances. She put a ham roll on each plate and went to the corner cupboard to get some crisps out. John's contribution to the household bills had enabled them to buy a greater selection of food and although crisps were hardly a luxury, it was still nice to be able to buy a good brand and have a packet each. The weddings still provided entertainment and provisions for the weekends, although they had started to dwindle now. Which on reflection, was a good thing, she thought, opening the packets and pouring the crisps onto the plates. She picked one up and popped it into her mouth as she went to put the wrappers into the recycling bin. Her heart jolted again as the car pulled onto the drive and she quickly finished chewing the crisp and picked up the plates. She hurried into the lounge and put the plates onto the dining table, and poured the jug of water into the glasses as quickly as she could, wanting to get to the door to meet them. Bill beat her to it, opening the door, laughing at something John had just said.

"How did it go?" she gabbled too brightly and Bill looked surprised at her tone. John came in and kicked off his shoes.

"Yeah, it was okay, considering."

"Considering what?"

"Considering I'm a muppet who shared too much information. I can't believe they offered it to me." John marvelled, taking his tie off and hanging it on the banister.

Ivy's eyes widened and she crossed to the where John stood and hugged him.

"You got it! Well done, that's wonderful!"

John felt a bit foolish as his mum clung to him, but as his father went through to the lounge, he managed to put his arm around her shoulders in return. Bill had sat down and took a sip of water from his glass.

"Are these just ham?" he called out as they came through the arch. Ivy looked confused and then registered his question.

"No, there's mustard in yours and tomato in ours…is that okay, John?"

"Oooh yeah I'm starving, thanks."

John sauntered across the room and took his seat at the table, a smile playing around his mouth. He was going to be working, out of the house, and being paid for it. He took a bite out of his roll and looked out of the window. The rain had stopped, but the sky was still grey and the room felt chilly. He made a mental note to turn up the thermostat later. John glanced at his mum and was surprised to see that she was looking guiltily at him. She tried to look away, but it was too late…John finished swallowing and then challenged her.

"What's up?"

Ivy was startled by the direct question and began to pull at her untouched roll, tearing off pieces of bread thinking she could eat, but the knot in her stomach filled the space. John took another bite, chewing slowly and staring at her. Bill, who knew what was coming, turned to stretch to where his paper had been left on the side of the chair. He opened it and became engrossed with reading, to avoid any side taking. Ivy smiled weakly under her son's scrutiny and started to speak.

"Well…you know Gladys and I visited Beryl?"

When he didn't answer, and continued to look at her, she carried on.

"She is very sick…far more poorly than we originally thought…I mean…I know terminal means you are very ill, but …well…she just looks…so…awful."

John finished his roll in one mouthful, still watching her and she decided to keep going, while his mouth was full.

"We got to talking about her final days…it's not suitable for her to stay at the hotel…partly the cost, but mainly the loneliness and care she is getting is well below standard. We just want to help her, you see….and …"

Here she faltered, unable to read what John was thinking and unsure of his response. He sat back in his chair, draining the glass of water and smiled in acknowledgement before speaking.

"I get it…you want her to move in here. It's understandable, you and Gladys can look after her…I don't mind moving out."

Ivy looked stricken and quickly answered him.

"Oh no, no, that's not what we were thinking at all, I don't want you to move out."

John frowned at her as she went on.

"No, it's whether she can stay at your old house."

She rushed the words out and then stopped, the sentence hanging in the air, reflecting John's jaw.

"My house? But I haven't even been back yet!"

"No, I know that, but I thought it would be a good thing for you to do, clear the house up a bit…you were going to do it anyway, before selling it."

John was still having trouble grasping the concept.

"But I hadn't envisioned it being this soon, and for a dying woman to live in…I mean, won't it smell of hospitals?"

That's the least of your problems thought Ivy, remembering the stench of the hot room, but she ploughed on.

"But it won't be for long…and the medical side of it would be better because she would be so well looked after. And I know Gladys and Beryl would be eternally grateful."

John suddenly put his hands together in front of his face, his forehead resting on his fingertips.

"You've told them, haven't you?"

Ivy, realising her mistake, opened her mouth to protest, but then, seeing raised eyebrows from Bill closed it again and swallowed. Her throat felt dry and so she took a sip of water, her roll now disintegrated on her plate; her hands had been working and fiddling without her even realising.

"How long do you think it will be for?" John ventured eventually.

"I don't know. I suppose I don't like to think about it."

"Well, you will have to, if you are going to help her. You need to be realistic, Mum."

Ivy realised he was conceding to the idea and tried to remember what Beryl had said…something about six months at Christmas, so that left her with three months. It was so weird to think that by Easter, Beryl would not be in this world anymore, it was just so sad. Her sadness showed on her face and John registered it and then made his decision.

"I suppose I could go over tomorrow and sort some stuff

out...it's about time. And if she is that bad, it's only right she has somewhere comfortable to finish...off."

He trailed off, unsure of the decent terminology and picked his plate up.

Ivy was full up, her throat swelled and her eyes filled with tears.

"Oh, that's lovely - I'll let Gladys know. She will be so touched. And Beryl can get out of that place and have carers to help and I can do my bit and..."

Bill held up his hand as John left with the plates.

"Spare our son the details dear, I'm sure you will manage to sort it out with Gladys and get Beryl the help she needs."

Ivy scuttled off to call Gladys and Bill smiled as he went back to reading the paper, another project to keep her busy. John took the stairs two at a time and went to lie on his bed. He lay there, processing what had just happened. He had agreed to sort out their home, now devoid of any life or love. It would be a painful, hard thing to do and the thought of it was making him feel uneasy. He closed his eyes and pictured his old lounge, the music system in the corner, the three-piece suite that Katy had insisted on saving up for, despite his argument that two armchairs would suffice as they never socialised. How obnoxious he was, he mused.... no wonder Katy had had enough. He could picture her on the sofa, curled up with a book, while he sat working on his laptop, barely registering her presence. John felt her loss even more now than he did initially. It seemed the better he got mentally, the harder it was to accept that part of his life was over. He wondered what she was doing now...

Chapter 24
Irritation Prickled

The carpark at Sainsburys was unusually busy as Katy pulled in. She contemplated coming back early the next day, as it was the weekend, but decided that she needed to get some food in, otherwise it would be another takeaway and she could already feel her jeans getting tighter. Having parked, she took her floral bag holder from the boot, pleased with her ingenious idea of bringing it with her, instead of ending up with copious amounts of carrier bags, gave her a sense of doing her bit for the environment. She took a pound out of her purse for the trolley and yanked it out of its slot. Taking the list out of her back pocket, she made her way to the door. The security man watched her as she came in, his huge frame leaning up against the customer services desk and she smiled, thinking how easy it would be for someone to shoplift, particularly if they were fit; they could outrun this specimen, with jowls like an orangutan, the closeness of his eyes adding to the effect.

Katy went through the aisles, checking everything on her list and putting the items in the trolley in an orderly way. She used to hate the way John threw things in, grabbing random junk food, just because it was on offer, laughing off her protestations that it wasn't on the list! She smiled faintly, knowing that memory was very early on in their relationship; towards the end, she did all the chores alone. She went to get some rolls for lunch the next day and then stopped herself, thinking that if Luke took her to meet his mother tomorrow, she wouldn't need it. She decided to suggest it again when she got back. They had been together eight months and it bothered her that she still hadn't met Agnes. She dropped the pack of rolls onto the floor and, annoyed with herself, bent down to pick them up. A sharp pain behind her breastbone caused her to press her hand on her chest as she put the rolls back on the shelf. She recognised the feeling from a few years before, when she had been particularly stressed at work and been diagnosed with acid reflux. She remembered taking Gaviscon, the chalky, salty, gloopy liquid, that eased the pain. Katy decided to find some in the medical aisle and double checked the list to make sure she had everything they needed. Hopefully Luke would make dinner tonight as she was feeling tired after such a long week and had put in some bacon and spaghetti for a carbonara. She found the Gaviscon and put it in the trolley and then went to wait in the queue. An elderly couple in front of her had arrayed their items in rows, neat and ordered and now they were getting their reusable bags out of a red square shopping bag that Katy was sure she can remember her mum using. She smiled as he took the heavy items for his bag and then passed his wife the lighter things. Her and Luke would be like that when they were old, she mused, he was so thoughtful and loving like that. The woman took her purse and paid as the man lifted the bags into their trolley. They both smiled at her as she finished putting her things on the moving belt and as they went to move off, her mobile went off. Their smiles faded as she grappled to get it out of her handbag and answered it.

"Hello?"

"Hi gorgeous, you ok?"

The cashier looked at her stubbornly, seemingly put out that she was daring to use a mobile phone while shopping. Katy gestured at her to start and spoke low into the phone.

"Yeah...I'm just at the checkout, so I can't talk."

Katy gestured again to the cashier to start and moved to the end of the belt, holding her phone under her chin as she pulled her bags out of her holder. The cashier was having none of it, taking a bottle of water out to have a swig and waiting.

"Ooh, did you get my peanuts?" Luke exclaimed.

A prickle of annoyance flitted over her throat but she managed to remain calm.

"No, I didn't...I hadn't put them on the list."

"Not to worry, I'll get some on the way to Mums tomorrow. I'll let you get on and see you later. I won't be out too late."

Confused, Katy stopped fiddling with the bags.

"What?" she snapped sharply, "Where are you going?"

"The pub with the lads from work...I did tell you." Luke chortled, all geniality, which only added to Katy's frustration. She put her hand over the mouth piece and directed her question to the cashier.

"Can you start please, I'm ready to pack."

The cashier looked dubious and started to put the things through roughly, causing Katy to grab and shove things in anywhere. She changed ear and kept her voice light an airy.

"Oh okay, I must have forgotten. We can chat when you get back."

Luke was laughing and had to ask her to repeat what she had said. She was really irritated now and felt drained.

"We'll speak later, okay? Love you."

Finished at last, she packed the Gaviscon carefully at the top of the bag.

"Yeah, laters!" giggled Luke, before ending the call. Katy knew she was being unreasonable but couldn't shake off the niggled feeling and slammed in the pasta pack, feeling the pressure ease with every new thing that got thrown. She stuffed the phone in her bag and took out her purse, still throwing things in the bags.

"That's forty-two pounds and fifty pence, do you have a Nectar card?"

"Erm, yes, somewhere…" she mumbled, trying to find the correct colour. After the Boots and Tesco cards had been rejected, she found the one she needed, but not before the elderly woman behind her had tutted and looked exaggeratingly at her watch. This caused Katy to get even crosser and she slowed her pace down, taking longer than was required to find her debit card.

Catching sight of the joint card she had had with John, a feeling of irritation prickled across her skin…another thing to have to sort out, she thought bitterly and as the cashier gave her a few vouchers, she took her card and stuffed everything back in her purse.

"Are you collecting the kids' vouchers?" The cashier asked this brightly and Katy shook her head, inexplicably struck dumb by the lump in her throat.

As the old woman behind her continued to stare, she put her head down and blindly made for the door, the tears initially blinked away now splashed off her face, running down her neck. She threw the bags into the boot and shoved the trolley back with its counterparts, fighting to get the pound coin out. She then turned and marched over to her car, ripped the door open and flopped down into the driver's seat and finally, let herself have a good howl. She didn't really know what she was so upset about. Luke only went out occasionally and it was her that had forgotten. Sorting the bank card out wasn't that bad, she reasoned, at least there wasn't children to sort out, or benefits to work through, no chasing him for money to pay for kids, it was easy really. Katy could never understand why couples got paid for having children, like come kind of reward system, surely those that didn't have them should be rewarded too, for not clogging up the earth with so many people. She looked out of the window, the rain reflecting the damp of her cheeks and watched as a young couple ran to get into the car next to her, laughing. The tears had stopped now and she was left feeling salty and sad. It gradually dawned on her why she felt so irrational. It was the seventeenth of the month, which meant her period would be due anytime. Smiling, realising that this was the real reason for feeling so overwhelmed, she instantly started to feel better. She waited until the couple next to her had pulled away before starting the engine. Driving home, she was glad that she would soon be back in the comfort of Luke's flat, cosy and able to relax. If Luke was home late, it wouldn't matter as she could have a bath get into her pyjamas and read, the bliss of some time to herself making her feel better.

* * * * *

John was glad that he was well enough to make the journey back to his house; the thought of having his mum or dad for company when he was unsure of his reaction filled him with dread and he had replied too brightly that he would be fine on his own. The medication was definitely helping, he could feel his nerve endings coated by it and things that used to really annoy him didn't bother him anymore. People cut him up and he just let them. They jumped the queue and he smiled and carried on waiting patiently. Nothing provoked him like it used to and he felt better about it, like he could cope with anything, which is why he felt a little more than disappointed as he got nearer the house and the familiar nag of anxiety began to ride up and down the inside of his chest.

He had brought some black bin bags with him, to try and clean up a bit. Knowing there were cleaning products under the sink meant he could just get on, assuming that Katy hadn't taken those with her. His mum had put some disposable gloves in, although he didn't feel he would need them. She had packed him some lunch, even though he had said he would pop out and get some food for lunch and dinner. He had to stay over and be there when Beryl came on the Saturday and it was pointless going back in between although he was beginning to feel unsure about sleeping in his old bed. By the time he got there, he was prickling with sweat and feeling nauseous. He pulled onto the drive and sat in the car, staring ahead, not wanting to look at the house and yet feeling a sense of home when he eventually did glance up. The ivy had grown up the side of it, without his careful attention to it, and the curtains were closed, giving it a certain lonely air. It was still a lovely looking house and he stayed sat in the car for twenty minutes before there was a knock on his window. He jumped and turned to see Brenda, the old woman who had been their neighbour for the last nine years, peering in at him. Fumbling with the door, he opened it as she stepped back.

"I thought it was you." she cooed, reminding him of a pigeon, especially as one of her eyes didn't quite look at him at the same time as the other and her greasy grey hair cut short added to the image.

"Hello," John smiled, before reaching in the back for the things he had brought to help him.

"Come to tidy up a bit, have you?" Brenda stated nosily, before adding "I can give you a hand, if you want, it's no bother."

John went to protest, but she was having none of it and followed him up the path to the front door. He would much rather have done this on his own, but she was already clutching the gloves and took the bags as he went to get his door key out. Having unlocked the door, he took a deep breath and stepped in, the aroma of a rubbish bin that has been cooped up for eight months hit them and they both wrinkled up their noses.

"Phew, that's a bit of a whiff," observed Brenda heading straight for the kitchen.

He was surprised that she knew where to go and even more surprised when she appeared with the bin bag.

"How did you know where my bin was?"

She smiled knowingly, her lips disappearing, revealing her yellowing teeth.

"I used to pop in once a fortnight and have coffee with Katy. Did she never mention me?"

He instantly regretted asking her and shrugged in a non-committal way, before unravelling the black bin bags and tugging one off.

"Well, I expect you were busy, always out working. Shall I stick this out the front, then? The bin men will be back Tuesday, so it should be fine until then. Might need to double bag it, mind, what with the smell."

He handed her the bag he had just torn off and took another one off. She opened it up and carefully placed the rubbish bag into the new one and tied it up expertly. For an older lady, she had surprisingly nimble fingers and John continued to stare as she went out the front door. He was still stood there when she came back in to wash her hands and she took pity on him. She realised he wasn't the same man that had left this house a few months before and that all the conversations she'd had with Katy couldn't be relied upon now. He was a changed man, she could see.

"So, do you want me to start on the bathroom?"

"No," answered John quickly, not wanting her in such a private place and yet not wanting to seem rude. "Thanks, but I'll start there…do you want to empty the fridge? I'm sure there is food in there that will need removing."

Brenda nodded before taking the bin bags from him and ripping one off before heading back into the kitchen. John went slowly up the stairs, the light where the sun came through the landing window lighting his way and at the top, he leant against the banister, his thighs aching with the effort. His anxiety gnawed at his chest, a caged animal desperate to get out and he stopped to take a few deep breaths; he had to push himself to keep moving forwards. The door to the bedroom was ajar and he steeled himself before pushing it open and surveying the scene. It was dark as the curtains were drawn and there was a musty smell in the air. The bed was neatly made up, although with a scattering of socks and t-shirts over it. There were deodorant and aftershave bottles knocked over on his chest of drawers and he was taken back to the day he had left, scrabbling about for clothes and toiletries in his haste to get to his parents, thinking he would pop back after a week or two.

He wished he hadn't left it so long, but knew it wasn't really something he could have tackled until now. Crossing the room, his shoes thudding against the hard floor, he opened the curtains. There was mould growing on the sealant and the inside of the window and John threw the roll of bags onto the bed, so that he could open the windows. The lock was stiff and he struggled to turn both locks, but eventually, they gave and he exhaled as he lifted the window up and a gust of cool, fresh air flew in. This seemed to revive him and he set his mind to work. He took the bin bags and flapped one open, before throwing the clothing on the bed into it too. Going through his bedside table drawers, he found piles of receipts and business cards, odd buttons and nail clippers, a tape measure that he had no idea was there and enough batteries to power a small village. He pulled the drawers out fully and tipped the contents into the bag, reasoning that he had not needed the stuff for eight months, so they obviously were of no real use to him. It was just stuff. He went around to what had been Katy's side of the bed and feeling a bit devious, checked her drawers. All empty, but he wanted to double check, to make sure everything was out before Beryl came in.

"Do you fancy a cuppa?" called Brenda up the stairs, startling him and he shut the drawer sharply and stood, crossing the room quickly to reply.

"Yes…please, if you don't mind, tea is in the…"

"I know," she called back, "I'll pop home to get some milk, won't be a minute."

John heard the front door close and then turned to sort out the chest of drawers. There were some trousers that he liked and so he took them out and put them on top, before chucking the rest into the bag. He contemplated donating the clothes to a charity shop, but knew they would be left in the boot of his car for months before being thrown away. Pointless. He cleared the wardrobe, knowing that he wouldn't need the suits and not wanting to take the shirts; too big anyway. Far too much stuff, he scolded himself. He reasoned that he had bought enough for his job, so why have any more? Another bag was required for these and he sat on the bed to get another one open. He couldn't believe that none of Katy's things were here anymore. How had he not noticed everything disappear? Being busy with work and pretty wrapped up in himself, he reasoned, so much so that there was nobody that he could call a friend in his life now… apart from Lisa, he thought ruefully as he stuffed the clothes in. Maybe he would meet more at work? Malcolm certainly seemed a nice guy, but then he was his manager and John never really thought you could be friends with someone who could fire you; it would feel shallow, being nice to them, as if you were creeping round them. Satisfied that the room was empty, he went into the en-suite, where there was a smell of damp and the fetid stench of death. He frowned and opened the little window, concerned to find that this was unlocked. He had often opened it to let out the steam, but had always locked it before leaving the house. Katy must have forgotten to do it on the day she left, he thought grimly, before bending down to pick up a hair bobble behind the loo. The smell grew stronger and he realised it must be the little pedal bin. Not wanting to see what the cause was and having a good idea what he would see, he picked it up and put the whole thing in the bin bag. The razors, shower gel and face balm went too and he realised the toilet needed a good clean; he would be needing the rubber gloves after all. John heard the door go and Brenda coming in and decided to leave the cleaning until he had cleared every room.

Popping his head round the door of the room Katy had used as a dressing room, he sighed. Apart from the full-length mirror in there, it was empty, the built-in wardrobe doors stood open, revealing a vacant space. The next room had a chair and ironing board in it, but nothing else, no knick-knack, no ornament to give it a homely feel. He began to feel a sense of despair, at this show home, where the two of them had existed, side by side, rarely together. Anything of beauty or value was gone. His office was the last room he needed to clear. Going into the office made him feel like an outsider observing somebody else's life. It just didn't seem possible that he had worked so hard, given everything, to this job. It had become his life and looking at it now, he loathed it. The in tray on the desk, piled high with paperwork, urgent stamped on most of them mocked him; how urgent can it really have been if nobody had come chasing him for it? He opened the bin bag fully and tipped the papers in. At the back of his mind, a little alarm bell rang, alerting him to the fact that he should probably be shredding this to destroy any personal information. Having wrestled with the thought, he thought better of it and pulled the papers back out and took them over to his shredder. It was already full and so he tipped the contents into the bag, before setting the top back on and switching it on at the wall. He took the papers and began to feed them through, a few at a time, not wanting to jam the machine but mindful of the need to get on with it. It whirred into life, gobbling up the sheets, turning them into piles of spaghetti. When the box was full, he emptied it and groaned inwardly…there was still so much to do. He did another boxful and then another, before deciding to have a break and deal with something else. He had just finished as Brenda walked into the room, jolting him again.

"Cup of tea for you," chirped Brenda, "I didn't know if you took sugar or not, I couldn't find any, so I guessed not."

He smiled briefly and took the cup from her outstretched hand. She looked around and said, "How are you getting on?"

He took a sip and joined her looking around.

"Well, there's quite a lot to do in here, so much paperwork

to sort out. I've done the bedroom," he added quickly, feeling the need to justify himself.

"I've finished the kitchen. You were right about the fridge, it was filthy, mouldy cheese and rotten veg. I switched it off and gave it a thorough deep clean, bleach and all, so it should come up nice and clean. There wasn't much in the cupboards but the stuff I found is now in a carrier bag by the front door."

John went from being embarrassed about the fridge, to feeling grateful for her help.

"Thanks, that's a great help."

She looked around again.

"Do you want a hand up here, or shall I do the lounge?"

"If you wouldn't mind, I'd like you to do the lounge," he suggested carefully, not wanting to upset her, but needing to be alone to sort out his past life.

"Okay, I'll get back to it then." she offered brightly and turned to go.

John watched her go stiffly down the stairs before getting up from where he had been squatting and put his cup on the desk. He went around and sat in his office chair, the familiarity of it like a hug. His diary was open, as always, marking the day that everything had changed. Thinking back to the meeting, when Simon had told him about his parents, he felt mortified at the recollection of swearing and storming out; that poor youth worker. He picked up the diary and began leafing through, remembering the meetings, the late nights, the time spent poured into this other life, horrified at the sheer number of appointments he had in one week, let alone one day. What was it all for? Putting the diary back and chewing his thumbnail, the feeling of sadness crept back up his chest, threatening to wind him, with a blow to the solar plexus. What was the point, all this getting together to talk, to eat, to drink, to network…where was his support network now? John realised that it had never existed, none of those in government had kept in touch with him, even those that he had worked hard to help achieve their goals. The celebratory meals shallow interactions, only for the moment he now realised, closing the book. He fingered it along the spine, wondering about shredding or chucking it in the bag, but instead left it on the desk, deciding he would take it home and burn it. He could do the same to the other papers, save him shredding them all. Opening the bottom drawer of the desk, he was appalled. Yet more paperwork, more ideas, policies that never made it off the drawing board, all those wasted days. Going over to the roll of bin bags, he tore another one off before taking the diary off the desk and putting it in and then suddenly, in a frenzy, opened every drawer, yanking the papers out and stuffing them in the black abyss, feeling a sense of cleansing, a burden lifting every time more was taken out.

By the time he had finished, he was warm, even in the coolness of the house and so took his fleece off. Chucking it on the chair, he went over to the bookcase that dominated the room; floor to ceiling and two metres wide, it held every book he had ever needed, the majority linked to his work. He took another two black bags off and started to throw some in. Most were destined for recycling, but there were a number he knew were valuable enough to sell on eBay and so they went into the other bag. He worked quickly, and by the time Brenda came up to tell him she had finished, he had emptied it and filled four black bags.

"You've done well," she exclaimed, looking around the bare room, the echo present now that there were no insulating books pressed up against the wall. "I've finished tidying the lounge as there wasn't much in there and gave it a good dust.

Shall I hoover too?"

John looked concerned.

"Oh no, I can do that, you have done more than enough."

She smiled warmly at him.

"I don't mind…and I wondered…well."

Brenda looked awkward.

"What?"

"Well, would you know how to use it? No offence, but I know Katy did a lot of the housework."

John felt the old irritation start up, but quickly squashed it down with a smile, realising she was right.

"Fair enough," he conceded, "I wouldn't. She didn't do a lot of the housework, she did all of it!"

They both smiled and she picked up the cup from the desk. As she turned to go, John spoke again.

"Thanks for the tea…and thanks for all your help, I really appreciate it."

The old woman turned pink with pleasure as he continued.

"It would have taken me so much longer if you hadn't popped in."

"Well, that's alright, I mean, it's what neighbours do, isn't it?"

John considered her and then shook his head.

"No, it's what you do. What have I ever done for you? Too busy to even say good morning."

He looked at the sacks of books, embarrassed and feeling awkward.

"I'm sorry it was like that. Hopefully, you will end up with some nicer neighbours when we sell."

She stopped smiling at this and looked concerned.

"Oh – I thought – I assumed you were moving back in?"

John looked surprised

"Oh God, no. I'm getting it ready to sell. Although I do

have someone moving in tomorrow."

"Tomorrow?!" she squawked before she could stop herself.
He raised his hand.

"Only temporarily…it's a friend of a friend, who needs
to stay somewhere. You won't know she is here." he lied,
knowing that Beryl would make her presence known and
trying not to feel too guilty about it.

"Oh, well…that's good that someone will be living here for
a bit, get rid of that smell – sorry, I don't mean to be rude."
she added hastily, mistaking his look for one of offence.

"That's alright," he conceded, relived that there was no
more to say on the matter.

Brenda went down the stairs and he finished tying up
the black bags. He looked around the near empty room
and realised that he was feeling better than he had earlier -
perhaps staying here wouldn't be so hard after all.

* * * * *

John wasn't feeling so great the next day. The night had
proven difficult and sleep had evaded him until the early
hours of the morning. Padding around the empty house had
felt alien and familiar all at once and the conflicting feelings
had fought all evening, keeping his eyes fixed open and
unable to switch off. He watched T.V for as long as he could
bear, hoping that he would fall asleep, but instead ended up
getting absorbed in a creepy thriller that left him on edge.
He looked online at house prices nearby, to try and gauge
how much he would be left with after the sale before going
up to the bedroom, the bed huge in comparison to his old
bed at his parents. He had slept fitfully, waking and seeing
the white wall, unsure of his surroundings and feeling sick, a
sense that he had done something wrong. Shivering, he got

up, throwing his clothes on quickly before making his way downstairs to switch on the heating. He knew that it would need to be warm for Beryl and went around checking the radiators, hoping that they would get warm and not need any tweaking. DIY was not really his thing and he didn't have long before they would be arriving.

He checked the clock on the oven, an hour fast having not been adjusted when the clocks went back, so it said 9.07am; this meant he had three hours until they came. Ivy had texted to say they would be there at 11.00 and bringing everything that Beryl needed in a van. Eric had agreed to drive it, so with his dad as well, there would be enough men to carry in the heavy stuff. John had been concerned at first that there would be too much, that his house would be packed with another person's things and that it would feel strange. But as he looked around the lounge, he realised this wouldn't be a problem; the three-piece suite stark against the backdrop of the empty bookshelf; hooks imploring for pictures to cover the sense of loss…even the carpet looked impersonal, beige, boring, crying out to have a glass of red wine spilled over it, or a dog to pee guiltily behind the sofa, memories stained forever.

Chapter 25
Is There Any Point?

Ivy had got into a routine of popping to John's twice a week, to help Gladys out with bathing Beryl and spending time chatting and cleaning up. John hadn't been back after the initial clear up and it was probably a good job. If he saw the amount of cleaning required, he would have changed his mind, regardless of the state of the patient. Beryl had grown increasingly thinner and could no longer walk unaided. The commode had been placed next to the bed, in the hope that she would make it in time, but often, the smell in the room revealed that her bowels, so often blocked to the point of desperate manual removal, had run to the point of falling out of her without her knowledge. She was past mortification now, allowing her sister to don the marigolds and remove the worst of it with wipes before stripping the bed and Beryl bare, fumbling in her hurry to get the dirty stuff out. Once the offending bedding was in a black sack, she would quickly put a fresh nighty on Beryl, before helping her pull on a pair of knickers…they had giggled about the size of them initially, proper granny pants that kept the belly button warm. But as the days went by and Beryl grew thinner, these flapped around her body and Gladys had to invest in some children's knickers. They had put her bed in the lounge, having moved the sofas into the dining room, leaving the armchair next to the bed so that Beryl could sit up if she wanted to. It meant that Gladys had somewhere to sit too, while they chatted, or watched television late into the night. Gladys slept upstairs in the guest room that looked as if it had never been used, so pristine was the furniture.

It had been a long day and she was exhausted, waiting on her sister hand and foot. It wasn't just the physical side of it. Beryl weighed next to nothing and the bed stripping was soon done – she had taken to just throwing the lot away, rather than try to wash it, the sheets being very cheap, thanks to Sainsburys economy range and the thought of having to deal with the mess turned her stomach – Ivy had suggested nappies, but Gladys could not bring herself to have that conversation with her sister…no, that was something for when the end was nearer, perhaps a carer could suggest that one. The physical side was okay to cope with…it was the emotional toll of seeing her sister, barely recognisable as the beauty from only a few months before. The pain of the past was swallowed up in the everyday knowledge that she was losing her sister for real, not just to another country for a few years, but forever, to never see her again and much as she wanted to ease her suffering, she didn't feel ready to let her go…not yet. She lay in bed and looked up at the ceiling, a sigh escaping from her lips at the thought of another day of care, of finding things to talk about, of just sitting while Beryl slept for hours, not wanting to leave her and yet feeling so bored and then guilty for feeling bored. She couldn't believe how John had been so kind as to let them use his house. He had certainly changed from the obnoxious, selfish boy he had been, not seeming to care about anything.

Perhaps Katy leaving him was the best thing that could have happened to him she thought as she shifted position in a vain attempt to stop her back aching. Ivy had told her that the therapy seemed to help and she had to agree. Gladys snuggled down and turned out the lamp next to the bed, the price labels still attached, confirming her opinion of a room with no use.

Gladys woke to a room full of pale sunshine, the glare from the white walls reminding her she had forgotten to pull the curtains the night before. Ernie always did it at home and so she wasn't in a habit of doing it yet. She got up and decided to have a shower as Ivy would be coming this morning. Picking up her watch to check the time, she gasped…it was already half past ten. A stab of fear hit her heart as she crossed the room to get her dressing gown from the back of the chair. Glancing at herself in the dressing table mirror, she was alarmed to see how wild and old she looked and quickly smoothed her hair down, before opening the door. She listened at the top of the stairs…nothing. She padded down in her mules and took a deep breath before entering the lounge, the door ajar as she had left it the night before.

Beryl was slumped to one side in the chair, apparently asleep. There was a strong smell of ammonia but not faeces, Gladys was pleased to notice and when she had crossed over to the commode, found it to be full. She passed a cursory hand over the bed – dry.

"I didn't wet it," croaked Beryl, "I got up like a good girl… twice."

Gladys smiled and turned to help her sister sit upright.

"Well, that's good, isn't it?" she chirped, trying and failing to not sound patronising.

Beryl harrumphed in answer and reached out for her water.

"Shall I get a fresh glass?" suggested Gladys, but Beryl waved her off before passing her the tablet pack to get out her quota for the day.

Gladys handed her the four she needed and she took them two at a time, her scrawny neck flickering as they went down.

"Listen I need to have a shower as Ivy is coming this morning to see you. Do you want me to freshen you up a bit before I go?"

Beryl surveyed herself and smiled ruefully

"Is there any point? One nighty looks the same as the next."

Gladys was secretly pleased and trotted off up the stairs. Halfway up, she suddenly thought what if Ivy turned up and she was in the shower, there would be no way for her to get in. Popping back down, she took the keys from the rack and unlocked the door, before putting the latch down. She went back into the lounge where Beryl regarded her with surprise, looking up from her magazine.

"I've left the door off the latch so Ivy can walk in, should be okay."

"I'm sure it will be fine…there's hardly anyone who would walk in and attack a defenceless old woman - the smell would send them packing."

Gladys chuckled and went back up the stairs to the bathroom. Mid shower, she could hear voices and stuck her head out of the flow. It sounded like Ivy and Bill had both come in and she hurried to get her hair washed. Finishing, she turned the water off and carefully got out, not wanting to slip on the tiled floor. She reached for her towel and wrapped it round, the heat from the towel rail warmed her skin, goose bumped as it was. Having roughly dried herself, she went out and stopped dead. The man's voice that was carried up to her wasn't Bill's...it was George!

"George?!" she cried, quite forgetting her attire, "Is that you?"

"Yes Mother, it's me," he replied, coming to the foot of the stairs

"Don't come up!" shrieked Gladys, making for the bedroom door.

"No fear," retorted George, "I'm going to put the kettle on...did you want a tea?"

Tears pricked her eyes and she fought to keep her voice light and airy.

"Yes please...I'll be down soon."

She heard him laugh at something Beryl said and closed the bedroom door. She pulled on her underwear and found her smart trousers and turquoise blouse that she had thrown in amongst the old clothes required for caring. Having got dressed, she took her comb from the table and flattened down her unruly mop. Applying a little lipstick, she felt ready to go down when the twinge of pain in both knees reminded her that she had her own medication to take. She took the co-codamol out of the pack and went downstairs.

Ivy was just coming through the door with a bunch of flowers when they came face-to-face.

"The door was open, so I came in," she said, "Did I see George's car out there?"

"You certainly did," answered George, coming up the hallway, "Lovely to see you, Ivy. Morning Mother...up at last?" he joked with a twinkle in his eye.

"I've been up, thank you, we just overslept a little, that's all."

"Aaaw, we can let you off just this once," he reassured handing her the cup, "Tea?"

He gestured to Ivy.

"Yes please, and for Bill, he's just trying to find somewhere to park."

George went back into the kitchen, leaving the two women alone in the hall. Ivy went to her friend. "How are you doing?"

"Don't," whimpered Gladys, filling up. "I shouldn't be feeling like this, I'm not the one dying."

The tears slid down her cheeks as Ivy reached for a tissue in her bag. The door to the lounge was closed and they could hear Suzie, George's wife chatting brightly to Beryl, who murmured in reply.

Gladys allowed herself to be enveloped in a hug from her friend and cried into the shoulder of Ivy's coat, leaving it damp. Bill came in and assessing the situation, moved wordlessly past them and into the kitchen, closing the door after him.

"It's bound to take its toll on you," she heard Ivy say, her words muffled against the back of her jumper, still being held by her friend.

Gladys stood back and Ivy gave her the tissue, watching her sympathetically as she wiped her eyes.

"I just want it to end…not to lose her, I'd give anything to have her well again, but she looks so awful and the cleaning and mess, it's just horrible and I know she hates it all too. I just wish we could have been better sisters, to have some good shared memories for me to hang onto when…when the inevitable happens."

Ivy nodded sympathetically, not sure what to say and turned to go through to the lounge, linking arms with Gladys, who dried her eyes on her sleeve. Fixing a smile on her face, she went through to where George was explaining to Beryl that his boss wanted to give him a promotion.

"The thing is," he went on earnestly, "I don't want it. I like the job, accounting is easy and I don't have any concerns. He wants me to be a partner, to manage people and I don't want the hassle…what do you think?"

Beryl had been regarding him with her eyes half closed, although dulled, they still had a shrewd look to them and she pushed herself up before clearing her throat.

"You know what you should do, really. You don't need me to tell you. If you flipped a coin and called heads or tails, heads you win, tails you lose, you know what the answer would be."

"I don't understand…" said Suzie, her puzzled face turning to look at George, who was smiling knowingly at Beryl.

"You mean the answer is what I would be wishing the coin to land on…either heads or tails", replied George, "It's true. I don't want a promotion, I'm happy and like the fact I have regular hours, no managing of anyone."

"Is it more money, though?" enquired Bill, who was blowing his tea and tentatively drinking it.

George turned to face him.

"Well, yes, but money isn't everything," he insisted quickly, passing a pillow to Beryl who smiled and allowed him to put it behind her back.

"I can vouch for that," she said drily, without a hint of bitterness, before picking up her magazine again.

Ivy broke the silence that followed.

"Can I do anything to help while I'm here? Clean the bathroom? Some washing perhaps?"

"There's not much to do today, we seem to be keeping on top of it." answered Gladys brightly, as Beryl steadily read her magazine.

"No bed wetting through the night," she muttered, "I seem to be getting better at controlling my bladder."

She turned and smiled at Suzie, who smiled back.

"Well, that's good," the young woman countered "And I have to say, you do look better than when we last saw you. You've even got some colour in your cheeks."

It was true, a rosy tinge had settled on her waxy cheeks and her eyes looked brighter and less sunken. Her hair, although grey was still growing and gave her an impish look.

"I feel a bit stronger today. Maybe later, I can sit outside in the wheelchair, take a look at the garden." she suggested, looking for confirmation at her sister.

"Oh yes, that's a good idea. Although we will have to wrap you up, as it's very chilly out there." warned Gladys, turning to pick up another blanket from the chair.

"We'd best do that while we are here to help get you in and out of the house safely." suggested George softly, turning to pick his jacket up from the table.

"If you can leave me to go to the loo for a minute, I can go out when I'm ready then."

The group hastily left the room, leaving Gladys to help her sister onto the commode. She was surprised at how strong Beryl's grip was on her arm and caught sight of the look on her face, as if she was in terrible pain.

"Are you okay?" she twittered anxiously and as quickly as the look had been there, it passed and Beryl was all smiles again.

"Yes, just tired, dear. Can you pass me the toilet paper?"

Gladys pulled some off and gave it to Beryl, before turning to pull her own coat on. She could hear the others at the back door, calling out to each other, before there were footsteps announcing the arrival of someone on the other side of the door. A low tapping was heard and then:

"Are you ready? I've got your chair."

George's voice carried through and Beryl manoeuvred herself back into her chair.

"I'm ready." she replied querulously and he came in, wheeling it in front of him.

Gladys was busy helping her on with her coat and scarf as he lifted her up and put her in the chair as if she was a child. Gladys took the blankets and began to pile them around her, wrapping her up, cocooning her against the cool of the day.

"Phooey, I'm all hot and bothered now," muttered Beryl, trying to loosen the covers. Gladys put them back on her and took her hat.

"You need to keep warm," she warned plonking the hat on Beryl, who tried to protest and was whisked away by George, revving the wheelchair up and wheeling her through the French windows. Once there, Bill helped carry the chair down to the garden and placed it gently down on the lawn. There were a few crocuses pushing their way thought the ground, and snowdrops dotted along the borders and around the only tree at the end of the garden. Beryl breathed in the cool air, her breath coming out again rapidly, the steam in front of her reminding her of the days in the school playground, the girls pretending to smoke, puffing out their visible air, trying to act cool. What she wouldn't give for a cigarette now, she thought, knowing that it would make her sick and yet craving the hit. She glanced down and saw a bush that looked dead, brown thin branches with little life and no buds on it.

"Is that a fuchsia?" she enquired, looking at Bill, who turned to follow her gaze down to the forlorn looking set of twigs.

"Yes," he answered, pleased to have something to say, "I think we bought it for John for their first wedding anniversary…looks quite dead now."

He bent down to touch it.

"Snap a bit off," she commanded.

Having looked at Ivy, who nodded, he did as she had asked.

"Now, is it green inside that twig?"

He peered at the bit in his hand closely.

"Yes," he uttered surprised, "It is."

Beryl settled back and pulled the blankets round her.

"It will bloom again in the summer, you watch if it doesn't and I'll see it and tell you I told you so!"

She sounded so strong in her conviction that nobody dared correct her, or told her to stop being ridiculous, she wouldn't be seeing another spring, let alone summer. Standing there, looking at her, triumphant and energised, there was such a sense of the old Beryl being back that they could hardly believe she was ill, let alone terminally so. Suzie placed her hand over Beryl's and looked around at everyone, grinning.

"It will certainly look beautiful in this garden in the summer. Let's hope there will be plenty of sunshine for us to enjoy our times outside this year!"

They all chuckled and felt grateful to each other for making a difficult situation a little better to bear. They didn't stay out too long, Gladys began to fuss over Beryl, who became quieter as the day went on. George brought her back in and put her into her chair again and she clung to him, feeling like a child who couldn't be consoled. He gave her a hug back and took her hands and kissed them.

"Get some rest. We will be back at the weekend to take you out again."

He kissed her on the forehead, mistaking the sadness in her eyes for tiredness and quickly slipped out of the room, taking Suzie by the hand. She was very tearful and they left, having kissed Gladys goodbye. Ivy and Bill hung back in the kitchen, Bill flicking the kettle on, wanting to do something of use. Gladys started to take out the Complan shakes from the cupboard and went across to the fridge. She poured the milk into the container to measure it and added the sachet, shaking it vigorously. A sound from the lounge startled her and she hurried in there, letting out a cry that brought Ivy in.

"Oh no, please…no…Beryl…BERYL!"

Ivy followed her and saw that Beryl was staring wide eyed at her, her mouth gaping open, unable to breathe, wordlessly working her mouth. Gladys held her by her shoulders, as if willing her to cough up, to clear her throat, so that she could breathe again. She slumped forward and although she did breathe again, it was laboured and noisy, like an old engine and they recognised it as the sound of departure, a final farewell. Gladys sat on the arm of the chair, cradling the sister who had caused their family the most awful heartache for so many years, living her life as she wanted to and ending it with nothing gained, no adoring family for her, just her only sister for company.

"It's not meant to be like this," she sobbed, stroking the side of her face, "I need more time with you…it's not fair!"

She was really crying now as Beryl seemed to relax into her, so much so, that Gladys thought she had gone to sleep. But as she prised herself away and held her sister against the chair, the dark liquid that oozed from the side of her mouth confirmed that Beryl had finally gone, left this world for the next; the fuchsia would bloom unseen by the glazed eyes of Beryl the rebel, the girl who travelled the world to find herself and ended her life with just that; herself.

Chapter 26
Terminating The Call

When Katy had woken up the first morning feeling sick, she put it down to her BPPV, the feeling of vertigo that she got upon waking that caused the room to spin and led to her feeling nauseous. She hoped that by getting up, it would ease, but it had got worse and she had vomited. Calling in sick, she was glad it was a Friday so that she had the weekend to recover. As the day progressed, she felt a little better and took sips of water that helped. Later, she felt well enough to eat a Rich Tea, cursing herself as she ran down the hallway, not quite making it to the toilet before it reappeared on the laminate floor. She went and grabbed some toilet roll to clean it up, gagging just looking at it and feeling wretched. Katy wished Luke was here, knowing he would be all concern and rubbing her back. But he had arranged to see his mum for three days this weekend, due to her arthritis being bad and so she was alone. Lying down on the sofa, she decided to sleep it off and spread herself out. As she looked down, she was surprised to see that her tummy looked bloated but, assuming it was part of the illness, soon drifted off to sleep.

When she woke up, she felt hot and sick again, retching before staggering to the toilet, dry heaving as her stomach was well and truly empty. What on earth was this…some kind of food poisoning? She thought back to the chips she had eaten the night before and promptly began dry heaving again, before sobbing on the toilet floor, the cool of the sink providing relief to her pounding head. She thought back to when she felt this tired and emotional - that night at the supermarket, crying over kids' vouchers, what an idiot, she thought, smiling at the memory of her sitting in the car. But then a cold fear gripped her stomach and she felt queasy again. Her period hadn't come when she got back that night, nor the night after…in fact, that was nearly four weeks ago and she forgotten all about it because of how well she felt. Now she got a sense of what was going on…bloated… feeling sick.

Oh, dear God, no. Please, not that.

After all the years of heartache and desperation, she was now desperate to not be pregnant. Being forty and in a new relationship wasn't the best backdrop for a new life, she thought, knowing that this is what everyone else would think. Don't get ahead of yourself, she told herself firmly and decided to pop to Boots to get a pregnancy test. She ended up buying three; they were on offer anyway, but she wanted to be sure either way. The woman behind the counter had looked at her and Katy was sure it was a look of surprise, almost 'What would you need with these?' type of look. But then she smiled kindly as Katy fumbled with her money and Katy immediately felt foolish, knowing she was being paranoid, and managed a smile as she thanked the shop assistant. She left the shop, beginning to feel nauseous again and light-headed and glanced back in the window. The shop assistant was pointing her out to a colleague and Katy stopped dead, turning to stare. They quickly turned away and pretended to be looking at the till but Katy had seen enough; she wasn't paranoid after all.

Feeling miserable, she got back to the car and sat down heavily. She retched and had to open the car door again, to release the water that had returned. Feeling hot, she drove home carefully, not wanting to make a mistake and was relieved when she was able to park right outside the flat. She grabbed the bag and went in, only relaxing when the door was closed and the cool of the flat soothed her. Jimmy came running and rubbed around her legs, but she almost tripped over him, so desperate was her attempt to get to the loo. She closed the door on his meows and put the toilet seat down so that she could sit and rest her head on the sink. The nausea subsided enough for her to be able to read the instructions and, having taken the first one out, cursing as the plastic took an age to rip open, she lifted the seat and held it in the stream, managing to pee on the end of the stick as well as all over her hand. Katy reached over to the sink to wash it and held the stick in the light of the sun. Were her eyes playing tricks? Or was that a faint blue line appearing in the window? She scrabbled to read the instructions again and saw that a blue line meant pregnancy. When she looked again after the allotted three minutes there was no doubting the dark blue line in the window; the two other tests confirmed it. She was pregnant.

But how? Katy had been so careful and assumed that being pre-menopausal would offer her some protection. If she was only a month, then it must have been around Christmas time, when she had a flu-like bug and diarrhoea. She had heard that the Pill wasn't always effective if a woman was ill, but had always assumed it was an old wife's tale. Her mind took her back to the consultant's room, all those years before, him telling her that she was perfectly able to have children, it was John that was the problem. And how she had kept that a secret, not wanting to hurt him, accepting that it wasn't meant to be. And now it had happened and after the initial shock, she could feel another feeling replacing it… excitement. Her chance to be a mummy to someone, to see a little person grow and be in her life. She put her arms across her belly aware of her negative reaction and hugged herself.

"It's okay…I'm going to love you…I just need time."

Padding through to the lounge and picking up her new iPad, she googled morning sickness and found out what she would need. By the evening, after a second trip into town, she had more Gaviscon, ginger thins, and some ready-made salad with hummus and crackers to eat. No glass of wine to wash it down, just a glass of milk that for some reason she wanted and that she found settled her stomach. Katy was still in shock and yet felt a sense of elation beginning to build in her chest, a sense of wonder at the way things had turned out. Having always wondered how it would feel to be pregnant, she was entranced; to have that secret knowledge, just her and the baby in cahoots. Seventeen years ago, when she had married John, she thought it would have been many years down the line after she had established her career. She certainly didn't expect to be in her forties, with a younger man as the father or to feel so dreadful; this thought flitted through as she ran to bring up the meal she had just wolfed down.

This was the biggest adjustment she felt she had to make… to feeling sick, being sick, knowing that it was a normal process, that at work she would be expected to carry on as normal. Katy was already feeling hungry again and went to take a ginger thin from the packet on the side. Jimmy came racing in from the bedroom, taking advantage of the fact she was in the kitchen, therefore prime position for getting him his tea. He curled around her legs, meowing loudly to get his message through. She turned to get his tin from the cupboard and absentmindedly opened it. The smell hit her and she staggered to the sink, treading on Jimmy, who yowled as he leapt out of the way, stunned. After heaving for a good minute, the room stopped spinning and she took a tea towel and wet it under the cold tap, mopping her brow. This helped and so she did it again, the cool water dripping down her face brought relief and the nausea subsided again. She turned to where Jimmy was eyeing her from the corner of the room, licking his leg and looking wounded.

"Sorry, Jimmy…come on, let's try again."

This time, she held her breath and managed to put his food in the bowl without vomiting, although she had to turn her head away and gagged a couple of times. She felt a sense of achievement as she left Jimmy to his dinner and went through to the lounge. Flopping down on the sofa, she picked up the remote and flicked the TV on. It was EastEnders, something she rarely watched. But something about the way the obnoxious woman on the screen was ranting at her daughter drew Katy in and she snuggled down, pulling the throw from the back of the sofa and covering herself. She felt drained, exhausted from the effort of the day and the emotional trauma and allowed herself to be drawn in to the inane lives of a soap opera. This morning, she thought to herself, I didn't know I was pregnant… and now I know. This thought filled her with contentment and she drifted off into a deep sleep, only waking when her phone rang three hours later.

Katy came around groggily, her head pounding, her stomach a bucket of squid and she got up, trying to focus her eyes in the semi-darkness. The light from the kitchen was on and she knew her phone was on the side in there, bleating out its little tune, kept loud deliberately so that she could always hear it, even from the depths of her bag. She looked at the screen and could see Luke's face beaming back at her…she loved this picture of him, taken when they had first got together, at a clandestine picnic on a visit to Cambridge…the way his fringe covered his eye, the light reflecting off his cheekbones and making him look even more lovely. Katy stared at it, knowing she should answer, but feeling too ill to talk to anyone, plus she knew she would blurt it out and she wanted to do it in a special way. She held the phone, willing him to stop the call and eventually, he did. She sat on the chair at the kitchen table and began to text him: 'Hi darling, I'm not feeling too well, been a bit sick and headachy, so have slept most of the day. Hope you've…'

A text came through and she touched the screen so that she could read it.

'Where are you? Have been trying to call all day. We need to talk.'

Those last four words stunned her and a cold fear now entered her heart. What did he mean, we need to talk? She only saw him yesterday; they could have talked then. Something must have happened, maybe his mum was ill. Relief washed over her as she realised that must be it. The fact he didn't text her and needed to speak to her must mean it is serious, she thought, poor Luke, trying to call her all day and getting no answer. Puzzled she looked at her call history and noted there were no missed calls except this one. She was worried about him now, concerned that he wasn't his usual happy self, he hadn't even texted a kiss or smiley face. Deciding that he needed her and that she should ring him now, regardless of how she felt, Katy took a deep breath. She went over to the plastic recycling bin and took out the bag of rubbish, leaving her with the perfect receptacle should she need to be sick. She pressed the screen so that Luke's mobile would ring. He answered it straight away.

"Hi…where have you been?"

"I've been in most of the day…my phone hasn't rung, maybe there's a fault on it. Is everything okay?"

Katy couldn't help sounding panicked, such was her desperation to know what was wrong. She heard him sigh and a thud and when he spoke, she knew he had gone into another room to talk.

"Mum's not well at all and the carer is rubbish, keeps on forgetting to come and help her get dressed in the mornings."

Feeling relieved, Katy sank back onto the pillows on the sofa and tucked her feet up beside her.

"Oh, poor Agnes, she must be so fed up."

"Yeah…she is. And being here has helped me to make my decision."

Katy's heart turned to stone as he continued with the words she knew were coming and yet couldn't quite believe she was hearing.

"I'm moving back in with my mum."

"What?" spluttered Katy, shock and outrage pulsing through her chest.

She heard him sigh before he went on.

"I've been thinking about it for a few weeks and seeing her like this…well, it's confirmed it really."

Katy was so stunned, she sat, unable to articulate anything and so Luke carried on.

"We haven't exactly been getting on, have we?"

"Haven't we?" she stammered, her voice tremulous, fighting to keep from crying.

"Oh, come on, you must have noticed the last few weeks,

the arguments…you don't need that sort of negativity…it's for the best."

Her feelings of reason began to come back and she felt angry as the tears coursed down her cheeks and sniffing loudly, reached to get a tissue.

"Look, I'm sorry, I didn't want it to be like this…"

"How did you want it to be?!" snapped Katy, furious now. "Did you think I would say 'oh that's fine, it's for the best'? I gave up everything to be with you!"

She knew she was shrieking but couldn't help it, the outrage poured out of her.

"Well, technically, your marriage was over…"

"Oh, shut up!" she screamed before retching into the bucket, the salty taste of tears and snot finally getting to her.

"Look, I'm sorry, if this isn't a good time, I'll call back tomorrow when you're feeling better."

She began to shake as the enormity of her situation finally dawned on her and decided that she might as well drop her bombshell as he had so easily tossed his grenade.

"I won't feel better tomorrow…I'm not ill…I'm pregnant."

She retched again and coughed, releasing the phlegm trapped in her throat and a rush of water came with it. She spat and used the tissue to wipe her mouth, still clutching the phone to her ear to hear his reply. Nothing.

"You can't be…" he answered pointlessly, "You're on the Pill. Look, I know you're upset, but this kind of shit isn't funny."

"This kind of shit?" countered Katy incredulously. "I'm not making it up! I've got three test results that confirm it and I can't keep anything down. Apparently, it happened a few weeks ago when we weren't getting along!"

Pressing the end call button, she threw the phone down and sobbed, angry, frightened and suddenly ravenously hungry. She really wanted cheese on toast and her mouth watered at the thought. Going through to the kitchen, she checked the bread bin. A mouldy crust was at the bottom and so she went to the fridge and checked the freezer compartment. There was a small loaf and so she took a slice and put it in the toaster to defrost it. She turned on the old grill and went back to the fridge for the cheese she knew would be in there as Luke had it most days in his sandwiches. At the thought of him, she began to cry again, her newfound joy at being pregnant had been crushed by his words, something she hadn't seen coming, had been totally unaware of. As she cut the cheese into slices, she thought back…had it been bad? She racked her brain, trying to think of every little detail, but there was nothing. They had the odd little disagreement over this and that, she liked things done a certain way, but they always laughed everything off, she was so happy. Or had been, she thought bitterly, the realisation that it was over finally sinking in. She gulped as she put the toast on the grill pan and laid the cheese on top as a thought began to process…she hadn't heard his reaction to her news. What if he changed his mind? Wanted to make it work, now a child was on the way? Even as she thought it, she knew, deep down that it wasn't right, that it couldn't be mended that a child would not sort it out. Katy had seen enough daytime television and celebrity drama to know that a child made no difference these days. A jolt went through her as her phone began to ring and she shoved the grill pan under the orange tubing and moved swiftly to where she had left it. Seeing his name, she snatched it up and pressed the answer button.

"Hello?"

"Hi…look, I didn't mean to be rude. I was just shocked, that's all…I didn't expect that."

She softened, although fought to stay firm.

"It's okay. I didn't expect you to say that we are over."

Katy hoped he would say he hadn't meant it, but there was silence down the line and she wandered back into the kitchen as the smell of grilled cheese came through. She bent down to get a small plate out of the cupboard and he spoke again.

"Well, it's obviously not ideal…I mean, talk about timing. But, like you say, it's only been a few weeks, so if you need any money towards it, then I'm happy to go halves."

Because Katy was trying to get her food out without burning her fingers, she didn't fully understand what he was saying until it was on her plate. Finally, her brain registered.

"Oh my God…you're talking about an abortion, I don't fucking believe it, how could you even think that?!"

"I just thought…that that was why you told me, to help you make a decision."

He sounded flustered and unsure and she was annoyed by it.

"Don't be so bloody ridiculous!"

She began to stuff the cheese on toast into her mouth, her hunger primal now, desperate to provide for the little one that he was discussing terminating.

"Well, it's just…it's not really something I have ever considered, I mean, I'm still young and all that and…I really don't want you to have my child."

Katy stopped chewing and suddenly felt fearful…could he stop her having the baby? Was there some archaic law that said if a couple were not in agreement, then a termination could be forced upon the woman? The next sentence revealed his real concern and she realised what she needed to do.

"I mean, it's not like I can afford a child."

Katy continued chewing and had a feeling of immense calm as she took another piece of bread out of the freezer compartment and put it in the toaster. Her stomach felt settled and she bent down to stroke Jimmy, his fur bringing an even stronger sense of peace as she sank down on the kitchen seat.

"Oh, I understand. Believe me, I won't come chasing you to provide for your child."

Luke tried to protest, but she wouldn't let him and carried on.

"I'm not interested in what you have to say. You've made your point, but there is no way I'm not having this baby. It's mine and I'll take care of it, without you."

She started to cut the cheese, holding the phone under her chin as he spoke.

"Okay, well that sounds fair enough."

She laid the cheese on the bread before putting it back under the grill and took the phone again.

"But I'll obviously need to find somewhere else to live… assuming you're not coming back yet?"

He coughed nervously before answering "Erm…yeah, I've paid the rent up to the end of this month."

Again, it took a while to register what he was saying.

"Hang on, that's tomorrow…you can't mean the end of January?"

"Yeah, I didn't want to come back to sort stuff out… thought it might be a bit…awkward."

Katy laughed bitterly and watched the cheese melt, turning from calm indifference to bubbling lava within seconds under the terrific heat.

"I can give you the number of the landlord, if you want to continue living there for a bit."

"Oh, would you, that is kind of you," she couldn't help

sniping, feeling stronger as she took another bite of her food.

Katy grabbed a pen and an envelope that she had opened earlier and scribbled down the number he said, her fingers marking it with grease.

"Well, I'm glad that's all sorted then." he confirmed, sounding like a man who had just got the deal of a lifetime and she couldn't help but feel irritation that he was just carrying on with life while she was left to carry the burden of heartbreak. She went to say goodbye when a sound from his end stopped her dead.

"What was that?"

"Just my mum," he mumbled hastily, "I need to go."

Katy heard the sound again and although she didn't want to go down the route of jealous madwoman, she felt she had to challenge him.

"Who is she?"

The sense of a curtain being pulled open to reveal a mystery prize began to build in her head and she held her piece of toast mid-air as a new and altogether terrible thought occurred to her.

"Oh please, no…your mum…it isn't your mum…you've been with…oh my God!"

"I need to go." he snapped abruptly before terminating the call and she let the phone slip down out of her hand and onto the table, the betrayal and foolishness hitting her full force, the thought of him and another woman, all those weekends, her playing the dutiful partner, him playing around, the bastard! Turning to see the plastic bucket, Katy got to it just in time to vomit half of her meal back up before crying, head in her hands as Jimmy jumped up onto the chair and nuzzled her head.

Chapter 27
Sacrificed In Exchange

Five months later – May

Life had changed for many of the people who lived in
the village where John had spent his teenage years. As the
season had changed from dark, dead and depressing to light,
warm and surrounded by the life of the garden, where Bill's
patience in setting seedlings into the ground was rewarded
by a riotous display of colour, so too, the lives of those
around him had changed for the better. Gladys had started
a pastoral role in her local hospital that dealt with a few
cancer patients, using her experience of caring for Beryl
as a backdrop to caring for those who were desperately ill.
George and Suzie had bought their own house, with the
large inheritance that Beryl had given him, weeks before
her death, keen to stop the taxman taking any of it. Ivy was
free of her anxiety that had troubled her for so long and
had started art classes, using the money that John paid in
rent. John had settled into his role as housing officer for the
council and found that he actually enjoyed it, even when he
couldn't solve the problem for the client. Just to know he
was trying to help was enough and Malcolm had become a

close friend, in and outside of work. The days of Parliament, although only a year ago, seemed a whole lifetime away and he never hankered back to that time. The therapy had helped enormously and Lauren was happy for him to meet quarterly, seeing the difference in his character and how work had played a vital part in his restoration. John liked to keep active, having realised how much he needed fresh air and time out. He had taken to having a forty-five minute walk every evening over the fields in the village and ending with a sit down on the bench in the park. Often Lisa would be walking Zippy and so she would sit with him and chat about how everything was going. She rarely mentioned Mike and the conversations over Christmas were not referred to. They almost had a dreamlike quality to John, the last time he had really been his old self; morphing from fat caterpillar, cocooned by ignorance, into a butterfly largely unrecognisable; he had his therapist to thank for that. He sat this particular evening, with the sun, which had been rather lacking of late, warming the back of his head and shoulders like a heat pack, giving him a sense of contentment. The new technique his therapist had taught him was an ancient one called mindfulness, a kind of living in the now. It was his favourite one so far and allowed him to cope with everything and anything that was thrown at him. John basked in the feeling of warmth and happiness, closing his eyes and letting himself feel okay. A dark shadow passed over his face and he lazily opened his eyes, sitting up quickly as he recognised the silhouette of Mike standing in front of him, his heavy breathing now audible, the smell of stale sweat and cigarettes wafting over to him in the heat.

"You seen Lisa?" he growled gruffly.

"No, I-er- no, I haven't…"

Mike smiled maliciously and took the cigarette he had

been smoking and threw it down onto the grass.

"She said you was a spaz," he hissed and then stamping on the smouldering end, he suddenly turned and moved at lightning speed, catching John unaware, snatching his collar upwards, causing John to grab hold of the bench to steady himself.

"You tell her she needs to get home…. she's got some explaining to do…got it?"

John nodded as Mike dropped him back onto the bench, all peaceful thoughts shattered, his nerves jangly, his stomach feeling exposed. Mike grimaced and sauntered away, whistling. John sat, shocked at the contact from such a brute, the adrenaline that had rushed to his defence, now redundant, flooding his body, causing him to shake uncontrollably. He folded his arms, trying to find something to hang onto, a thought, a word, a technique, anything to stop him feeling so weird. He couldn't focus and so just sat, unable to do anything. He had been there for half an hour before he noticed a movement in the bushes to the right of him. The park had a path all the way round it, lined by bushes, to give it a lovely garden feel. But now, it just looked ominous and John wished he had managed to muster the energy to go home, the jolts of anxiety still flickering in his chest. Squinting, he could now see a figure making her way towards him. It was Lisa, he could tell by her walk, although she was clad in back and wearing a dark hoodie with the hood up. She stayed close to the hedge as she made her way to him, the darkness as dusk fell shielding her from exposure.

"Are you alright?"

She spoke in a stage whisper and John sat up, realising his buttocks had gone to sleep and his legs ached.

"Yeah, I'm good, thanks," lied John, "You?"

She looked around and then sat down.

"I'm great. But I'm leaving…which is why I've come to see you."

John looked puzzled and turned to look at her. In the light of the lamppost, she had a brightness to her eyes and he had to admit, she looked well. Her hair, although tucked up under the hood had escaped to one side, giving her a young, pretty look and she was wearing makeup that brought colour to her pale face. There was no evidence of any bruises, that he could see.

"Are you moving away?" he enquired, rubbing his thighs to get the blood circulating again.

"Yes – but Mike doesn't know. He can't know. I've been given a place in a refuge two hundred miles from here, a chance to start again."

She was speaking earnestly now and he was suddenly aware that she had moved closer.

"Oh." he exhaled dumbly, as she took his hand.

"Come with me! This is a chance for the both of us to start afresh!"

John felt like he had been slapped in the face and sat back abruptly, snatching his hand out of hers. Lisa looked confused and then, realising her error, studied the ground in front of her, not wanting to look at him. He immediately felt guilty and began to try to make amends.

"Look, Lisa, you are a lovely girl…don't get me wrong."

"Don't! Just…don't."

She inhaled sharply.

He felt miserable.

"I'm sorry."

They sat in silence, uncomfortable in each other's company. John could see the moths flitting round the light, banging into the glass over and over. It seemed they never learned; the pain of contact overruled by their desire to get closer. At last, Lisa exhaled.

"No, I'm sorry. I shouldn't have assumed anything…I just thought, after all the chats we had and Christmas."

She swallowed, before clearing her throat.

"I thought you had felt it too."

John stared at her as she turned to look at him. She really was very pretty, he thought, I must be mad to not fancy her.

"I'm just a mess at the moment, that's all." he admitted finally, cracking a tired smile. "I don't have enough energy to look after myself, let alone anyone else."

Lisa smiled back and sat up. She held out her hand to him and he shook it formally.

"I hope it works out for you…and that you find someone to look after you properly." he recited awkwardly, feeling like a bit part in a soap opera.

Lisa laughed roughly.

"Anything will be better than what I've had to put up with for the last few years."

They sat in silence, though this time it was more comfortable. A thought suddenly occurred to John.

"Where's Zippy?"

Lisa smiled and a look of pure love came over her face.

"My sister is looking after him for me. Once I've got myself sorted, and am renting privately somewhere, he can come and live with me again."

"Oh, well that's good."

"Right…I best be off then," she exclaimed brightly "Sure I can't persuade you?"

John smiled and stood up.

"No, it's fine. You go and find the life of adventure. I'll stay here, with my parents, working in a council office…it's such fun." he murmured, sarcasm dripping from every word.

She laughed and then checked herself, looking round.

"He's already been here, looking for you." he stated matter-of-factly, feeling ashamed of his weakness in the face of aggression.

As if she sensed what had happened between her now ex-partner and the man she had hoped would be her new partner, her eyes widened before she turned to walk back the way she had come.

"I'll go this way then. My friend is picking me up in ten minutes from the other side of the river and then I'm off. He won't be able to trace me anywhere."

She spoke solemnly and he knew she was still fearful. He leant forward and gave her a sideways hug, surprising her.

"All the best, then."

John turned to walk away. When he had taken a few steps, she called out.

"Thanks for everything…goodbye."

He turned and watched as her figure disappeared behind the hedge and then carried on across the park. He walked along the main road back to his parents' house and passed Lisa's house, where he could see the lounge lit up. Through the curtain crack, he could see Mike, walking around, obviously realising that she wasn't coming back this time for a good hiding. Mike paced across the room and opened the curtain suddenly, catching sight of John standing by the gate. The face looked angrily at John, but John felt no fear… no anxiety…just a calm feeling came over him, that Lisa was now safe from this vile man and he did something he had never, ever done. John took a step forward and stuck his middle finger up at the man now gaping at him through the glass. He smiled and turned away, listening as the banging on the glass and shouts became fainter. His mum's policeman friend would come in handy with this situation, he thought, realising that he had after all been a witness to the damage

Mike had inflicted on Lisa. If it meant Mike wouldn't pursue her, then it was worth it.

He was humming 'Zip-a-Dee-Doo-Dah' as he came into the house, the smell of toast in the air, his father's nightly ritual that was now his own. Taking the bread out of the bread bin and popping it in the toaster, he looked through the archway, into the lounge, where his parents sat, watching TV, snuggled together and he felt a pang, an ache of something that he had thought would be his, a regret of the foolish recklessness he had shown, losing the only woman that he cared about. He knew that it was just an excuse that he couldn't look after himself, using it as a reason to avoid a new relationship…he simply wasn't over Katy. He missed her. Missed her smile, missed her cooking, missed her conversation, missed her humour, missed her quirky films, missed her being beside him and more than anything, missed the Katy that he had sacrificed in exchange for the power of being an MP. Katy had long gone before she had broken up with him and he couldn't believe he had traded that woman, that body, that amazing creature for being a somebody… who was now a nobody.

The feeling of happiness that had come with him into the house, now evaporated, leaving him feeling deflated and he took his toast up to his room to eat. He had work in the morning and he knew he needed to get a good night's rest after all the excitement.

* * * * *

John felt tired as he got into his car to drive to work, the antics of the night before had an almost dreamlike quality to them and although he was pleased for Lisa, he wished he hadn't needed to be involved with the situation; everything was so draining. He put his 10CC album into the CD player and sang along 'I'm not in love, so don't forget it'. Humming the tune and feeling a resonance with the man who clearly was still in love, he sighed. He felt gloomy but almost enjoyed the feeling, knowing Lauren would say it was a good thing to be feeling something as deep as this. He drove the thirty minutes it took to get to work, thinking about the day ahead. A full day, a morning of tenants hoping to be taken on by the housing association, putting their case forward and bringing the number of points with them, like some kind of voucher. He pulled into the carpark and parked in his space, pleased that the sun was shining as it lifted his mood.

Taking his bag out of the boot, he went up the steps and through the glass doors. Every day he observed his reflection and was starting to like what he saw again. Walking had helped build up his legs, as had using his mum's static bike in the conservatory. Gardening and doing press-ups and sit-ups every morning had strengthened his upper body and he had lost the paunch that had threatened to spill over his jeans. He had even managed to purchase some slim fit jeans that Malcolm had recommended he get, as pulling bait for when he was ready to get back into the dating game, although he still felt that this would be a long time coming. John nodded to Claire as he came in and said 'Morning!' to her and smiled. She smiled back and handed him a clipboard with the printout of today's clients for him to peruse. He took it through to his office and decided to make himself a coffee first. Malcolm came through the doors backwards, holding a French stick, a pot of St Agur dipping cheese and some pate and grinned at him.

"I've bought breakfast…do you want to do the drinks and I'll slice the bread?"

Claire swung around on her swivel chair and laughed.

"I've seen it all now, a fine romance this is turning out to be!"

Malcolm laughed easily and John smiled again and flicked the kettle on in the side office. Taking down two mugs, he felt a sense of peace settle in his chest at the thought of easily sharing some food with a friend, who enjoyed his company and made him laugh. He had never had this experience before either in work or out - everything had been a competition and he knew he had been difficult to manage. Not anymore, he thought ruefully as he put two teaspoons of coffee in each cup. He needed the caffeine today, he reasoned as he went through to his office, to find Malcom already in there, setting up a napkin with bread, a slice of pate and leaving the dip for him to help himself. Malcolm studied him as he sat opposite and started to eat the bread, taking sips of coffee to wash it down.

"You look really well, John."

John guffawed and shook his head, still chewing.

"People will talk." he said raising his eyebrows and Malcolm chuckled.

"I'm serious…you look nothing like the scrawny, timid, messed up bloke that came for an interview six months ago."

John stopped chewing and feigned a hurt look.

"Is that meant to make me feel better? Because as counselling skills go, I think it's fair to say you are crap!"

"You know what I mean…you look better, fitter, as if you like it here."

John considered him and ripped a piece of bread off and dipped the end into the cheese.

"I do. Some of the people are lovely," he said pointedly before biting the bread and chewing. "It would be a perfect job if it wasn't for the clients."

Malcolm laughed again.

"Oh, they're not all that bad…and you do help them."

"True, I suppose."

John finished eating and drank some more coffee, the list still untouched on the desk. He was about to have a look at it when he heard someone come through the glass doors. He checked his watch…it was only 8.30am and the first appointment wasn't until nine. He looked at Malcolm, still stuffing his face and was about to say something rude when he heard her. The voice of his dreams, the voice that had settled in his mind for so many years, the voice he had silenced by his selfish ambition; her voice, his beloved Katy.

"Are you okay?"

Malcolm had glanced up and seen the shock frozen on John's face and mistaken it for illness. John didn't answer, just stood and slowly walked across the room to the open door. Peering out, he knew what he was expecting to see, but still couldn't believe his eyes. She stood with her back to him, leaning over the desk and pointing to something that Claire had written down in front of her. She was saying her name and sounded impatient and from where John was standing, she seemed to be awkwardly leaning forward as if something was in her way. Aware of his presence she turned to see him and they both went 'Oh!' as if the wind had been knocked out of them and the colour drained from their faces. Malcolm appeared at the door, hurriedly wiping his face, and watched as John realised the reason for her ungainly movement and she took in the fact her ex-husband was now her housing officer.

"You're pregnant!" he exclaimed stupidly and Katy flushed and began to get flustered.

"I'm sorry- I didn't know it was you here…is there someone else I can see?"

She turned to Claire in desperation and Malcom, being

quick on the uptake, crossed over to her.

"Hi, I'm Malcolm. John is our only Housing Officer, but he is very good at it and I'm sure he can sort out any problems you may be experiencing."

"You're pregnant." he stated again, his brain not quite able to process such an incredible fact on top of her being there.

"Well, yes, obviously, that's why I'm here" she replied crossly and folded her arms on top of the bump.

"Look, why don't you go into his office," suggested Malcolm, all smiles, "Sit down and I'll make you a nice cup of tea...how about that?"

Katy turned to look at him and offered a small, grateful smile.

"That would be lovely...two sugars and milky please."

As she caught sight of John's surprise at the request, she muttered 'Coffee makes me sick!' before walking through the door and sitting where Malcolm had just been. John felt like he was in a dream as he watched her go and Malcolm came close.

"I take it this is your wife?" he whispered and John glanced at him, still stunned.

"Ex-wife...I can't believe it."

He continued to stare at the back of her seated form until Malcolm gave him a little nudge.

"Get in there...you need to be professional and treat her like any other client." he commanded wisely and asked Claire to make the tea, before disappearing into his own office.

John clenched his hands together and released them as he felt the tell-tale tingling of panic start to flood his body. He gave himself a mental pep talk as he walked in and took his seat. She is just like any other client, she needs my help, she is going to be a single mother, she is just like any other client…her breasts look amazing.

The weight gain around her hips suited her and her complexion was smooth, with a hint of rose on her cheeks. She looked utterly beautiful and his heart ached. He wanted to touch her cheek, to hold her close and tell her everything would be all be alright, like he had all those years before when the doctor had told her she couldn't have children… but this just didn't make any sense…how could she be pregnant? He had sat for a few minutes studying her and she mistook his adoration for mockery. Katy set her face in the hardened mask he was more used to seeing before she spat the words out.

"Okay, enough of the gloating," she snapped, her eyes glittering, "Luke has left me. Gone to live with someone else. Not part of his game plan, having a child…bloody ironic, isn't it?" she finished, sitting back in the chair, her tummy pushed even further forward.

John was mesmerised by it, thinking about the baby inside, the miracle and the sheer callousness of Luke, the man who had taken his prize away. The fact that it was really himself that had been the cause of her heartache for many years eluded him. She was eyeing him warily and he realised he needed to speak.

"Right, well, I'm sorry you are in this position…" he began, looking at his computer screen.

She looked at him incredulously, but said nothing. Claire came in with the tea and Katy thanked her and had drained it before she had even closed the door on her way out.

"Oh, it's so hot in here, I can't cool down, it's so frustrating," she growled, struggling to get her blue cardigan off.

Her breasts seemed to grow as she writhed about and John willed himself to look away, not wanting to get caught out.

She was too busy faffing about thankfully and he took the opportunity to look at his list. Her name was at the top. If Malcolm hadn't bought breakfast, he would at least have been prepared to see her, would have got himself together enough to speak professionally to her without the need to keep looking at her chest…she did look amazing though.

"I've got you down as needing a two-bedroom flat." he observed as she finally settled down in her seat.

"That's all I can afford to rent. I lost my job over…a misunderstanding"

Katy stumbled over the words and he couldn't hide his surprise. She had loved her work and he knew how hard that must have been for her.

"And the redundancy pay is pittance. I was hoping to have got something else by now, but unfortunately, nobody wants a pregnant forty-one-year-old, funnily enough…"

John smiled at her sympathetically before looking at the paperwork again and she glanced at him, wonderingly. He was so far removed from the man she was in the process of divorcing; she began to think he was on some kind of drug. He hadn't made one snide comment, or been critical or judgemental. Then her sensible head came back to lead and she realised this was his job, he was trained to deal with situations like hers and she couldn't help but feel a bit disappointed, without really understanding why.

"There will be some money coming your way after the sale of the house" he uttered quietly, not sure if this was very professional, but wanting her to know provision was coming.

She sat forward, interested.

"Oh? I thought you still lived there…there are often lights on and people around."

He looked embarrassed and she jumped to the wrong conclusion. Of course, that's why he was so much nicer…he had met someone.

"Well, not anymore," he said firmly, "so once it's been cleaned thoroughly, it will be put up for sale. You should get quite a good chunk of money."

Katy was surprised at this - considering he had just split up with someone, he seemed very happy about it. She bit her lip.

"I didn't think you were for sharing out the cash…the solicitors said."

"Yeah, but – that - that was different," he spluttered hastily, "You weren't on your own…or pregnant. I can see if we can get you something ASAP, certainly before the baby is born and then, once the money from the sale of the house comes through, you can either privately rent or buy a small place."

She eyed her cup wistfully and he caught her gaze.

"Would you like another drink? Claire can get it for you."

She smiled, nodding and settled back in the chair again.

"Only if it's not too much trouble." she replied softly and his heart seemed to explode, causing him to cough, trying to clear the feeling.

He picked up the phone on his desk and pressed the number for Claire, who was more than happy to make another drink, wanting to get another look at the woman who had left such a lovely guy like John. He started to type up notes on the computer and Katy relaxed, knowing that at least her housing would get sorted.

"When is the baby due?" he asked without looking at her.

"September 11th," she said, looking down at her bump. "I'm huge already though."

He turned and looked as though he was going to say something, but then seemed to think better of it and went back to typing. Claire came in and brought her drink, smiling at her before asking if John wanted another one. He turned and smiled and said, 'No thanks' and Claire smiled back and for a moment, Katy felt a flash of jealousy. She was astounded and quickly took a sip of the tea, feeling ridiculous. Her hormones were obviously playing up and she took another sip, satisfied that's all the blip was, confirmed when John stood suddenly, to inform her that her time was up and that he would let her know when something became available.

"You are on the list, now, so it shouldn't be too long. Hopefully before the baby is born."

He looked at the bump and put his hand out and for one strange, sublime moment, she thought he was going to touch it. Instead, he took her hand to shake formally and went to open the door. She went to pick up the cup to take it out, but John reached forward and took it from her, their fingers connected and he felt a jolt go up his arm and through his heart.

"Thanks for all your help. I need to go to the Benefits Office too, to see what I'm entitled to, at nine forty-five."

"Claire can show you where that is."

He spoke abruptly and turned and went back into his office and closed the door, leaning against it, so he could hear Claire graciously offer to take her in the lift and listened as they walked away. John went over to the screen and looked at her file. Her name, date of birth and mobile number were the only things filled in. He didn't know why, but he had some crazy notion that she wouldn't be needing housing. John could feel himself obsessing over her, wondering what sex the baby was, how she was coping when she was sick, if she slept well. He was swinging from hating Luke for treating her so badly to wanting to shake the blokes' hand for bringing her back to him and then crushing despair at the thought of her not being in his life. Hurrying her out, he couldn't stand being in the same room as her, the pain, like an open wound rolling around his chest, made him want to cry. He felt like weeping and looked to see when his next appointment was…half an hour. He suddenly felt drained and wanted to go home but he knew if he did, there would be too many questions from Ivy - how would she take this news?

He put his head in his hands and groaned…it was going to be a long day.

* * * * *

Ivy had just put the toad in the hole in the oven when she saw John's car pull onto the drive. He was home early and she wondered if everything was alright, as she peered through her kitchen window. She saw John sitting in his car, with his head in his hands, not getting out. Concerned, she went out into the garden to find Bill tidying up the beds, clearing the weeds that had sprung up during the last few weeks of sunshine and rain.

"I think there's something wrong." she announced to Bill, who didn't even look up.

"In what way?" he murmured, using the trowel to work the dandelions out carefully.

"Well, John is home already but he is still sitting in his car. What shall I do?"

"Just leave the poor boy alone, I'm sure he is alright and doesn't need you fussing around him." replied Bill pragmatically, taking a seedling from its little box and placing it into the newly weeded bed.

Ivy went back into the house, still unsure. She went to the kitchen window and was alarmed to see John slumped over his steering wheel and knew she couldn't leave him to it. She wiped her hands on her apron and took it off, before going to the front door. Going to the passenger window, she knocked. John didn't respond at first and so she knocked again. He reached across and opened the door for her, before continuing with his pose of deflation. She sat in the seat next to him and shut the door. After a few minutes of silence, she was aware of the snuffles that revealed that he was crying. She felt her own tears prickle and reached for her handkerchief. Finally, she could bear it no longer.

"Whatever is wrong, John?"

He let out a such a howl of sadness that it made her jump and fearful of his answer.

Wiping his eyes across his sleeve, he spoke in a shaky voice. "Oh Mum...I've seen her...I've seen Katy!"

This was not what she was expecting him to say and her own tears were momentarily stopped.

"Oh...and what did that madam want?" she quipped hotly, not at all pleased with the effect that Katy still had on her son.

"She's not a madam...she's lovely and beautiful and...oh Mum...she's pregnant!"

John turned to her and reached out for a hug and Ivy grabbed him and put his head over her shoulder, astounded at what she had been told and still confused by it all.

"But...I thought...she couldn't...I don't understand." Ivy bleated, feeling foolish.

John drew back from her and wiped his eyes with his thumbs, running them down his trousers before taking a deep breath.

"It was me," he answered looking straight ahead, the tears stopped, his voice hoarse with sadness. "I assumed it was her, but it was me. I don't think she meant to get pregnant... and Luke left her, he didn't want to know...it seems he was cheating on her for most of their relationship."

He blew his nose, calmer now, the emotion spent.

Ivy snorted and began to say 'Well, that serves her right' when John raised a hand to shush her. He flicked the dust from his dashboard as he carried on.

"She has to find somewhere else to live…she was my first client this morning…I don't know how I made it through the day." he finished ruefully.

"Oh Johnny!" she said, incredulously, "My goodness, that must have been awful."

He pinched the bridge of his nose, and took a deep breath as Ivy put her hand on his shoulder.

"I just couldn't believe my eyes…not only was she there, but pregnant…and she's lost her job. I need to get the house sold so she can have half."

Ivy slid her hand down his arm and looked at him sceptically.

"Now hold on a minute, this isn't your problem, she left you. It's not for you to fix it."

John fiddled with his keys, not looking at her.

"I know," he admitted at last, "But I can't help it, Mum. I want to help her."

Ivy looked out of the window, feeling helpless, not knowing what to say. She suddenly remembered the dinner and opened the door, turning to look at him as she got out.

"Come on in for dinner. We can talk about it with your Father, see what he has to say about it."

She slammed the door, forgetting that his car was a newer model that didn't need much pressure to close it, but instead of being cross, he smiled at her through the window and opened his door. John was feeling calmer now, the excitement of the day dissipating as the familiarity of being back in his place of safety flooded his senses. He took his bag out of the boot and closed it, pressing the fob to lock it before following Ivy into the house. The smell of sausages filled his nostrils and his stomach contracted at the thought of food…he realised he hadn't had lunch. Hanging his bag over the banister, he went through to the kitchen, where Ivy was plating up the meal. He flicked the kettle on for the gravy and spooned the gravy granules into the measuring jug. Bill came in from the garden, slipping his boots off at the door before pulling his slippers on.

"You'll never guess who John saw today." remarked Ivy, taking over from John and stirring the gravy before picking up two of the plates.

"You're right, I'll never guess." Bill replied, glancing over to catch John's eye. Seeing John looking dishevelled and completely out of sorts he retracted his statement.

"Actually, I bet I can…Katy?"

Ivy dropped the spoon with a clatter and turned to him.

"How did you guess? Did you tell him?"

She directed this to John who merely shook his head as he loosened his tie.

"Well, John looks like he has been through the wars and you obviously know the person, so Katy is the obvious choice."

"Oh, alright, Sherlock." joked Ivy as she went through the arch to put the plates on the table.

"How is she?" asked Bill, washing his hands.

John picked up his glass of water and took a swig before answering.

"Pregnant…and homeless."

Bill stopped and turned to look at him.

"Oh…that is a turn up for the books. And how does that make you feel?" he said with a twinkle in his eyes, causing John to laugh out loud.

"God, you sound like my therapist!" John chortled, carrying the last plate through to Ivy, who was coming back for the gravy.

As she came back to the table, Bill sat down and asked the question again. John shrugged before cutting into a sausage and taking a bite. Ivy took her napkin and shook it out before putting it on her lap. She glanced at Bill and took a sip of water before attacking her meal with vigour.

"Well," she sniffed, "I do think this is a bit of a 'serves her right' moment…she did cheat on you and obviously thought very highly of herself, to go off with a younger man."

John considered her and shrugged, reaching out for the salt before sprinkling it over his mashed potato. He put some sausage into the mountain of mash, causing a rivulet of gravy to cascade down the path he had created, before taking it all off the fork with his teeth, the scraping on the inside setting his teeth on edge. He chewed quickly, the sausage hotter than he had expected and reached out for his water.

"I don't blame her," he stated finally, having washed the molten lump down with the cooling liquid, feeling it burn as it slid down his esophagus, "I was pretty awful."

As Ivy went to protest, he fixed her with a questioning look.

"Oh, come on, I was horrible!"

He felt awkward as both his parents were looking at him and he knew he needed to say more.

"And not just to Katy. I know I was a terrible son…I can't even explain what was going on, or why I behaved the way I did."

He trailed off, fiddling with the pepper shaker and Bill coughed uncomfortably, not enjoying the intimacy of the moment. Ivy however, lapped it up.

"It's alright, darling," she gushed, "We all did things back then that we regret. It doesn't matter now…today is all that matters, that we are all together and happy again." she finished, going back to eating her meal.

John had cleared his plate and sat, thinking about what she had said. Was he really happy? Yesterday he had been, hell, even this morning, eating breakfast with Malcolm (was that only this morning?), he had felt content, that finally, life was becoming pleasant, he had friends, a job that was the right balance in terms of fulfilment and challenge, it had all seemed to be coming right…and then Katy. Just the thought of her now made him ache with the desperate sadness of wanting something you know you cannot have; the albino craving sunlight; the butterfly child craving a hug; the diabetic craving jelly babies and the nut allergy sufferer desperate for a Snickers; the impossibility of it just made it worse. John suddenly had an idea. Katy had filled out forms…she must have left a contact number! He would at least be able to contact her. He got up from the table and walked over to his briefcase. Sitting down on the sofa, he pulled it onto his lap and clicked it open, frowning as he thought about what he was about to do.

"I'm just making a cuppa," called Ivy through the doorway, "Did you want one?"

John stared ahead, taking a few seconds to realise she had spoken to him.

"Erm…yeah, that would be nice…" he murmured before taking out Katy's file. He hesitated before opening it, feeling uncomfortable about looking at a client's file outside of work and the reason he was looking at it. He knew it was unethical to be taking private information and, wrestling with his gut that told him to leave it, he snapped it shut. It could wait until after the weekend and then he could call her with a house related question…at least he would have the opportunity to talk to her, without feeling guilty. Malcolm was such a nice bloke, he didn't want to screw things up.

Ivy brought the tea through and set it down on the side table, before going back for her own and sitting in her favourite chair. Sometimes she just liked to sit in her lounge and survey the family scene; Bill reading the paper, the light from the lamp glinting off his glasses, causing them to wink as he moved his head. John, usually watching television, or using his phone, engrossed. They all looked so well; she knew that John was so much better and with summer coming, she looked forward to them all going out as a family again. Her eyes clouded over briefly as she thought of Katy. Ivy sincerely hoped that Katy's arrival in John's office wouldn't undo all the good that had been done over the last year.

John was so excited Sunday evening that he couldn't sleep. Just the thought of speaking to Katy again caused him to feel a flutter in his chest, like the first time he had fancied her and he kept grinning at the thought. In his imagination, they were together, planning a future, preparing for the baby. Then he would come back down to earth and despaired that he wasn't even able to get a handle on how he felt. That was the downside to therapy, he decided, it pulled out all these emotions and left them floating too near the surface, to be hooked out by circumstances or someone, dripping the mess all over life. Talk about heart on your sleeve…more like soul on your skin, spread over so that at any given moment, anything could happen to the third degree. He turned over onto his side…although he favoured sleeping on his back, he liked the idea of pretending that he was snuggled up with Katy, putting his arms out round her, leaving space for the bump.

Chapter 28
Love Collided

It was a bright, sunny morning as Katy made her way out of her friend's house, moving slowly down the stairs and out onto the street. She pulled the door closed behind her, checking that she had her key before going along the pavement to where her car was parked. She was wearing a new dress, floral and cut sympathetically for someone feeling huge; the floaty material fitted over the bump neatly and was perfect in the heat. Already she was sweating and glad her legs were free and feeling cool. As she got in the car, she noticed that her ankles were swollen and felt annoyed – it kind of ruined the look of summery prettiness, having flabby ankles, she thought crossly as she put her seatbelt on. She wondered how much longer she would be able to drive, the pedals already felt too far away, her hips at full stretch, the bump leaning against the steering wheel. Stretching across for her handbag, she groaned as the baby wriggled and kicked her bladder. Katy undid the clasp, found her diary and pulled it out. The appointment for the scan had been made at the beginning of her pregnancy and she wanted to double check the date, having already turned up to two midwife appointments a week early.

Katy looked at the page and the words swam in front of her eyes, causing her to feel nauseous She became aware of her head throbbing and so turned the key in the ignition, to open the window. The fresh air helped and she checked the page again, happy that she had got the right day. Having started the engine, her phone rang. Taking it out of her bag, she frowned. It wasn't a number she recognised and was about to end it when she realised it was a landline and might be important. She slotted the phone into her hands-free kit and answered the call, pulling out of her space.

"Hello?" she snapped as she came up to the junction at the end.

"Oh, hello, Katy, it's John here…your housing officer."

Katy couldn't help but smile at the absurdity of John's words as she checked both ways.

"Hello again…is everything okay?"

"Er, yes, all fine here."

There was a silence on the line and Katy glanced at her phone to make sure it was still connected. The sun was glaring and she reached her hand down to get her sunglasses from out of the door.

"So…is this a courtesy call for something, or…"

"Sorry, yes, I mean, no it's just…I wondered…about a landline phone number."

Katy was feeling irritated, the sun too bright, her head pounding and John making no sense.

"I'm sorry, John, I really need to go, I'm driving at the moment…oh shit!"

Katy felt like a bomb had gone off in her head, complete with sparks of light and managed to pull over, before vomiting over her lovely new dress. She slumped forward, her head tight, like being held in a vice, her eyes closing, a hissing sound in her ears blocking out everything, or nearly everything…in her dreamlike state, she could hear John calling her name. She was aware her passenger door was being opened and a female voice was asking her if she was alright. In her mind, she was yelling 'Do I look alright?!' Externally, she looked unconscious, and the woman, who had seen her erratic driving and had stopped to make sure she was okay, used the phone in her hand to ring for an ambulance.

"What's happened?"

The male voice made her jump and she reached for the now unconscious woman's phone and spoke into it.

"Hello?"

"Who is this? Is Katy alright?"

"My name's Megan and I've just seen this woman pull up, right, and she's like, fainted or something, she looks like, really sick, I mean she's actually been sick, like…."

"Oh God…uh… where are you?"

Megan looked up the road.

"I'm in Sherwood Avenue, like heading for the ring road… I've phoned for an ambulance…I did my first aid last year on placement, so, like, I've checked she's still breathing and all that shit…"

"I'm on my way" commanded John, not wanting to hear anymore.

By the time he got there, the paramedics had just finished putting Katy into the back of the ambulance. Her car had been moved off the road and he pulled his up behind hers and tried to get out without undoing his seatbelt. He pulled against it and finally snapped it off before getting out, running to catch up with the paramedic, who was now closing the back door on her.

"Please…I need to see her. Is she okay?"

The paramedic turned and put his hands out reassuringly.

"Are you her partner?"

John swallowed before replying.

"Yeah…is she okay? And the baby?"

"Suspected pre-eclampsia, we'll know more at the hospital…do you want to follow in your car?"

"Come on, we need to move!" shouted the other paramedic as he poked his head out of the window.

John felt dazed as the paramedic patted him on the arm and ran around to the front to get in. He ran himself, wanting to get in the car as quickly as possible, knowing he was going to have to put his foot down to keep up with the ambulance, which had already pulled off, the siren wailing. John started the engine and pulled off quickly, not seeing the motorbike until it was almost touching his car, the screech of tyres and an angry shout made him look in his mirror. The biker had regained control and zoomed up alongside him, angrily gesturing. He felt a whirlwind of emotion well up in him as he wound down the window.

"I'm trying to follow…my wife…she's in there…I'm sorry!"

Instantly, the angry look was replaced by one of concern and the biker nodded.

"No worries mate, you go on, I'll follow."

John shakily got going again, catching up with the ambulance as it weaved its way through the traffic. He couldn't remember whether it was legal to speed behind an ambulance but he didn't care. He knew nothing about what was wrong, if the baby was coming, whether the baby would survive being born early or if Katy's life was in danger; he just wanted to be there for her. Tears pricked his eyes and he swallowed hard.

"Stay strong, John, stay strong…" he murmured, blowing

out quickly as a car pulled out on the ambulance. It went around and John followed, the biker still with him, urging him on.

* * * * *

Katy could hear a beeping sound as she regained consciousness, her eyes seemingly welded shut, the red slash indicative of the fact that she was in a bright room. She could feel crisp cotton against her face and so knew she wasn't at home…no, not home, that wasn't right, she didn't live at the flat anymore…Becky's house then…but no, the covers were unlike these. Her brain hurt, as if using it had been such an ancient experience, it had gone rusty, squeaking into motion. Her head pounded and she wanted to go back to sleep, but she had such a sense of urgency to work out what was going on, that she couldn't switch off. She sniffed the air and disinfectant entered her nasal cavity and, in a rush, she knew. Forcing her eyes open, the brightness stinging, she could see a blurry white room. When she was able to focus, she saw the drip in her hand and instinctively used her free hand to check the bump. Still there, she thought, before trying to move. A pain shot through her buttock and she winced, attempting to turn onto her other side. Less painful, but still hampered by the monitor strapped to her belly. Her left arm was rhythmically tightening, to the point of being uncomfortable, before release came with a beep. A nurse came in with a jug of water and went to the left of her, before placing it on the melamine table next to her bed.

"How are you feeling?" she asked gently, studying Katy's pale face.

"My head aches…" Katy began as the nurse looked at the

machines next to her.

"That's normal with pre-eclampsia," stated the nurse and seeing the look of alarm on Katy's face quickly added "But we have managed to get you under control, so try not to worry."

Katy tried to sit up and let out a moan as the pain in her buttock flashed again.

"What is that?" she groaned, rubbing her haunch and the nurse, who had now finished with her notes, took Katy's wrist in her hand.

Checking her fob watch, the nurse answered without looking at her.

"You've had three steroid injections for baby's lungs. We didn't know if your little one would be making an appearance at that stage, but thankfully, your blood pressure dropped back to a more normal range and, looking at the readout, it's staying that way."

Katy reached out for the beaker and the nurse took it from her and poured the water in, before handing it back.

"Your husband will be happy to hear you are awake," commented the nurse as Katy choked on the liquid, coughing so hard the water dribbled from her nose, the nurse pulling tissues from the box and handing them to her.

"Are you okay? Did it go down the wrong hole?"

"What do you mean, my husband? I'm not..."

"Oh sorry, partner then, I thought he said he was your husband. He's been here all night, bless him and just popped out to get some lunch."

Katy took this information in as she continued her drink, puzzled by the idea that John would be here. She felt anxious and tearful at the thought of him being here in her hour of need. It didn't make any sense.

"I'll go and see if he is back, shall I?" the nurse queried

kindly, before leaving the room briskly.

The heat in the room was stifling and she could feel the sweat running down the side of her body. She felt mortified that John would be seeing her looking and smelling this bad. She tucked her chin in and inhaled…yep, absolutely awful, plus she had no idea how bad she looked. Katy felt a kick and a wave of emotions flooded her, relief, anxiety, and love collided and left her wanting to howl.

A knock at the door made her heart jump.

"Come in." she gurgled, coughing to clear her throat as the door opened.

John came in looking dishevelled and exhausted, carrying a carrier bag. He seemed uncertain as he made his way to her side, standing awkwardly next to her before smiling.

"How are you feeling?"

Katy said nothing, just stared at him.

His smile faded and he looked at the bag in his hands.

"What are you doing here?" she croaked, coughing and reaching for her drink.

"I thought…I heard you…on the phone. I was worried."

Taking a sip of water, she swallowed and closed her eyes. Of course. She had been talking to him just before it all went pear-shaped.

"I see," she managed at last, before turning her attention to the bag. She was feeling hungry and hoped he had brought some food in.

"What's in there?"

Glad to lose the focus for a minute, he opened the bag and rummaged through.

"Well, I got myself a sandwich," he said as he began to unload it onto the bed, "And I got you a ham and cheese baguette – hope that was okay."

Katy snatched it up and used her teeth to open it, before

taking a huge bite, all thoughts of decorum and grace forgotten.

John's smile returned.

"I'll take that as a yes, then…" he chuckled before returning to the bag, "There's some grapes, a packet of Maryland cookies and a bar of Fruit and Nut…I wasn't sure if you still liked it, or maybe had gone off it."

"No," she said quickly, reaching to take it from him.

He looked embarrassed as he passed her the still full bag.

"There are just a few bits in there I thought you might need."

As she pulled the bag towards her, dropping the chocolate onto the bed, she stopped short.

"What are these?"

She pulled out the colourful square package and looked across at him. John flushed and ran his hand through his hair.

"The shop assistant said they would be a good idea."

Katy put them onto the bed and then revisited the bag, pulling out a tiny, white babygro. They both stared at it, the beep of the machines providing a sympathetic symphony.

"I'm sorry…I thought it was cute…you don't have to keep it."

Katy's eyes filled with tears as she took it off the hanger.

"I love it," she squeaked, her voice distorted by the emotion. "It's the first thing she will wear."

John sat forward, interested.

"You're having a girl? I thought as much, I could just see you with a girl!"

He stopped himself, feeling foolish.

"Sorry, it's none of my business."

Katy looked at the things that surrounded her, tried to assess her feelings but couldn't. Too much going on, too many unanswered questions. Mistaking her silence for annoyance, he rose from the bed.

"There's a magazine in there for you to read. I wasn't sure how long you would be in for."

The tears were rolling down her face now and she reached across for the tissues, pulling a handful out and wiping her face. Suddenly, the door opened and the nurse breezed in. She smiled as she took in the scene of domestic bliss.

"Ah, you made it back, then," she directed at John, who was searching through his pocket for his keys.

"Yeah, just got a few bits. I need to get back to work."

He crossed over to the door and held it open.

"Will you be back later? Visiting starts again at seven tonight." the nurse explained, taking Katy's wrist again and consulting her watch.

"Gosh, your heart rate has gone up, young lady." she laughed and Katy smiled weakly.

John hesitated in the doorway, unsure of what to say. Katy took in the worn-out look, the stubble, the dropping of everything to be there, the gifts that were so thoughtful, the sense of a piece of life falling back into the perfect slot and caught his attention with a wave.

"Can you come back at seven? I need some clean underwear."

She giggled and was rewarded with a grin from John, whose heart had just ignited.

"Of course. I'll see you then."

He left the room and floated back to the car, full of hope.

The nurse finished checking Katy and then spotted the bag of goodies.

"Aaah, I love the outfit," she commented, holding it up.

Glancing down at the bed, she spied the coloured package.

"Did he buy these for you too?"

She held up the packet of sanitary towels and Katy nodded.

"Wow, there's not many that would think of them. You've got a special one there."

Katy placed her hand on her bump and feeling a peace descend, lay back on her pillow.

"I know…he is amazing."

The nurse left her alone and she looked at the things John had bought and thought about all the time he had spent with her and for the first time in a long time, she felt cared for. She was looking forward to seeing him; not thinking about tomorrow, or what might or might not happen, just now, this time.

THE END

Carolyn Aldis was born in 1974 in a house in London and had a vivid imagination from an early age…her story telling got her out of many scrapes. In 1997, she married her husband and the ensuing family life with four daughters took up most of her creative time.

When Carolyn hit 40, she decided to have a gap year and the result was this book (and a much happier Carolyn, who finally knew what she wanted to do when she grew up.)

When not writing creatively, Carolyn can be found drawing, painting, baking, walking, singing and hanging out at her local church in Peterborough.

Keep up to date with Carolyn at:
youtube.com/@carolynaldis
&
thethoughtsofafruitcake.wordpress.com

Printed in Great Britain
by Amazon